"Just tell me this—why are you here?" Annie asked.

"I think that's pretty obvious, isn't it?"

Annie took a deep breath. "Do you want her? Do you want Bella?" She died ten times before he finally answered.

"I never knew I had a daughter until I received your letter. The second I could, I came here and saw her. What would *you* do in my place?"

Her heart turned over in her chest. "I'll fight you."

"I expect that."

"You'll never win," she responded.

"No. I'm afraid that's not true." Gray's eyes burned into hers. "The fact is, Annie, I never *lose.*"

Dear Reader,

I'm not going to waste any time before I give you the good news: This month begins with a book I know you've all been waiting for. *Nighthawk* is the latest in Rachel Lee's ultrapopular CONARD COUNTY miniseries. Craig Nighthawk has never quite overcome the stigma of the false accusations that have dogged his steps, and now he might not live to get the chance. Because in setting himself up as reclusive Esther Jackson's protector—and lover—he's putting himself right in harm's way.

Amnesia is the theme of Linda Randall Wisdom's *In Memory's Shadow*. Sometimes you *can* go home again—if you're willing to face the danger. Luckily for Keely Harper, Sam Barkley comes as part of the package. Two more favorite authors are back—Doreen Roberts with the suspenseful *Every Waking Moment,* and Kay David with *And Daddy Makes Three,* a book to touch your heart. And welcome a couple of new names, too. Though each has written elsewhere, Maggie Simpson and Wendy Haley make their Intimate Moments debuts with *McCain's Memories* (oh, those cowboys!) and *Gabriel Is No Angel* (expect to laugh), respectively.

So that's it for this time around, but be sure to come back next month for more of the best romance reading around, right here in Silhouette Intimate Moments.

Yours,

[signature]

Leslie Wainger
Senior Editor and Editorial Coordinator

Please address questions and book requests to:
Silhouette Reader Service
U.S.: 3010 Walden Ave., P.O. Box 1325, Buffalo, NY 14269
Canadian: P.O. Box 609, Fort Erie, Ont. L2A 5X3

AND DADDY MAKES THREE

KAY DAVID

Published by Silhouette Books

America's Publisher of Contemporary Romance

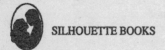

SILHOUETTE BOOKS

ISBN 0-373-07784-X

AND DADDY MAKES THREE

Books by Kay David

Silhouette Intimate Moments

Desperate #624
Baby of the Bride #706
Hero in Hiding #725
And Daddy Makes Three #784

KAY DAVID

is a native Texan who has recently returned to her home state, along with her husband of twenty-two years, Pieter, and their cat, Leroy. She holds undergraduate degrees in English literature and computer science, as well as a graduate degree in behavioral science. Her careers have varied from designing jewelry to building homes, but her first love has always been writing. She has also been published under the name Cay David.

Prologue

Annie Burns gripped the arms of her chair and stared at the doctor facing her. They were sitting in the waiting room of the hospital and the doctor was talking. At least, Annie *thought* he was talking. His mouth was moving and sounds were coming out, but Annie didn't hear them. She was still trying to absorb the first words the physician had delivered....

"I'm sorry, Annie, but she didn't make it. I'm very sorry...."

Annie continued to stare at the physician. One thought echoed over and over in her mind: twenty-seven-year-old women weren't supposed to die.

They had too much life ahead of them, too much to do. There were men to be loved, children to be raised, lives to be fulfilled.

Twenty-seven-year-old women weren't supposed to die.

Especially not one who was your best friend and had been since first grade.

"I...I don't understand," Annie finally managed to get out. "What happened in the labor room—" She broke off abruptly, her heart leaping into her throat. "The baby? Oh, God, is the baby okay—"

"The baby's just fine. She's small, but that's probably because she came early. I suspect about a month premature. She'll be perfectly all right, though."

"But Monica..."

The doctor shook his head, regret in the movement and some anger as well. "If she'd had some prenatal care, someone would have caught the problem in time, but as it was, we didn't know until it was too late. By the time we saw what was happening, there wasn't anything we could do."

Annie couldn't speak, couldn't cry, couldn't do anything but stare.

"Eclampsia is like that," the doctor went on. "The blood pressure shoots up and the toxicity level of the mother goes sky-high. Did she say anything to you about blurred vision? Headaches?"

"No, but there wasn't time. She just showed up at the house, upset and everything...."

"Is there anyone to call? Some family, perhaps?"

"No!" Annie said instantly. "Th-there's no one to call. Her parents are both dead."

"What about the baby's father? Shouldn't he know?"

Yes, he should. But he won't. The image of Monica's face—when Annie had suggested the same thing—shot into Annie's mind.

Monica had simply called late that morning and said she was in town, could she stop by? She spoke as easily as if she and Annie had seen each other last week instead of more than four years ago. With anyone else, Annie might have been irritated. August was one of her busiest months for Riverside, her bed-and-breakfast in the hill country of

Texas, but Monica wasn't just anyone. And besides…it was a typically Monica thing to do. The impulsive redhead didn't believe in long-term planning.

So right after lunch, when Annie had opened the door of Riverside, she'd expected to find Monica on the front porch. But not in the condition she was. Clearly in distress, she was bent over, one hand gripping the front door for support and the other wrapped protectively around her stomach.

"Oh, God! Monica!" Annie had cried. "Come inside…I'll call C.G. We'll go—"

"No! Absolutely not!" Monica abandoned the door and grabbed Annie's arm instead, digging her fingers into the skin so deeply that the bruises still showed. "You have to promise me, Annie. Promise me right now that you won't call him. He…he made his choice when he divorced me! He…he didn't even want a child and—" She broke off abruptly, then started again, speaking even more vehemently. "I don't want him anywhere near this baby. Not now. Not ever."

"Divorced…" Annie managed to get the one word out, then shook her head. It didn't matter. Not now. "We'll talk about that later," she said, her voice rising in panic. "We have to get you to the hospital. Right now!"

Monica stared at Annie with pain-crazed eyes, her voice a screech of wildness. "I'm not going anywhere till you promise me," she screamed. "He knew about the baby, but…but it didn't matter. Th-that's why I came here, Annie. I'm not going anywhere till you promise you won't call him."

There was nothing else Annie could do. "All right," she cried. "I promise—now can we get you to a doctor?"

Nodding once, Monica collapsed into a tiny heap on the steps of the porch. Annie screamed for Maggie, her sister, and together they managed to get Monica to the car. In the back seat, cradled in Annie's arms, Monica came to only once. Her green eyes locked on Annie like twin lasers. All at once, she seemed lucid and completely in control of herself. "He's a horrible man, Annie. He's cold and unfeeling, and he doesn't know the meaning of love. He wants to control everything and everybody. Don't ever trust him. You'd want to—don't look at me like that, I know you would." She closed her eyes and took a sharp breath. When she opened her eyes again, they seemed greener, more intense. "Just don't. Don't *ever* trust him."

Annie's arms tightened around her friend. "I don't understand, Monica. The last time we talked, everything was fine—you were in love, you—"

"He fooled me, Annie. I thought he..." She gasped, grabbing her stomach. She stayed that way for a second, then her body began to tremble and shake. She managed to get the words out through clenched teeth. "If anything hap-happens, I want *you* to r-raise my baby. Promise me you'll do that, Annie. Please..."

Suddenly terrified, Annie shook her head. "Please, Monica—calm down, sweetheart. *You're* going to raise this baby, and I won't have you even thinking otherwise. Please believe me...."

That had been four hours ago.

It seemed like a lifetime.

Now Annie looked down at her hands. They were shaking. She couldn't control them, just as she couldn't control her emotions. Grief, anger, confusion rolled over her in waves.

The physician spoke again. "I'll phone him, if you like. Just give me the man's number and I'll call him."

Annie raised her face and looked into the doctor's exhausted but still concerned eyes. At least here was one thing she could handle.

"That's not necessary," she said quietly. "I'll take care of everything."

Chapter 1

Five years later

The late afternoon sunshine angled through the open door and covered Annie's rolltop desk in a stripe of warm brightness. She hardly noticed. Instead, she concentrated on the forms spread out before her. In two more months, Bella would be starting kindergarten. It didn't seem possible…but it was. The truth lay before Annie, a series of boxes to fill in, answers to circle and squares to check.

And the toughest question of all was the first one.

Parent or Other.

Annie's pencil hovered over the first word. In the last five years, on countless forms, she'd been grateful to simply circle the word 'other.' Having Bella in her life, seeing her grow day by day, watching in awe as Monica's daughter turned into a unique and special person had been all Annie wanted. She'd felt privileged just to be able to have that experience. But it was getting harder and harder to circle that word.

She wanted more.

She wanted to be Bella's mother in *every* sense of the word. Legally, emotionally, spiritually. She wanted the acknowledgement that she and she alone was responsible for this child. She wanted to adopt Bella and be her parent, not her "other." It was time to let the world recognize what everyone in Timberley had accepted for years.

Bella was hers.

Annie dropped the pencil on her desk and leaned back in her chair, rubbing her forehead with a moan of frustration. The same problem that had always been there was *still* there, though. Money. Adoptions were terribly expensive and in the past five years, the price had not gone down. She hated to think that an issue as basic as funds was keeping her from doing something so important, but the reality of the checkbook was as obvious as the reality of the forms before her. Running a bed-and-breakfast right cost money. Every month an emergency seemed to pop up that she hadn't expected. The money she tried to put aside for legal fees was forever getting sidetracked...to the plumber, to the electrician, to the mortgage. She'd had to make a choice; having a steady income by building her business so she could feed them both and keep a roof over their heads, or paying the costs of a legal adoption. When it came down to it, Annie had decided Bella's present security was far more important than the comfort a simple piece of paper would bring Annie.

But the situation was changing. The older Bella got, the more questions, they were going to have to face, questions that only a parent could answer. A *parent,* not a guardian. Like the form Annie was looking at right now. Like the nosy questions Bella had cried over the day before.

Annie had been sitting right where she was now when

the gate leading from the front yard to the back had squeaked, then slammed shut. Expecting Bella, Annie had jumped up from her desk and hurried to the back door, a smile on her face.

The smile had disappeared a second later as she took in the little girl's disheveled appearance.

"My God! What happened to you?" Opening the screen door and dropping to her knees, Annie looked at the child in dismay.

Bella raised her eyes. One braid was completely undone and her red hair—the same shade as Monica's—had escaped to fly around her face in a tangle of curls. The bow was missing. The pocket on her T-shirt hung down, the stitches ripped out, and a long streak of dirt decorated her right cheek.

"I got in a fight," she said, her head hanging down.

Annie's hands went over the little girl's arms and legs. "Are you hurt? Are you bleeding?"

"I'm okay," Bella mumbled, toeing the edge of the tiles on the terrace. A second later, she raised her face, a fierce expression darkening her eyes. "But Billy's not."

Her initial fear fading, Annie rocked back on her heels and tried to hide her amusement. Billy Tiggnerr had moved into the neighborhood last month, and the six-year-old boy was already the scourge of Riverside Drive—or at least the scourge of Bella and her best friend, Rose, who had been the sole rulers prior to his arrival. "What happened?" Annie asked.

Bella kicked at the tiles a second longer, then she raised her face to look at Annie. The child's green eyes—also exactly like her mother's—were filled with tears, and Annie was amazed. Bella was a tough little kid, and she almost never cried. "He...he said..."

"He said what?" Annie prompted gently.

"He said you weren't my mother!" The tears spilled

over and ran down in two tracks on Bella's face. "I told him you were, too, but he said his mommy said you were my guard, not my mother. I told him guards were for jails, not kids.

"It's not true, is it, Annie? You aren't my guard, are you?"

"Oh, sweetheart!" A flash of anger at the gossips came over Annie as she wrapped her arms around the little girl and patted her on the back. The Tiggnerrs were new and obviously someone had been explaining the situation to them—but not too well, it appeared. "We've talked about all that before—don't you remember?"

Bella shook her head, her voice muffled against Annie's collar. "No," she sniffed. "Tell me again."

Annie rubbed circles on the child's back and spoke softly. She'd told the story a hundred times but she didn't mind telling it again. She'd always wanted Bella to grow up knowing the truth about herself. "Well...your first mommy and I were very best friends—just like you and Rose—and she came here, to Riverside, when she was sick, right before you arrived. She asked me to take care of you for her because she couldn't." Annie moved the little girl back from her so she could see her face. "And I promised I would. I said I'd love you and take care of you and feed—"

"Feed me chocolate-chip cookies every day!" Bella grinned as she finished the statement, the tear tracks on her face already drying.

Annie grinned back. "That's right," she said, nodding her head. "Chocolate-chip cookies every day!" A surge of love came over her as it always did when she thought about how lucky she was to have this child. Annie leaned forward and kissed the grimy cheek.

"And then you took me to the courthouse—" Bella prompted.

"I took you to the courthouse and the judge made me your guardian—*not* your guard. Remember what I said a guardian was?"

Bella nodded. "Like a guardian angel."

"That's right—someone who loves you and watches over you."

At this point, in the past, Bella had usually been satisfied. But it wasn't going to work that way now. Annie could see the shadow of more questions darkening the child's expression.

"But…I…I want you to be my mommy. I don't want an angel anymore." She puckered her lips into a pout and crossed her arms. "I want a mommy. Rose has a mommy and that's what I want, too!"

Annie's heart cracked open. There was nothing she wanted more herself. It was almost as if Bella had read her mind. She smoothed a strand of red hair away from the porcelain forehead. Then, taking a deep breath, she spoke again. "Well, if you really feel that way, how about if I adopt you?"

Narrowing her eyes in obvious suspicion, Bella pulled back and looked at Annie. "'Dopt me?" she said. "What's that?"

"It's a legal thing," Annie explained. "It means that I'd be totally responsible for you just like your real mother would have been and no one in the world could ever say I'm not your mommy…because I would be." She paused and searched the child's face. "Would you like that?"

With a relieved look, Bella nodded her head vigorously. "I'd like that a lot," she said. "Because I love you, Annie."

Emotion welled inside Annie's chest, choking her with its power. She couldn't possibly love Bella more, even if she'd given birth to her, but the love between them had only grown as Bella herself grew. Love that had no ending, no beginning. Love Annie couldn't measure and couldn't possibly describe.

Her throat closed tight, but she answered. "I love you, too, baby. Just like your mommy did. And I'll always love you. No matter what. Always. I want you to remember that, okay?"

Annie's heart was so full, she could almost feel the sensation. She leaned over and kissed Bella's brow, taking in a deep breath of that indescribable childish sweetness, complete with grime and a day's worth of play. The smell brought forth a surge of protectiveness.

Bella nodded again. "Then I think we should go ahead," she'd said seriously. "Go ahead and do the 'dopting." And then she was off. Running out the door. All her problems solved and nothing else to worry about.

Closing her eyes now, Annie prayed it would be that simple.

And knew it wouldn't be.

Slipping a white apron over her head, Maggie Burns stood beside the refrigerator door and glanced over at her sister. "How many do we have this morning?"

Blankly, Annie looked up from the rolltop desk in the corner. She'd been sitting there—in the kitchen of Riverside—since 5:00 a.m., trying to make sense of her budget but worrying instead about the phone call she'd made early last week to Loring Shaver, her attorney.

She'd told him to go forward with the adoption.

And he'd told her what that meant. *Exactly* what that meant.

He would have to locate Bella's father, Monica's ex-husband. Then he would have to convince him to relinquish his parental rights.

If the man couldn't be found, then other steps would be

taken—costly, more time-consuming steps. It was a night-mare come true for Annie, but she had no other choice.

"How many do we have?" Maggie repeated her question and held the egg carton out for Annie to see. "I need to know how many eggs to use."

"We have two couples. The Boatwrights in the Sam Houston suite and the Williamsons in the Alamo Room. But go easy on the muffins—the Boatwrights are newly-weds…we probably won't even see them till this afternoon." Turning back to her desk, Annie picked up her pencil, but ended up gnawing on it instead of writing with it.

Maggie opened one of the cabinets and retrieved a bowl, then she threw Annie another glance, this one filled with concern. "You've got to ease up, Annie. Worrying about the situation isn't going to make things happen any faster."

"I know." Throwing the pencil to the desk, Annie stood. "But what else am I supposed to do? It's been a week since Loring sent the letter. We should have heard something by now."

Cracking the eggs one by one, Maggie shook her head. "You know how those kinds of things go. It'll probably take a lot longer. Where's your patience?"

"It's gone." Annie walked to the coffeepot beside Maggie on the counter and poured herself a cup. "Now that I've decided to go forward, I can't relax until everything's resolved and she's mine—officially. I want to be Bella's mother in every way."

"A piece of paper isn't going to make you her mother any more than you already are, and besides, when have you required a license? You've been mothering everyone and everything around here for the past thirty-two years."

"Thirty-two years? I think you're overestimating things a bit, aren't you?"

"Nope. Not in my opinion." Maggie cracked an egg on the side of the bowl. "You probably jumped out of Mom and told the doctor to take a break."

Annie laughed. "Am I that bad?"

"Yes." Maggie smiled. "But I'm not complaining."

Annie met her sister's eyes and silently acknowledged what she was saying. Maggie had just gone through her second divorce. Terrified of living alone again and completely daunted by the aspect of moving away from the Texas hill country to look for work, Maggie had been on shaky ground. Annie had solved both problems by having a sudden and urgent need for help at Riverside. An extra employee was the last thing she could afford, but she'd immediately offered her baby sister the cottage out back and a job.

Annie smiled at her sister now. "I hope Bella feels the same way."

"She does, and you know it. She told you herself just the other day." Maggie added a dash of Tabasco to the eggs.

"I know that, but it's just..." Annie let her voice die off.

"What?"

She looked at her sister over the rim of the coffee mug. "It felt weird telling Loring to write the letter. I felt like I was betraying Monica somehow."

Maggie made a scoffing sound. "That's ridiculous. She wanted you to raise Bella."

"Yes, but she definitely didn't want me to contact Bella's father. She made that more than clear."

"She wasn't a lawyer. She didn't know you didn't have a choice."

Annie nodded. In her head, she'd been over the argument a thousand times, but she still felt disloyal, guilty and nervous all at the same time. Just last night she had dreamed about the day Monica died, about the promises she'd extracted from Annie. She'd sat up in bed, drenched with perspiration, her heart pounding, the image of a faceless man carrying Bella away into the darkness haunting her. "I just hate knowing I'm going to have to deal with the man."

"What do you think he'll say?"

"How can you gauge a man's reaction to something like that?" Annie sipped her coffee and looked over the rim to the window and the river that formed the boundary of her yard. It was July and hot, Texas-hot. Diamonds of light danced on the water and it wasn't even 7:00 a.m. yet. "How could a man not want his own flesh and blood to begin with? I don't understand any of it."

"People dump their kids all the time—we've grown into a society that doesn't care, don't you know that?"

"I disagree. If you trust people and expect the best, then that's what you get. If you criticize and think the worst, then guess what happens?"

"This isn't a matter of expectations, Annie. They were married for five years. Monica knew what she was talking about." Maggie began to beat the eggs. "He must have been a good-looking son-of-a-gun, though. He certainly swept Monica off her feet. Remember when she called you—right before they got married?"

"How could I forget? I'd never heard her so excited, so happy. I thought..." Annie looked down into her coffee cup, then finally back up at her sister. "I thought she'd finally be content. Obviously he wasn't what he seemed."

A splatter of yoke hit the toaster. "That appears to be a problem with a lot of men. Know what I mean?"

Annie's voice turned dry. "I'm afraid I do."

She'd been married once—for five long years when she'd lived in Dallas and had been working at the Ritz. For five years, she'd thought things would work out, that

he'd change, become the man she'd wanted him to be, but
finally, feeling like an idiot, she'd awakened and realized
he wasn't ever going to be any different. Larry Suller
didn't have a warm bone in his body. What she had mis-
taken for quiet dignity was, in reality, cold disregard—for
anyone and everyone. His business was the only thing he
really cared about. They could be lying side by side in the
bed, and Annie would feel that he was somewhere else—
a place she didn't know about and to which he'd never
invite her. Those five years had been the loneliest five
years of her life.

And that was one of the reasons Bella meant so much
to Annie now. Annie wasn't like Maggie. She didn't give
her heart away easily, and the marriage to Larry had been
nothing but pure disaster. She'd never make that kind of
mistake again. Never marry. Never fall for a man who hid
himself from her. Never let herself be hurt again.

Never.

All her love would go to Bella.

Annie pushed open the heavy mahogany door and
stepped into the cool, wide hallway. The smell of potpourri
hung faintly in the air, and the gleaming oak-plank floor
shimmered in the sunlight passing through the fanlight
over the doorway. Everything was perfect, as usual, but
for once she didn't stop to admire the way Riverside
looked. All she could think about was the meeting she'd
just had with Loring Shaver.

The attorney had still heard nothing. Nothing at all.
He'd written Bella's father more than two weeks ago and
so far he'd heard nothing. Annie fought the bubble of
panic threatening to rise within her. What if the man hadn't
received the letter? What if he never answered? What if…

She stepped out of her black high heels and let them
fall to the side with a clunk. Peeling off her jacket, then

running her hands through her short brown hair, she tried to stifle the thoughts beginning to assail her. Panic would do nothing. She had to stay calm, stay focused. Before she could manage a concentrated effort to forge ahead, the front door swung open behind her. Annie turned around with a smile on her face.

Instead of Bella, though, a man stood in the opening, a ribbon of sunshine streaming in behind him. Stepping inside without hesitation, he firmly closed the door and came toward Annie. His steps were forceful and every movement he made gave the message that he was definitely in control. When he spoke, his voice was low and pleasant, but as commanding as the rest of him appeared to be. "Hello. We faxed you last week for reservations. I'm—"

"Mr. Kingsley!" Horrified that she'd actually forgotten about the man, Annie spoke quickly and stepped forward. How in the world could she have forgotten? William Kingsley had faxed Riverside and requested the largest suite she had—for an indefinite stay! With what she hoped was a dazzling smile, she held out her own hand. "Yes, of course. I'm Annie Burns, the owner of Riverside. Welcome to Timberley."

He took her hand and focused on her, his dark eyes soaking up every detail of her appearance with a startling intensity. From the top of her tousled hair to the bottom of her red-painted toenails, he inspected her. She felt like something under a microscope.

"My friends call me Gray," he said in the same low voice.

"What a lovely name," she said quickly, trying to cover up how flustered she was. "Then Gray it is." She tried not to stare, but it was impossible not to. He was a most intriguing man. Not movie-star handsome, not drop-dead gorgeous, but striking. Striking in the kind of way that kept you from making sense when you talked to him. "I...I have your suite ready," she finally managed to get out. "Do you have a better idea of how long you'll be staying?"

His gaze never left her face. "I'm not sure. It all depends…"

Maggie appeared at Annie's side. The man turned his eyes toward her, and some of the pressure went with them.

Annie introduced them.

"Depends on what?" Maggie asked in a friendly voice.

"My business," he said smoothly. "I'm an oil and gas consultant and I have clients here in Timberley. I've rented a small office in town and I'll be staying as long as they need me."

Annie held her breath—Maggie was prone to asking more questions than necessary when people checked in. Time and time again, Annie had told her the private lives of their guests were none of her business, but Maggie usually ignored Annie's warnings. This time she stayed silent, though, and Annie knew why. Something in those dark, probing eyes made it clear he was the kind of man who *asked* questions—not answered them.

He looked down at Annie. "That won't be a problem will it? If I turn into a long-term guest?"

She should be so lucky as to have problems like that, especially now with the legal bills adding up. "We'd be happy to have you as long as you like. Come to my office and we'll get you checked in." She began to walk back down the hall, the tall man following. "As you requested, I've put you in the largest suite. You have a private bath, a king-size bed, and a view out the back toward the river. I'm sure you'll like the room—it's the most comfortable one I have."

And it should be. It was her bedroom. She didn't make a habit of renting it out, but it was the only room she could give him. He'd specifically mentioned in his fax that he didn't know how long he'd be there. Her other suites were booked for the weekends from now until after Christmas. She'd be sleeping in her office for a while, but that was okay. She'd learned to be flexible running a bed-and-breakfast.

She sat down at her desk, opened the registration book, and pushed it toward him. "If you'll just fill this out…"

His hands moved easily over the form as he completed it, and Annie couldn't help but notice how well-shaped they were. Long, tapered fingers with spotless nails, masculine and strong-looking. Hands made for working, for creating, for protecting.

Before she could begin to imagine those hands doing something else, Annie pulled her eyes away and let her gaze go to the rest of him. A thin gold watch decorated one thick wrist, but there were no rings. Not even any thin white lines where former rings had rested. His dark double-breasted suit was as expensive as his watch—well-cut and elegant. Just like his black hair. A little on the long side, but razor-shaped and hanging as smoothly over his collar as only a fifty-dollar haircut could manage. And those eyes—my God, those eyes. They reminded Annie of a set of black opals she'd seen once at Tiffany's in Dallas. Incredible.

"Does the room have a phone, Miss Burns? Miss Burns?"

"Uh…yes. A…a private line." She smiled at him and wondered how big of an idiot he thought she was. She scribbled out the number and handed it to him. "Here's the number if you'd like to give it out. Shall I put your charges on your credit card?"

He took the number from her then removed a gold-embossed money clip from the pocket of his jacket. "I prefer to pay cash, but I'll pay for a month in advance."

He peeled off a handful of bills and gave them to her. "Will that do?"

Payment in advance? It would more than do. "Of course," she said as casually as she could, accepting the money and slipping it into her desk drawer.

He rose easily from the chair, his long legs unfolding. "I'll be installing my fax machine on your phone line, if that's all right with you."

"No problem." Wishing for the heels she'd discarded earlier, Annie stood as well and moved around the desk. She wasn't a short woman, but he made her feel that way. She looked up at him. "If you need anything else in that direction, just tell me. We don't have many business guests so I may not be in touch with exactly what you require."

"I'll let you know." Again the dark stare intensified. "You stay pretty busy here?"

"Yes. Most of our weekends are booked through the year, especially in the summer."

He looked around her paneled office. She'd furnished it with second-hand pieces from Duncan's on the Square, a local antique dealer. They weren't extravagant things, but she felt they blended well in the old house. She found herself wondering if the man in front of her agreed.

"It must be expensive. Setting up a place like this." He raised one dark eyebrow. "How long have you been in business?"

"About six years, give or take."

"You opened Riverside—all by yourself?"

Annie was accustomed to the questions of her guests— most of them were curious about the old house and the surrounding area. His questions were more than curious, though, they were probing. Just like his eyes. A tingle of uneasiness feathered over her. There were secrets in those dark depths. Secrets and emotions and passions that he worked hard to suppress. She instantly told herself she was being silly, but the impression refused to leave. Clearing her throat, she finally answered his question. "It was my dream for a long time to have a B&B. I'd worked for a large hotel chain in the past and it wasn't what I wanted."

As if sensing her growing disquiet, he nodded then smiled and started to move. "Well, I'm taking up too much of your time. If you'll just show me my room…"

"Of course." She turned and led him back into the hallway, but before they could head up the stairs, the front door flew open. Annie glanced over her shoulder, then stopped and smiled.

Bella bounded through the open doorway. She wore a short denim jumper and a smudge on one knee, and as always, her startling resemblance to Monica was the first thing Annie saw…especially today. Her hair, as wild and tangled as Monica's had been at that age, hung around her face like a red halo, and her eyes, green and huge, dominated her oval face.

"Hello, sweetheart," Annie called out. "Did you have fun down at Rose's?"

"It was great!" She ran into the hallway, the door slamming behind her. "They have a new puppy. He's black and white, and his name is Harry. He's s-o-o-o cute, Annie. Can we have a—"

Annie interrupted the flow of words. "You can tell me all about it later, sweetheart. Right now, why don't you say hello to Mr. Kingsley—um, Gray. He's our newest guest."

Bella nodded, then came closer to the stairs. The bright sunlight behind her set her hair on fire. "Hello."

She spoke politely, just as Annie had taught her. "Welcome to Riverside."

Smiling her approval, Annie turned to the still silent man beside her. "This is my daughter, Bella. She's five and…" Annie raised her eyes to his, then her smile began to fade and her words slowly died, shock replacing all her other emotions.

His face had drained completely of color, and he suddenly looked ill. Very ill.

Chapter 2

Alarmed, Annie stepped toward the man and spoke at the same time, her hand going to his arm. "Are...are you all right? Would you like to sit down?"

He seemed to shake himself mentally, and a second later, his face regained its color. Annie dropped her hand from his arm, suddenly feeling foolish and wondering if she'd imagined the whole thing—if her own stress was somehow catching up with her in a weird kind of way.

"I...I'm sorry," she sputtered, "I...I thought..."

He turned away from Bella and looked at Annie, his dark eyes sweeping over her. "You thought?"

She laughed lightly and put a hand to her head. "I think I'm losing my mind—that's what." She smiled down at Bella. "Why don't you go see if Aunt Maggie's finished those chocolate-chip cookies and I'll show our guest to his room?"

Bella was running down the hall before Annie even finished speaking. She turned to the man beside her once more. "Shall we go upstairs?"

His eyes never left her face and he didn't move for several seconds. Finally, he nodded and she led him up the stairs. She wondered for a long time later what had really happened.

"Is he married?" Maggie sprawled out on the couch in Annie's office. It was late. A bowl of popcorn sat in her lap, and her hand went from it to her mouth as the television murmured softly beside her, the talk show ignored.

Reaching over the clipboard she held in her own lap, Annie stretched toward the bowl and grabbed a handful of popcorn. "I didn't ask," she said, "And I'd appreciate it if you didn't, either."

"What makes you think I'd do that?"

"Oh, let me see...maybe because you tend to be nosy and personal with all our guests?"

"I haven't done that in a long time. I've been really good."

"This is true." Annie didn't look up from her papers. She was trying to study her monthly budget. "So keep it up."

The television rattled on for a few more moments, then Maggie spoke again. "Where's he from?"

"I have no idea."

"You didn't read his registration form?"

"No."

"Why not?"

Annie glared at Maggie and didn't explain how many times she'd thought about doing that very thing during the day. Instead, she gave her sister the same reason she'd given herself hours earlier. "I have better things to do than investigate our guests—like run a business. I'm bidding on the Chavez wedding, and I have to plan a luncheon menu for thirty next week—not to mention trying to balance my stupid books and worry about Bella's situation, too.''

''Where's the register?'' Maggie rose and went toward the desk. ''Center drawer, like always?''

Annie made a sound of disgust and reached for more popcorn, pointedly ignoring her sister's actions. A second later, she heard the pages of the register flipping, a tantalizing sound.

''Hmmm.'' Maggie's hum filled the office. ''Now *that's* interesting.''

Annie stayed quiet.

''Wow. I wouldn't have thought *that!*''

Annie was a statue.

''Now, I would *never* have—''

Annie jumped up. ''Oh, give me that!'' Pulling the book toward her, she ignored Maggie's victorious laughter.

There was an address in Oak Cliff and nothing more.

No phone number, no next of kin, no nothing.

Maggie grinned. ''Gotcha.''

Annie snarled once, then flopped back down on the couch.

Maggie propped her chin up on her hand. ''You *are* interested, aren't you?''

''No.''

''Oh, come on. There were sparks shooting off the two of you when I walked into that hall.''

Horrified, Annie stared at her sister. ''Are you crazy?''

''He's a good-looking man—and those are heavy-duty eyes, that's for sure.''

''You noticed too?''

''I'm divorced, Annie, not dead.'' She leaned back in the chair and grinned. ''I say go for it.''

''Get real…I've got enough on my mind right now. A man is the last thing—the *very* last thing—I'm interested in.'' Shaking her head, Annie stood up from the couch and met her sister's stare. "Now why don't you get out of here so I can go to sleep?"

Annie measured carefully, pouring the fine white flour from the bowl into the cup for the second time. With her mind on everything but the cake she was making, she'd had to throw out the first batch of batter. The way she was going, she'd have five wedding cakes for Mrs. Chavez to taste, but none of them would be edible.

Loring had called Annie this morning and told her he'd finally received notification that their registered letter had been delivered. Someone at Powerplay Engineering—the company Bella's father supposedly owned—had signed for it. They might be getting somewhere now.

But the waiting—it was so nerve-racking!

Maggie entered the kitchen with a load of towels and headed for the nearby laundry room. "Aren't you finished with that cake yet?"

"I'm fine-tuning the recipe." Annie rubbed her cheek against her shoulder then blew at her bangs. It hadn't gotten any cooler, and the kitchen was steaming.

Maggie reappeared. "Well, if all else fails, you can always serve some of Mrs. Dawson's cookies."

Annie tilted her head toward the plate on the table. "Have you tried one?"

"And break a tooth? I don't think so." Maggie picked up one of the oatmeal cookies and sniffed it suspiciously. "I don't understand why you keep buying her stuff. You're throwing away money."

"What I am supposed to do? Tell the poor woman no one can eat her cookies because they're hard as rocks?"

"That would be a start."

"Oh, Maggie, get real. I couldn't possibly do that and you know it. Selling those cookies is the only reason Martha Dawson is still around and kicking at eighty."

"I thought she was ninety-five if she was a day." Maggie tapped the cookie against the table. It made a hollow sound.

"Well, it doesn't matter how old she is, and it doesn't matter that no one can eat them. She thinks we're leaving them on everyone's pillows at night and it gives her a great deal of pleasure. For the little bit it costs me, I'm not going to break her heart and tell her the truth. Besides, I've got other things to think about."

Maggie looked at Annie sympathetically. "What'd Loring say?"

Annie explained it all, then finished up by complaining, her frustration too big to contain. "If he's gotten the letter, the least he could do is call us. I guess Monica was right, though. He obviously doesn't care about anything. The man's a real bast—"

"Excuse me?"

Annie and Maggie turned together. Gray stood on the threshold of the kitchen looking totally out of place in a well-tailored pin-striped suit. Annie blinked and wondered how much of their conversation he'd heard.

"I need another light bulb." He held one up. "This one seems dead."

Maggie shot forward. "No problem—I'll go get it." Smiling widely, she took the bulb from him then went out the door...where she stopped and pointed her finger at Annie, then at the coffeepot.

Annie glanced over at the man who seemed to fill the kitchen with his presence. "Would you like a cup of coffee?"

"That'd be great. Thanks."

She dusted her hands on her apron and moved toward the coffeemaker on the opposite counter. The only time she'd seen him during the past week was at breakfast, and with a start, she realized how unusual that was. Most of the time she sought out her guests, talked to them, made sure they were enjoying themselves. As she poured his coffee, she wondered if this avoidance was an offshoot of her preoccupation with Bella, or a deliberate attempt on her part to keep out of his way. Something told her it was the latter—this man made her uneasy, very uneasy.

And she knew why, of course. He was way too attractive, and she tried to avoid men who drew her to them as much as this one did. Once again, though, the impression swept over her that there was something more to him than just what she saw. Something he was hiding. Feeling ridiculous, she argued with herself. She didn't even know the man, for God's sake...why would he be concealing something from her?

Trying to ignore her feelings, Annie turned and handed him the cup with a smile. "How's the room? Everything okay?"

"Everything's perfect." He stared at her over the rim of the mug, his lips full and generous where they met the porcelain edge. Coming through the nearby window, sunlight hit the square line of his jaw and put black sparks in his hair. Everything about him gave off an aura of power and control. Annie wondered if he was aware of this effect—if he practiced it—or if it was simply an innate part of him.

He sipped his coffee and acted as if he noticed nothing unusual about her inability to breathe. "I usually have a hard time away from home," he said. "The beds aren't long enough, but yours fits me perfectly."

She fought the image his words conjured and tried to regain her composure. "I...I'm glad you're comfortable. That's our goal."

He nodded and the silence grew for a moment before he broke it again. "How's your daughter? I haven't seen her around too much."

"She's fine...and thanks for asking. Actually, I usually try to keep her out of everyone's way."

"Why is that?"

"She can be pretty rambunctious. Not everyone enjoys that when they're on vacation."

"She didn't seem that way to me when we met. I thought she was exceedingly polite."

"Well, thank you." Despite her mixed feelings about Gray Kingsley, his unexpected compliment felt good. Annie smiled, then felt her expression slip. "I...I hope I've done a good job with her, but..."

"But what?"

She rolled her hands into the kitchen towel that was tucked in the waistband of her jeans. "I don't have much experience in the child-raising department, and I'm always afraid I'm going to goof it up somehow." .

"She's your only one?"

Annie thought of keeping it simple, of simply saying yes, but something made her say more. "She's not really my daughter...I mean...well, I'm not her birth mother."

He nodded thoughtfully. "She's adopted?"

"Not exactly."

He waited.

"It's kind of complicated," Annie said.

His dark eyes studied her for a moment. "I'm not in a hurry."

Annie could see he was genuinely interested. "Well, her real mother—her birth mother—was my best friend. She passed away while giving birth to Bella, and I've raised her ever since."

A shadow passed over his face. It darkened his eyes even more and gave the secrets hiding in their depths more credence. "I'm sorry your friend died. That must have been...rough."

"It was terrible," Annie said simply. "Even though it's

been more than five years, I still miss her like crazy. We hadn't been able to spend a lot of time together prior to her death, but it didn't matter. We were best friends. Had been since first grade, even.'' She smiled. ''But I have Bella and I'm about to adopt her—formally, that is.''

He seemed to hesitate for a fraction of a second. ''There's no father?''

''There's a father....'' Annie heard the bitterness creep into her voice. She hated the sound. ''But he's—''

At that moment, Maggie bounded back into the kitchen. ''Here you are,'' she said with a smile, handing him the light bulb. ''Is there anything else you need?''

He shook his head and said thanks, then turned once more to Annie. ''I hope things work out.''

With his words, Annie realized she'd broken one of her cardinal rules. Never burden the guests. People didn't come to Riverside for that, and she'd made it a policy a long time ago not to let her personal life overflow into her business life. Now she couldn't believe she'd told this man everything that she had. She mentally shook herself and murmured her thanks, suddenly embarrassed. A second later he was gone.

''So, did he ask you out?''

''Are you nuts?'' Annie turned to Maggie and frowned. ''Why would he ask me out?''

''You're cute, smart, nice...shall I go on?''

''What is it with you? Why have you suddenly decided I need to be fixed up?''

''Well, for one thing, he's good-looking as heck, and for another, how many men like him do you meet? Are you going to stay single forever?''

''I might.''

Maggie just shook her head. ''You'd better think again, sister. You're getting a daughter. She's going to need a father.''

Annie stared at Maggie, her mouth dropping open. "A father? That's the craziest thing I've ever heard you say. I can raise that child by myself. What on earth makes you think—you, of all people—that I need a man to help me do that?"

"Maybe because I *am* who I am." Her voice turned serious. "Haven't you ever wondered why both of us married the wrong kind of man? We didn't have a father around us. Grandmama did a great job raising us, but we only had women around. Bella's in the very same situation that we were in…and frankly, I'm not sure it's such a good idea."

"Her situation isn't at all like ours was. How can you say that?"

"Oh, Annie, think about it…when Mom and Dad both died, where did we go? To Grandmother's. And who lived there? Grandmother—Gramps was already gone. Now here we all are again—you, me, Bella…. There isn't a man around for miles." Maggie's eyes filled with something unusual for her—earnestness. "I think you need to think about it, Annie. Don't set up Bella to make the same mistakes we did."

The storm had been building all day. By late that night, dark clouds hovered over the horizon and an eery stillness lay over the river. Annie was a bundle of nervous energy and useless anxiety. After putting Bella to bed, she went down to her office and dropped onto the couch, the phone clutched in her hand.

Loring answered on the second ring and listened patiently as she told him how she felt. Finally he broke in. "You have to give it some time, Annie. We just got the notification back. The man could be out of the country. Maybe his secretary signed for him."

"How long do we have to wait?"

"As long as it takes—unless you want to spend more money."

"That's not an option." She twisted the phone cord and stared out at the black sky. "I don't have it to spend. I'm saving everything I can right now to pay for the adoption itself."

"Then let it ride a little longer. Maybe he's thinking about it. If we have to serve him to get him to agree, then we'll have to serve him, but let's try the low-budget way first. Give it some more time."

"There's nothing else we can do?"

"Not right this minute. Be patient."

Annie's anxiety rose another notch as she hung up the phone and stared out the window. She didn't want to give it more time. Every day the situation remained as it was, her nervousness inexplicably increased. She felt a disaster hovering, like the storm outside. She could practically *taste* it. The waiting had another effect as well. It gave her too much time to remember Monica's warnings...and the promise Annie had made, the one she was now breaking.

A huge crack of lightning broke across the western part of the sky and, as if on cue, the rain began. It wasn't a subtle, late-summer soaking, either. With a military-like precision, the drops battered the French doors leading out to the garden. It sounded like gunfire.

A moment later, the lights flickered once, then twice, and an instant after that, everything went off. The silence was deep and complete as the old house shuddered into quiet darkness.

Annie sat still for a second, then she rose wearily from the couch and felt her way to the door. She'd have to go into the kitchen and try the breakers. If that didn't work, poor Mr. Planter would have to come out again. He was already doing her repairs for next to nothing. If this situation required his electrical skills, he was going to have to wait for even that.

She stumbled down the hall and made it into the kitchen. The flashlight she kept in the drawer by the door was dead, but she had candles sitting around everywhere. This wasn't an unusual occurrence. She lit the two candles waiting on the table, then made her way to the corner of the kitchen and the breaker box against the wall. Opening the door, she stared at the black panel and waited for a flash of light to augment the candles and what little moonlight the clouds were allowing through.

She realized later that the sound of the rain, pounding harder than ever on the roof, must have muffled his approach. At the time, it seemed as if he simply materialized beside her.

"May I help?"

Annie jumped and let out a small scream before she realized who stood beside her. For a moment, all she could do was shake her head. Seconds passed before she regained her voice. "Gray! I...you...you scared me," she finally managed to get out.

"I'm sorry."

He'd obviously been in the shower. His hair was wet and finger-combed back from his face. He wore a shirt, but it was completely unbuttoned. Jeans hung low on his slim hips. He stood so close she got a whiff of the special English soap she put in all the rooms.

"I thought I'd check your breakers when the lights went out. I didn't mean to frighten you."

"How'd you know where they were?"

"I noticed the panel the other day."

"That's very observant of you."

"I'm an observant kind of person."

She felt his stare in the dark. If he'd been blind and

running his fingers over her face, she couldn't have experienced the sensation more.

It was strangely erotic.

"May I look?" His words broke the impression and, nodding silently, she stepped out of the way. His hand went up to the panel then stopped just short of touching it. "The breakers look okay, but they feel a little warm. Let's give them a minute, then I'll flip them one by one. That might do the trick."

The rain had subsided into a steady downpour. Annie moved away from him and felt her way to one of the kitchen chairs. She sat down weakly and cursed herself for being so aware of him. He took the chair beside her, closer than she would have liked, and then the silence between them grew. It wasn't a comfortable, easy silence, either. It seemed thick to Annie, thick with sensations she neither wanted nor understood. Thick with secrets. Thick with tension.

Before she could think about it more, she half rose from her chair. "I should check on Bella—"

"She's fine. I heard her snoring when I passed by her end of the hall."

Annie sank back down. "For a little kid, she can really saw some logs. I hope it's not bothering you."

"I went to boarding school, Miss Burns. I sleep better when I hear snoring."

She nodded once. "Please...call me Annie."

"All right, then...Annie."

Inside the room, silence returned, while outside, rain continued to hammer the roof. And still she could feel his stare.

"Would you like something to drink? There's milk in the fridge, or I have some brandy."

"I'm fine, thank you."

More silence.

"How's your work going?"

"Very well."

Even deeper silence.

"You don't have to sit here, you know," she finally blurted out. "I can handle this. I have problems with the house all the time and I handle them just fine. It's part of being the owner, and I can do things now I never used to know how to do." She knew she was babbling, told herself to shut up, but she couldn't seem to stop. She had too much going on, too much of everything and the conversation with Loring had served to bring it all to the front. Now this. "I can repair the water pump and caulk the windows and just last week, I learned how to clean out the septic tank. I—"

"I've been wondering ever since we talked the other day about the child's father."

Surprised by his words—and his observation—Annie blinked, her hand going to her throat. Before she could say anything, he continued.

"You seem to have a pretty low opinion of him. I couldn't help but wonder why."

"I have the same opinion of him that anyone would." She paused, remembering. "My friend told him she was pregnant, but he still refused to acknowledge his obligations. I don't think that's right."

The only sound in the room was the pounding of the rain. Finally he spoke again. "How do you know that's what happened?"

"My friend told me."

"But he's out of the picture now, isn't he? Does it even matter any more?"

"He isn't out of the picture...not at all. I need his permission to adopt Bella, and frankly, I'm very worried." Annie looked at him through the flickering light of the candles. "Bella's been my daughter for five years. I've raised her all alone and I promised her mother I'd keep it that way."

The silence turned deep again, and for a few minutes they sat there, Annie lost in thought, the man beside her forgotten. She was more than worried—she was petrified—and until now she hadn't even let herself fully think about what it would mean if Bella's father refused her request. She'd been afraid to think about it.

He spoke unexpectedly, his voice deceptively soft. "A child needs a father."

Annie answered automatically. "Not the one she has."

"Are you sure?"

"Absolutely. Bella's mother was very adamant. She said her ex-husband was a very controlling man who was heartless and cold. He didn't care that she was pregnant and he basically refused to acknowledge the fact." Annie held out her hands. "What kind of child needs a father like that?"

"Is that a philosophical question or a real one?"

"It doesn't matter, does it? There's only one answer."

"There's always more than one answer," he said quietly. "If you look hard enough."

Annie shook her head, a thread of irritation going through her. "Not in this case. He wanted nothing to do with her. If you ask me, that means he forfeited his right to be concerned now."

"They were married at the time?"

"Yes, but they divorced shortly afterward."

"Maybe he didn't believe her. Maybe he didn't think it was his child. Maybe she'd lied to him before."

Annie's back stiffened at his presumptuousness. "You're talking about a friend of mine. I don't think you understand the situation."

"Perhaps not...but I stand by my statement. A child needs a father. All children do."

There was something in his voice, a catch, a deepening,

that made her stop for a moment. Was this part of the shadow she saw in his eyes, the secrets he held so close to his chest? "Do you have children?" she asked without thinking.

His face took on the now familiar stony look, and his answer was quick. "No."

It must be something else, then, she surmised. Had he lost his own father when he was young? Had he experienced that gut-wrenching pain that shoots through you like a bullet when someone comes up and says "There's been an accident...." She wondered, then firmly pushed aside the memories. "I'm perfectly capable of raising this child by myself. It's what her mother wanted, and it's definitely what I want. If you understood the situation..."

Before she could finish speaking, the house sprang back to life, the lights coming on, the refrigerator humming. Annie was instantly aware that she had on nothing but her robe and smeared makeup. He hardly seemed to notice.

"I *do* understand," he said, his voice tense and tight. "Better than you can imagine." He rose slowly, towering over her and the table, his presence made even stronger by the width of his chest and the energy that seemed to hover around him like the electricity still popping outside. "Children need a father, their *real* father, and people who think otherwise are fooling themselves."

Chapter 3

"I'd like to have the actual ceremony in the garden. It will be cooler by then, and I think it would make for a lovely setting. We could put up a large tent under the big pecan tree and with the river in the background, it'd be perfect." Annie turned to the woman at her side, just in time to see her swipe the corner of her eye with a lace handkerchief. "Mrs. Chavez? Are you okay?"

"Yes, yes," the woman answered. "I...I think that'd be perfect. It's just that Yolanda's our only child, and I can't believe she's actually getting married. I...I'll be all right, just give me a second."

"Of course," Annie murmured. To give the woman privacy, she looked away and down toward the bottom of the yard where Bella was playing along the low stone wall that separated the grassy area from the river beyond. She was singing and running a stick against the stones. Beau, Maggie's golden retriever, was walking with her, his sturdy body on the other side of the wall, between her and the water, almost as if he were guiding her away from any potential harm. The water wasn't a foot deep in the river at that point and Bella knew she was not supposed to pass the wall even though she could swim perfectly fine, but Annie understood the dog's concern. She felt the same way about Bella, just as Mrs. Chavez felt about Yolanda. Protective. Concerned. Loving. It didn't matter who—or even *what*—you were. When you loved someone, you loved them.

He might be the most compelling man she'd ever met, but her latest guest didn't know what he was talking about. The only thing children really needed was love. Where it came from wasn't important.

Annie turned back to the woman beside her. "Okay now?"

Mrs. Chavez nodded once then followed Annie as they walked farther away from the terrace. "We can have the reception out here—on the lawn—or if you prefer, we can set up tables in the living room and open all the French doors. Then people can wander in and out as they like after they prepare their plates."

Mrs. Chavez nodded, her black hair gleaming in the hot sunshine. "I can see it exactly." Her voice became more excited as she got into the spirit of things. She began to describe Yolanda's dress in great detail. It would look even more stunning out in the open, she said, the hand-sewn pearls more obvious.

Nodding in agreement, Annie continued to listen until the sudden crunch of tires pulled her eyes away from her client and toward the house. Gray's large black Mercedes was pulling into the circle out front. Deliberately, she turned around so her back would be to the house. Bella was bad enough—Annie didn't need him as a distraction, too. But as if she'd called it up, of course, an image shot into her mind. An image of him wearing an open shirt, with wet hair and a hard pulse at the base of his neck. It was an image that had haunted her last few days as much as his unwanted words.

"If you think that would be all right?"

Annie realized too late Mrs. Chavez was asking her a question. She smiled down at the short, plump woman. "I...I'm sorry, would you mind repeating that? My mind was jumping ahead to...to the color scheme, and I wasn't listening."

The woman began to speak again, something about salmon mousse and the heat, and then Gray rounded the corner of the house. He paused at the edge of the terrace and looked toward the river at the base of the yard, shading his face with his hand. Sometime in the last few days, he'd changed his wardrobe. The thousand-dollar suits had disappeared, and now he wore what the local men favored— jeans and an open-neck shirt. Somehow they looked a lot different on Gray than they did on Eddie, the guy who lived across the street.

"But I'm not sure. Do you think it'd be all right?"

This time Annie was trapped. "Uh, well, if you think so." She smiled again. "You're the boss."

"Well, I'm not sure yet. Yolanda thinks it might be too much, you know. She doesn't want people talking."

"I understand." Crossing her arms, Annie tried to listen. From the corner of her eye, she watched Gray traverse the yard. "We wouldn't want that, no, no."

Mrs. Chavez looked properly concerned. "Do *you* think it's too much?"

"Well..." Annie drew out the word as long as she could. Gray had reached the lower part of the yard and Beau had spotted him, just as Bella had. Jumping the wall, the dog headed straight toward the man, a goofy canine grin on his face. *Traitor,* she thought illogically. She looked back at Mrs. Chavez. "Anything done in moderation isn't ostentatious, do you think?"

The little woman nodded her head vigorously, her double chins moving up and down. "Exactly," she cried. "That's exactly what I told Yolanda. Why don't you work that into the bid? Then we'll decide, depending on the cost."

Great. She had absolutely no idea what the woman was talking about, and now she was going to have to bid on it.

Annie lifted her eyes just in time to see Bella run up to Gray. He bent down to be on her level, then together they threw a stick toward the river. Sailing over the wall, just as the piece of wood had done seconds before, Beau was instantly after the treasure, splashing into the current and grinning even bigger than before as he retrieved it and headed back up the yard. Gray laughed and Bella joined him, his deep tone mixing beautifully with her high, childish voice. Their heads went together again and Annie could see them talking. She would have given her right arm to know what the subject was.

"Well…if that's all…" Mrs. Chavez looked up at Annie questioningly.

Annie tried to refocus. "I think that's it. Unless, of course, you have any more questions about anything?" *Or you'd like to repeat one or two you already asked…just in case I wasn't listening.*

"No. Mail me the bid and Johnny and I will talk it over. We'll let you know as soon as possible."

The minute Mrs. Chavez's car disappeared, Annie started toward the bottom of the yard, her curiosity killing her. Before she could get off the terrace, Bella bounded up, Beau wet and messy romping along beside her. "I'm going fishing, I'm going fishing."

"Whoa there," Annie said, grabbing the little girl as

she tried to run past. "Just what do you think you're doing?"

"I'm going fishing," she cried. "I asked Gray to go
with me and he said yes." She started singing again. "I'm
going fishing, I'm going fishing...."

Not bothering to hide her surprise, Annie sent her gaze
over Bella's head to the tall man standing behind her. Despite his words from the other night, Gray hadn't struck
her as the kind of man who felt comfortable around children. Once again, though, she had the distinct feeling there
was a lot about him she didn't know, a fact that intrigued
her, yet made her nervous at the very same time. She put
the thoughts aside and turned to Bella. "You know you're
not supposed to bother our guests, sweetheart," Annie began gently. "How many times have I—"

"It's not a problem," Gray interrupted. "Really." He
smiled down at Annie, one side of his mouth going up a
little more than the other. Quite attractively, she noticed.
"If I hadn't wanted to go, I would have declined."

"It *is* okay, isn't it, Annie?" Bella hopped from one
foot to the other. "We can go, can't we?"

Suddenly glad she didn't have to make the decision,
Annie pulled her eyes away from Gray and looked down
at Bella. "But have you forgotten already? Today's your
haircut day, remember?"

They'd been planning the event for weeks, Bella alter-
nating between let's-go-right-now and I'm-not-so-sure.
Her face fell, then she raised her hand to the end of her
long red hair. "Oh, no... I..."

Gray made it easy. He kneeled down and looked at her.
"Hey, I'd hate to stand in the way of a lady and her
beauty-shop appointment." He paused, looked thoughtful,
then spoke again. "You go on to the beauty shop with
your...mom."

Bella didn't notice the hesitation, but Annie did.

"Can I take you another day?" Bella said.

"If your mom says okay."

"Okay, then we'll do it later." Totally confident of getting her way, Bella turned and looked at Annie, grabbing her hand and pulling. "Let's go to the beautiful shop. Let's go…let's go."

Laughing, Annie tugged her hand away. "You go get my purse and wait for me in the car. I'll be right there."

Gray met her eyes when she turned toward him. They were as unsettling in the bright daylight as they had been in the candlelight a few nights before. "I'm sorry she bothered you," Annie started. "I've tried to keep her from doing things like that but she's just naturally friendly. Please don't feel obligated…."

"It's okay. I didn't mind."

"Well, you will if she keeps insisting…and she may. She definitely wants things *her* way." Annie shook her head. "I have no idea where that comes from. Her mother wasn't like that…not at all."

His face registered nothing. All he did was nod.

"Well…" Annie hit her notebook against her leg. "I…I guess we'd better be off then…to the beautiful shop." She gave him a smile, then started up the lawn. She was three steps away when he called her name. She turned and looked back at him, but the sun had dipped behind him, and she could see nothing now of his face, but shadows.

"About the other night…"

She stiffened. "Yes?"

"I just wanted to let you know—I'm sorry I butted in. I was way out of bounds, and I should have kept my feelings to myself."

She realized immediately what he was doing. It was an apology but for what he'd *said*, not for how he felt. She told herself that at least he was making the effort—a lot of men wouldn't even back down that much. The tightness in her shoulders eased.

"I...I shouldn't have burdened you with all of it anyway," she said. And she shouldn't have. For hours after their conversation, Annie had berated herself for doing the same thing she'd fussed at Maggie for—telling the guests personal details. She still couldn't believe she'd done it...and she still had no idea why she had.

She saw the outline of his head as he dipped it in acknowledgement. "She loves you very much."

"And I love her...but it's an easy thing to do. She's a beautiful child. Anyone could love Bella."

"Even her father?"

Before Annie could answer, Bella called out. "Annie! Annie! Are you coming or what?"

Annie turned and waved. "Just a minute." Then she looked once more at the man in front of her. He'd stepped closer to her, halved the distance between them. Now she could see his face. It wore a look of persistence.

"You said anyone could love her. Do you think her father would love her if he knew about her?"

In the distance a turtledove sounded, his soft, plaintive cry carrying across the river. Overhead, a light breeze ruffled a nearby oak tree, sending a shower of leaves down on them.

Something tugged at Annie, told her not to get involved, not to continue, but it was too late. She looked into his dark eyes and spoke. "I suppose he'd have to want to, wouldn't he? Isn't that how love works?"

Gray stepped even closer. The shadows in his eyes were troubled and even darker than usual, the secretive cast in their depths more obvious than ever before. "In my experience—no." He paused and looked out over the river, then brought his gaze back to her face. He wore an enigmatic expression and anxious uneasiness rippled over her

when she took it in. "You can't control love. It's like a
bad houseguest. It comes when you least expect it and
stays when you want it to leave."

"I've got good news and bad. Which do you want
first?"

Annie lifted her head and stared at Maggie through
bleary eyes. She hadn't slept well all week, and the more
time that passed since Loring had received notification
about the letter, the worse it got. When Annie finally did
sleep, her dreams were full of disturbing, recurring images—someone calling out for help, heart-wrenching cries,
a man with a concealed face who wouldn't talk to her.
And when she wasn't facing *those* monsters, her dreams
had been full of someone else—Gray. She couldn't believe
it. The man was a perfect stranger, and she was having
dreams about him she'd be embarrassed to reveal in the
confessional. What was wrong with her?

"Give me the bad news first," she said.

"Mari just called. Her mother's sick again and she can't
come in."

Annie groaned and dropped her head into her hands.
"That's the fourth time this month. I can't run a business,
be a caterer *and* clean all the rooms, too."

"Well, you won't mind as much after I tell you the good
news. Mrs. Chavez phoned right afterwards. She loved everything you showed her the other day—including the
cake—and she wants to book Riverside for Yolanda's
wedding. 'With all the extras,' I believe were her exact
words."

Annie released the breath she'd unconsciously been
holding and sat back in her desk chair, relief flooding her
at the news. "Oh, thank God! That wedding's going to be
the biggest thing to happen in Timberley for years. I'll be

able to handle a good part of Loring's bills with it, and we should get tons of referrals.''

"It's already brought one. A Mrs. Meyers called right after Mrs. Chavez hung up. Said she was a friend of the Chavez family and she wants to have a shower here for Yolanda. Some time next month.''

Annie grinned. ''Well, with news like that, I suddenly don't even mind scrubbing toilets.''

And she didn't, she realized a few minutes later as she lugged the cleaning supplies and fresh linens up the stairs.

But none of the jobs associated with the big old house bothered her. She loved dusting the antiques and making the mirrors gleam. Getting up early to start breakfast was never difficult, and she actually looked forward to the summer rush. Owning Riverside had been a dream for so long that the realities of hard work didn't matter, especially now. She'd been scared to branch out into social events, but she'd had to do something to earn some extra money. Loring certainly wasn't cheap.

Tapping on the door of the first suite she came to, Annie waited a few minutes, then unlocked it and went in. Most of her guests were neat and considerate people who seemed to realize they were staying in a private home. It didn't take twenty minutes to clean and straighten the room. In short order she did two more suites, then right before noon, she came to the last door in the hallway. Her bedroom. Gray's room.

She hesitated, then knocked firmly. Only silence greeted her. She knocked once more, then opened the door and called out. ''Hello? Anyone home?''

The room looked untouched. Everything was in its proper spot and the furniture gleamed. Not only was the bed made, but the curtains were pulled back from the windows and tied perfectly. The only signs of habitation were a pair of men's loafers peeking out from under the bed and a book about the stock market lying facedown on the handmade quilt.

Somehow she wasn't surprised.

With the feeling she was trespassing, she walked into her own room and set down her bucket of cleaning supplies. He'd hooked up his fax machine to her phone and a folder of papers rested beside it. She resisted the powerful urge to go over and look at them in the hopes of understanding the secrets she knew he hid. Maybe his business wasn't doing so well... Maybe he'd come to Timberley to drum up *more* business... Maybe... She cut the speculation off in midstream. This was *his* room, *his* privacy was at stake. She might be experiencing some weird obsession with the guy, but that didn't give her the right to snoop. To resist further temptation, she grabbed her bucket and headed for the bathroom.

Things were pretty much the same in the spacious bath. Neat. Orderly. Spotless. She picked up a bottle of his aftershave and sniffed the top. A flip of something happened low inside her stomach as the fragrance reached her brain. She set the bottle down—quickly—and let her eyes examine the rest of the room. Except for a row of his toilet articles along the edge of the countertop, there were no personal clues about who he was. No photos, no letters, no quirky bathrobes stolen from ritzy hotels. Vaguely disappointed, she picked up the towels he'd already used and refolded, then turned to grab her bottle of spray cleaner. Before she could discharge the first squirt of cleanser, the phone sounded.

She waited for the fax machine to start, but nothing happened. It was obviously a call and not a fax. She debated for only a moment, then turned and walked briskly into the room. Picking up the receiver, she spoke. "This is Riverside. May I help you?"

There was a slight pause, then a woman's voice spoke,

her tone almost desperate. "I...I'm trying to find Grayston Powers. Is he there by any chance?"

Annie frowned. "Grayston Powers? We don't have anyone registered by that name."

There was silence, then, "Oh, my God...I...I mean Gray, um, Mr. Kingsley."

Annie spoke slowly, the woman's obvious mistake over Gray's name confusing, her attitude disconcerting. "Mr. Kingsley isn't here. Would you like to leave him a message?"

"Just tell him to call his company in Dallas, Powerplay Engineering. Please."

"I'll see that he gets the message. But tell me—" Before Annie could say more, the woman hung up.

Slowly, Annie replaced the receiver, a sense of unease coming over her. Something was wrong. The woman on the other end of the phone had been too nervous, too...weird. Why had she called for Grayston *Powers?* Gray's last name was Kingsley...wasn't it? Pondering the confusing call, Annie let the back of her mind go to something else the caller had said that sounded strange. Powerplay Engineering. *Powerplay Engineering.* Why did that name sound so familiar? Annie printed the name, forming the letters slowly and saying them as she wrote.

"Powerplay Engineering."

She was halfway to the bathroom when it hit her. She gasped and groped for the chair beside the nearby desk.

Powerplay Engineering!

She stared at the note still clutched in her hand, her heart racing against itself, beating inside her chest with a rhythm of panic and overwhelming confusion. Feeling as though all the air had been sucked from the room, she struggled with the effort to breathe, to make sense of it, but she couldn't. All she could do was remember Monica's warning. *You can't trust him, Annie. You just can't trust him.*

* * *

"Are you sure?" As if she didn't believe her, Maggie stared at the note Annie had ripped off the pad upstairs. "Maybe it's a mistake, maybe—"

"Maybe nothing!" Annie thrust her right arm into her jacket and struggled to pull it on. "He had a folder of papers sitting beside the machine. I looked at them. He owns Powerplay Engineering! In Dallas! What are the chances there are *two* companies called Powerplay Engineering in Dallas?"

Maggie looked confused, her hazel eyes taking on a brown cast. "But Annie, wasn't Monica's husband named C.G. something or other? I distinctly remember her saying it once because I commented on it and she fussed at me."

"It *was* C.G.—C.G. *Powers.* That's the name on the letter Loring sent out. Obviously our guest made up some kind of name using parts of his real name. Gray— Grayston. Powers to Kingsley. Who knows! He's a rat! I can't believe this!"

"Maybe you should call Loring—"

"I just talked to his secretary. He's not there." Annie managed to get the rest of her jacket pulled on, then she grabbed for her purse and headed for the front door, Maggie right at her heels.

"Where are you going?"

Annie never broke stride. "To the bastard's office, where else?"

"Oh, Annie, I don't know if that's a good idea. Don't you think Loring should handle—"

"No!" she cried. Her fingers tightened around the doorknob, then she yanked the door open, bright sunlight flooding the hallway and blinding her for a second. "I'm going to handle this." Anger rolled over her in waves. Burning, raging anger.

She welcomed the feeling. Because the alternative was terror.

*   *   *

The one red light in town was green, and it didn't take Annie five minutes to find the office of Gray Kingsley— or whatever in the hell his name was. She roared into the parking lot of the small strip center, killed the engine of her Jeep, then jumped out.

A second later, Annie yanked open the door and stormed through the reception area of the two-room office. In the rear office she could see the corner of a desk and a pair of long, stretched-out legs resting behind it. She headed straight for the back, then stopped dead in front of the desk and slammed her open palms down on the wooden top. "Just what in the hell do you think you're doing?"

His dark eyes regarded her with an eerie calmness. Slowly he acknowledged her with a tilt of his head. "Annie." He turned to the startled man sitting across from him in a wooden chair. "Mr. Stanley—do you know Annie Burns?"

Speechless, the older man did nothing but nod his head, his own eyes wide with obvious surprise at Annie's sudden appearance. "Ye-yes, I do. How...how are you, Annie?"

She threw a curt glance toward the longtime Timberley resident, a wealthy oil man. "I'm just fine, Stan." She'd known him since she was five years old. Her grandmother had been a big friend of his. "I think you'd better leave, though. Mr. *Kingsley* has some business with me he needs to take care of. Right now."

"Of...of course." The older man jumped up, grabbed his Stetson from the hat rack and nodded once in Gray's direction. "I...I'll call you later, Gray."

Gray's eyes never left Annie's face. "Absolutely, Mr. Stanley. I'll be waiting to hear from you."

The door swung shut a second later, and the only sound in the tiny room was Annie's hard breathing.

"You'd better have a damn good reason for coming in here and being rude to a potential client of mine," he said, his voice tight with the obvious effort of keeping himself in check.

"I have better reasons for *my* actions than you have for yours. You've been lying to me, and I want to know why."

Terrified, but more angry than she'd ever been in her life, she drew a deep breath and ignored both her shaking knees and the pull of his bottomless black eyes—those eyes whose secrets she now understood.

"Start talking, *Mr. Kingsley*. I want to know just when in the hell you planned on telling me who you really are."

Chapter 4

His face could have been carved in granite. Not a muscle twitched, not a line moved. "How did you find out?"

"Your office called while I was cleaning your room. I recognized the name of the firm." She paused, her heart ticking madly against her chest. "The woman who called—she asked for Grayston Powers. Who...what..." She couldn't even finish her sentence.

"My full name is Clarence Grayston Powers," he said quietly.

"Clarence Grayston..." An enormous lump formed in her throat. She spoke around it. "C.G."

"That's right." He paused for a moment, then his voice dropped another notch. "C.G. Powers."

"And William Kingsley is..."

"My assistant," he finished for her. "I had him call and make the reservations for me."

In the back of her mind, Annie had almost been hoping she'd been wrong, been confused somehow, but watching him now as he told her the truth, the reality of everything sank in. This man was Monica's ex-husband, for God's sake! And Annie had actually been attracted to him! Her fingers gripped the edge of the desk. All she could think of to say was "Wh-what should I call you?"

"Gray will do," he answered wearily.

She stared at him without saying a word, then her knees gave way. She sank into the chair behind her. "Why? Why didn't you tell me who you are?"

He stood up slowly and went to the window on the other side of the room. For a few long seconds, he stared out into the parking lot, then he turned and faced her squarely. "I had to see what kind of person you are. I wanted to check out the situation before you knew who I was."

"To check out the situation?" Annie's voice quivered, low and angry, as her shock slowly faded and her anger returned. "I guess I should have expected something like this from you. Monica told me not to trust you, but I just didn't listen, did I?"

He shot her a look, his jaw clenching visibly.

She spoke quickly, before he could say anything. "You don't need to check out anything. All you need to do is sign those papers, then get out of our lives. You don't need to get involved any more than that."

His voice was low and determined as he crossed his arms and stared at her. "I am involved, and I can't just walk away. Not now."

"Why not? You did before."

"You don't know what you're talking about."

"Are you trying to tell me you didn't know about Bella?" Annie snorted, a sound of disgust. "Don't do it, if you are. You knew Monica was pregnant. She told me you did. I *know* the story."

"You know the story." He repeated the words without

inflection, then spoke again, even more slowly. "*All* about it? *Every* detail?"

Instantly uneasy, Annie couldn't suppress her automatic flicker of nervousness. Monica sometimes left out pieces of stories, especially pieces that didn't fit her perception of who she was. This had been too important, though, too critical a situation for her to have done that. On the other hand, they hadn't had much time that horrible day. She'd died so quickly....

He didn't wait for Annie's answer. "I'm sorry you're upset, but I thought it was best that you didn't know who I was. At least, not right away. Especially considering the fact that there's a child involved."

"And you want me to think you care about that?"

"Frankly I don't care what you think—but it *is* the truth. I'm a stranger. I didn't think it was a good idea just to appear out of nowhere and tell Bella I'm her father."

Her chest closed in on itself, and suddenly Annie couldn't breathe. She listed her hand, felt her heart tripping, wondered if this was real or if she was having some kind of horrible nightmare.

He stayed where he was for a few more minutes, then she heard him circle her. He moved in front of her and rested a hip on the edge of the desk, his eyes never leaving her face. His dark, endless eyes. The eyes she'd been dreaming about, for God's sake. "Are you all right?"

No—she wasn't all right. She was dying, slowly, inch by inch, starting inside in the general vicinity of her heart. She didn't answer...couldn't answer.

"I'm not the monster you think I am," he said finally.

"You don't know what I think of you."

"Oh, I've got a pretty good idea. Let me see...I think the words were 'controlling, unfeeling, heartless.' Am I right or did I leave something out?"

Annie flushed, remembering the earlier conversation. "Just tell me this—why are you here?"

"I think that's pretty obvious, isn't it?"

She licked her dry lips. "Do you want her? Do you want Bella?"

The words lay heavy and jumbled in the tension-filled air, and although she'd asked the question, Annie didn't really want to think about his answer. About what it could mean. About what it might take from her. As if sensing her reluctance, he stayed quiet. She died ten times before he finally answered.

"I never knew I had a daughter until I received your letter. The second I could, I came here and saw her. What would *you* do in my place?"

Her heart turned over, a painful flip that cut off her air and threatened to bring her down. "I'll fight you."

"I expect that."

"You'll never win."

"No. I'm afraid that's not true." His eyes burned into hers, and she felt her world tilt to the side. "The fact is, I never *lose*."

Maggie found Annie an hour later, down by the river. Her face was swollen and red, her hair was in a tangle, her blouse was wrinkled and splotched. She was shivering and crying and hysterical, but she didn't care. All she could think about, all she could focus on was one single thought. *He wanted Bella.*

He wanted Bella.

Maggie kneeled beside her, took one look, then wrapped her arms around Annie. "Oh, sweetie," she murmured, "oh, sweetie."

The tears resumed in an angry flood Annie couldn't hold back. By the time she finished, Maggie's shoulder was soaked. "I...I'm sorry," Annie hiccuped. "I...I've ruined your blouse."

Maggie glanced down at her sodden T-shirt. "My God, you have! And to think I paid $9.95 for this at Target, too!"

Annie smiled for a second, then the tears came again. At length, she managed to get herself under control, or at least the appearance of control. "I...I'm sorry," she repeated.

"Why are you apologizing, you nut?" Maggie pulled back and looked in Annie's eyes. "You have every right to be upset." She handed her a tissue, then waited for Annie to finish wiping her eyes. "What did he say?"

"He...he didn't deny a thing. He said he wanted to check out the situation, then he was going to tell us who he was."

"And...Bella?"

"He wants Bella, Maggie. He wants her!" The tears started afresh.

Maggie held on and waited for the storm to abate. When it slowed, Maggie spoke again. "Have you called Loring?"

"He...he's coming over this evening, after dinner. That's the earliest time he had open."

"What are you going to do?"

"I'm going to fight Grayston...Powers. What other option do I have?"

"Are you sure that's the best thing to do? A long legal battle? Everyone all upset?"

Annie jerked her gaze to her sister's face. "Of course, it's the best thing to do. It's the *only* thing to do. Surely you aren't suggesting—"

"I'm not suggesting anything, I was just asking—"

"Don't even say it. Don't even *think* it," Annie snapped back. "The man's an irresponsible, cold, uncaring person.

With her last breath, Monica told me not to trust him, and he proved her point exactly by not telling me who he was."

"He had a reason."

"But not a good one." A flash of illogical anger came over her. Illogical and uncontrollable. "This is the only home Bella has ever known—we're her family, Maggie! *I* am her mother!"

"And he is her father!"

"Well, he's not a good one, that's obvious. Should I remind you of everything Monica said? Whose side are you on, anyway?"

"I'm on Bella's side. That's the only one that counts around here and you need to make sure you're on that side, too." Seeing Annie's expression, Maggie's face grew softer. She reached over and put her hand on her sister's shoulder. "You're upset, Annie. You're scared, worried...you've immediately jumped to the conclusion that Gray is going to take Bella and run away. You need to calm down, then you need to sit down with Gray—and with Loring—and the three of you should talk this out. Divorced people face custody battles like this all the time and they work things out. You can, too."

Annie was shaking her head before Maggie even finished talking. *Sit down with Gray...talk it out?* Had her sister lost her mind? "There isn't going to be any *'working out,'*" she said heatedly. "Bella is *mine*. That's how Monica wanted it, that's how I want it, and most of all, that's how Bella wants it. There will be no other solution than that, and if Grayston Powers—or anyone else—thinks differently, they're going to be sorely disappointed."

Getting through the afternoon, Annie fought to keep herself under control. She had guests checking in, produce deliveries to receive, Mrs. Meyers and her shower to plan.

It was a nightmare. To top it all off, Bella, who had been with a friend down the road all day, came back cranky, which turned into teary, which then went into exhausted. By the time Annie fed the little girl dinner and got her in bed, she wanted to crawl in beside her and pull the covers up over her own head. She couldn't, though. Loring was waiting downstairs. She'd heard him come in while she was tucking Bella into bed.

"Read me another story," Bella demanded.

"I can't, sweetheart." Along the little girl's brow, Annie smoothed a strand of red hair. The instant she took away her fingers, the curl sprang back out. "Mr. Shaver's downstairs. We have to talk."

"What about?"

The question was a delaying tactic, and Annie half rose from the bed, determined to ignore it. Then something clicked inside her and she thought about what she was doing. What if she were never to have this tucking-in task again? What if she never heard "one more story" or "tell it to me once more," ever again? The thought wrenched her heart, and instead of leaving, she sat down again and hugged Bella tight. "We're going to talk about the adoption," she said, rubbing the little girl's back. "Remember that?"

Bella nodded. "So you'll be my mommy."

"That's right." Annie smiled. "You still want me for a mother, don't you?"

Bella rolled her eyes as if she were thinking.

"Well…"

Annie acted like she was going to slug her, then they both dissolved into a fit of giggles. Beneath the laughter, though, Annie held back the threatening tide of tears. God, how could she possibly let this child go? It couldn't happen. It just couldn't happen.

As if sensing the undercurrents, Bella looked up at Annie with a serious expression. "You know I'm going to start school pretty soon."

"Are you?" Annie looked puzzled. "I'd plum forgotten!"

Bella looked uncertain for a moment, then giggled. She'd talked of nothing *but* school for the past few weeks, and Annie had indulged her.

"I don't know," Annie continued. "I think you might be wrong about that. Kindergarten doesn't really start *this* month, does it?"

"It does!" Bella pulled at a lock of her hair. "Don't you remember? That's why we went to the beautiful shop."

"Oh, yes…I'm sorry. I'd forgotten."

"Well, I need supplies," Bella went on. "Rose's dad is taking her tomorrow to Wal-Mart. They're going to buy notebooks and pencils and everything." Her face turned uncertain. "Can you do that or is that just a daddy job?"

"I think I can handle it," Annie said, her voice earnest. "But just exactly what is a daddy job anyway?"

Bella's expression turned irritated. "You know what daddy jobs are—it's like mowing the grass and washing the car…daddy jobs."

"And who said this was a daddy job?"

"Rose. Her daddy takes all her brothers and sisters shopping every year for their supplies. It's a daddy job." She looked at Annie with suddenly troubled eyes. "I was afraid since I didn't have a daddy I wouldn't get any new pencils."

Since that morning, Annie had been trying not to see a resemblance between Bella's green eyes and Gray's black ones, Bella's straight nose and Gray's slightly crooked one, Bella's small lips and Gray's more generous ones. Annie had finally convinced herself there was no similarity, none whatsoever. Now, though, with that one expression, Bella tore that decision to hell and back. The serious look in those green eyes was so similar to Gray's, so indistinguishable from the one Annie had seen earlier in his gaze, that it stole Annie's breath in one fell swoop. Everything came crashing in on her.

She managed to pull herself together at the very last second. "I...I think we can find you some new pencils. And a few other things as well. But you need to go to sleep now, and I have to go downstairs." With a full heart, she stood, then smoothed the pink blanket over the Winnie the Pooh sheets. Holding back tears, she leaned over and kissed the smooth, sweet brow. "Sleep well...and remember I love you."

Standing beside the bed, the open window sending in a humid breeze, Annie watched the child a minute longer, then she turned and headed for the door.

She had a battle to fight.

From his vantage point by the river, Gray watched Annie turn and go. Every night at this time she went into Bella's room and sat down on the bed. For half an hour or more, he could hear her voice, sometimes laughing, sometimes soothing, always loving. Not a night went by that she didn't tuck in the child and have a final goodnight kiss.

He'd watched her every night since he'd arrived at Riverside, and every night had been the same. Bella didn't go to sleep without Annie telling her, "I love you."

What in the world would that feel like?

He closed his mind to the past, to the place where he'd never felt that kind of love, and turned instead toward the present.

What was he going to do?

The tragic look on Annie's face this afternoon had given him a momentary twinge of guilt over his actions, but he'd also known he'd had no other choice. He'd had to judge for himself, without anyone knowing who he was, what kind of woman would be willing to take on the upbringing of a child to whom she had no real ties. In his opinion, people weren't that altruistic. Not in this day or time. And if he'd known nothing else about Annie Burns except that she had been the best friend of his ex-wife, Gray would have known *for sure* that she was running some kind of scam.

Like attracted like.

Or so he'd thought.

So far, Annie Burns hadn't been at all what he'd expected. The other women he'd met who had been friends of Monica's were sophisticated, materialistic, concerned about appearances and not substance. Annie, he was finding out, was just the opposite. She appeared to be as loving and caring and genuine as anyone he'd ever met.

Was it real?

He stared into the river and at the flickers of silver darting just under the surface. When he'd received her letter, it had been more than a shock. It had been a nuclear strike. The idea—the very notion—of him having a daughter had sent him reeling. Sure, Monica had called and told him she was pregnant. Annie had been right about that. What she didn't know, obviously, was that Monica had said the same thing before. And had been lying.

He remembered the first time as if it had happened this morning. He'd been shocked, of course. They'd only been dating a few months, hadn't even talked about marriage at that point, but then Monica had come to him, crying so beautifully, the tears gliding down her smooth cheeks like polished diamonds. She'd told him she was pregnant, and his rush of shock had been quickly replaced by thrilled happiness. He'd always wanted a family, wanted children so he could be a better father than the one he had had.

He'd picked her up and swung her around the room, yelling and screaming. Then immediately stopped and gently set her down, scared to death he'd somehow upset the baby.

A few weeks after they'd married, Monica had told him the truth. Crying again—so hard that it'd broken his heart—she'd confessed. Unaware of how little his mother's opinion meant to him, Monica had been afraid the older woman would object to her. Scared that he would do nothing without his mother's approval, Monica had lied about being pregnant.

He should have divorced her right then and there, but he couldn't. There had been a vulnerability in her eyes, a terrified expression that had hinted at how needy she was, and he just couldn't let her down as someone else so obviously had done before him. Although he hadn't understood her completely—or himself either, at that point—he'd felt compelled to carry on with the marriage and try to give her the perfect family she so desperately wanted.

Clearly Annie didn't know all this history, and something had stopped him from telling her. That's why he hadn't believed Monica when she'd called him that last time, though. He'd fallen for that trick before.

But the last time obviously hadn't been a trick.

All he'd had to do was take one look at Bella, and he'd known she was his. In appearance, of course, she looked exactly like Monica, but he'd known the minute he'd laid eyes on the child that she was his. Instantly. There was something about the way she held herself, the way she moved, that confirmed it for him. Crossing that sunlit hall the first time he'd seen her, she'd been so obviously his that his heart had almost stopped. Sometime in the past ten years or so, he'd simply come to accept that he was never going to have children. He would never remarry, so he'd never have a child, a family. That was just the way it was going to be.

Then he'd gotten the letter. And the minute he'd seen Bella, Gray's entire life had changed.

He turned around and stared into the living room windows. The lights were on and he could see Annie perched on the edge of the couch. She was talking earnestly to a man seated in a nearby chair, waving her hands and trying to convince him of something. He was obviously the lawyer. Gray headed toward the lights. He had a battle to fight.

"I'll do whatever it takes," she was saying. "If I have to sell Riverside, it doesn't matter. I'll make a living somehow. I'll wait tables—"

"Ahem." Loring cleared his throat, then nodded his head. "Uh, Annie—"

Her irritation mounted. "Are you listening to me, Loring—"

"He's trying to tell you I'm here."

Annie jerked around at the sound of Gray's voice, flinging one hand over the back of the couch as she turned, the other going up to her throat in surprise.

He crossed the threshold of the open French door and came to a stop in front of Loring to shake hands. Gray was taller, more intimidating, and appeared a hundred times more capable than the small-time country attorney she had hired. Annie tried to tell herself looks were deceiving, but in this case, she was terrified they weren't.

"I was explaining to Loring who you are," she said stiffly. "I was also telling him I have no intention of quitting. I plan on adopting Bella whether you like it or not."

Gray moved toward the silver coffee service she'd put out on the table nearby. Without saying a word, he poured himself a cup of coffee, added sugar, then sat down in the chair beside Loring. When he finished stirring his coffee, he took a sip then glanced first at Loring and then at Annie.

"Then let me make my position just as clear," he said quietly, distinctly. "I have no intention of relinquishing my parental rights. I intend to take my daughter and return to Dallas." His black gaze never left Annie's face. "Bella is my daughter. And you will not be adopting her."

Annie felt ill.

A thick awful silence filled the room. "I don't think you understand—" she began.

"I understand perfectly. You *want* Bella. She's been with you since she was born, and you have very close ties with her." He smiled, almost sadly it seemed. "But I'm her father. Her *natural* father. If we went to trial, any court in the country would award that child to me." He turned to Loring and raised one eyebrow. "Am I right?"

"Of course not," Annie started. "That's ridiculous—"

Loring held up one hand. "Annie, as much as you don't want to hear it, Mr. Powers could be—"

Annie made a sound of disbelief, her gaze fastening on the attorney. "Don't even think it, much less say it, Loring. I'm paying you to *help* me, dammit—"

"And that's what I'm trying to do, Annie." The first note of exasperation came into the attorney's voice. "I'm saying you could sell Riverside, you could sell your car...you could sell your soul, and it wouldn't bring enough money to get you the answer you want. The courts favor natural parents."

Annie sat back in stunned silence. She couldn't believe it. This couldn't be happening. "But he abandoned her—"

Loring turned to Gray. "Were you married when the child was conceived, Mr. Powers?"

"Of course—and I didn't abandon her or her mother. I...had reason to believe that there actually was no child. Obviously I was wrong, and I've come now to take her."

Annie stared as Gray spoke. His face was a mask, no emotion on it whatsoever. She turned to look at Loring, a terrible hole forming in her heart. "How can he do that? I raised her. I'm the one who brought her home from the hospital. I changed her diapers, I sat up with her, I did it all." She didn't mean to keep going, but the words wouldn't stop. "*I've* been that child's mother—he hasn't even been around!"

"To the courts, I'm afraid it may not matter—"

"Oh, it matters, all right." Gray's deep voice broke into Loring's gentle words. "Half her childhood is gone. I'll never see her first step, her first tooth, hear her first word...how do you think that makes *me* feel?"

Gray set down his coffee cup and stood. Annie could do nothing but stare. For a moment she thought he was going to leave the room, and she prayed that he would. She didn't want to hear his words, didn't want to be touched by his loss. He'd brought it all about himself, hadn't he? A storm of thoughts raged through her mind as she watched him turn around, then stand behind the chair, gripping the back of it as though his life depended on it.

"There are things about my marriage you don't need to know," he said tightly, "but I'll tell you this. Monica was *not* the person you thought she was—just like I'm not the person she probably described to you."

"Right now the only thing that matters to me is Bella," Annie replied quickly. "She's the only important thing in this whole affair."

"That's right." His voice dropped, became even more calm, even more demanding. "She *is* the only important thing here, and I intend to see that she spends the rest of her life knowing that her father loves her more than anything in the world. You can't give her that—only I can." Tension gathered in the room like a summer storm. It was a tangible, solid mass that suddenly smothered Annie in a layer of disbelief and shock.

"I won't take her immediately," he finished in a quiet voice. "I'll let her get used to the idea and then—"

"You won't take her at all," Annie interrupted in a voice as hard as her resolve. "In fact, I want *you* out of here. *Right now.*"

A flicker of anger lit in his eyes. "If I leave, I'll take her with me. *Right now.* Is that what you want?"

Annie stared at him a second longer, then felt her expression collapse. Rising from the couch, she turned away from him, a wave of disbelief washing over her. This couldn't be happening. It couldn't. Except for her labored breathing, silence filled the room.

"It doesn't have to be this hard," he said softly.

She let his words hang in the quietness. Then, slowly, she regained her composure. Turning around, she moved silently toward him, stopping close enough to see the few touches of gray along his temple. Her voice sliced through the room like a sword. "I don't give a damn how hard you make it. I love that little girl. I *am* her mother. I'm not going to let you take her and walk out of here. Not without giving it everything I've got."

"You don't know what you're getting into."

"Whatever it is, it's worth it to me." Annie stared into his eyes. Their magnetism came over her once more, but she fought the tug with cold resolve.

And at that very moment, an idea buzzed into her mind. It was a long shot—very long—but at this point what did it matter? She had nothing to lose. She turned to Loring, her heart suddenly pounding. "We don't know he's the father. They were married, sure, but that just means they were married. What if he's not Bella's father? He wouldn't have any more right to her than I do then, would he?"

Before Loring could answer, Gray spoke. His voice and

his expression held an icy fury. "I *am* her father. How could you possibly think—"

"Are you sure? Are you absolutely positive?" Annie pinned him down with her gaze, but there wasn't even the remotest flicker of hesitation when he answered.

"I have more rights to that child than you ever will." The control in his voice was pure, pure and absolute. It was all Annie could do not to shiver when the cold, steely tones ran over her. "And that's all I need to be sure of."

"Then let's do a blood test."

"No." His answer was instantaneous. "I don't want Bella to have to go through that. Not after everything else."

Loring stepped to Annie's side. "The paternity would have to be without question, Mr. Powers."

"Those tests can be unreliable."

"Then we'll do DNA," Annie shot back.

"The courts do accept those." Loring spoke with authority.

"I'm not letting her go without being positive on this point. I can't believe you wouldn't feel the same way. Wouldn't you want to know—for sure?"

"I *am* sure." He narrowed his eyes and stared at her. "If you insist on this, you're making a big mistake."

Was he talking about the test or something else? Like taking him on? "I'm willing to take that chance. For Bella's sake."

She wasn't sure, but she thought there was a second of admiration in his eyes at her persistence. Then his gaze hardened once more. "All right. But I'll make the arrangements."

This was going to be a fight to the finish, she realized instantly. "No. *I'll* make the arrangements. I am her legal guardian." She took a deep breath and plunged ahead.

"And you will *not* tell her who you are until those results are back. I insist on it."

His gaze weighed her words, and at that precise moment, Annie realized just how accustomed Grayston Powers was to being in control. The aura of power that hung over him wasn't just an illusion created by expensive suits and a practiced voice. Other people did what he told them to—and they usually did it without question. He wasn't in the habit of being the one ordered about. She didn't know how she knew this—his expression remained unchanged—but something had shifted in his eyes. Something unyielding and assertive.

This man would do anything he had to do to get what he wanted.

"All right," he said in that same low, deceiving voice. The words held concession, but not his expression. "You can do your test, and I'll stay quiet, but I want something in return."

Her gaze never wavered, but her nerves sounded bells of alarm. "What?"

"I want to be part of her life while we're waiting for those results. I've lost five years of it already. I don't intend to lose more."

"What...what do you mean exactly?"

"I want to do things with her, I want to be there when she needs me, I want to be part of her life...and I don't want any grief from you about it, either."

Annie's jaw tightened. Let him into Bella's life? Let him share with her all those wonderful things that had been Annie's alone until now? The thought turned her inside out. On the other hand, if he was the man Monica had said he was, he'd get bored easily. What interest would he have in schoolyard problems and playground upsets? She could put him off; then, after one or two incidents, he'd probably forget all about it. A whispered voice in the back of her mind argued the point, but there was nothing else Annie could do. Right now. "You promise you won't tell her who you are?"

He shook his head. "Not until the results come in. The minute they do, though, I'm telling her the truth. I'm telling her and then you'll help me prepare her to move to Dallas. Agreed?"

A hole formed inside Annie as his words sank in. She was going to lose her daughter—the only child she'd ever loved. Unless she could think of something else to do, this man was going to take her baby and leave. Part of her wanted to rush out of the room, grab Bella and run away. The logical part of her counseled patience. If she had time, she could come up with a way out of this. The compromise would give her breathing room, if nothing else. Most important, Bella still wouldn't know what was going on. It might be the only chance Annie had. After one measured moment, she met his eyes then nodded once. His footsteps echoed when he left the room.

Chapter 5

Over the next few days, it was all Annie could do to keep herself together. She felt numb and at the same time, sensitive to every moment, every second.

She was mad as hell...and scared to death.

Every time Annie looked at Bella, she wanted to cry, and every time the little girl stepped out of Annie's view, she wanted to scream, "Come back!" She couldn't stand for them to be apart for the shortest time, and even though she knew it wasn't good, Annie found herself clinging to Bella, their good-night tuck-ins growing longer and longer, their idle chatter over breakfast taking up half the morning by the time the last crumb was gone.

Gray's presence made it worse. When he wasn't on the phone taking care of business, he was talking to Bella or sitting outside with her or watching her run and play in the yard. He wasn't forward or obtrusive with his attentions—just consistent. And just as consistently, Bella rewarded him. She grinned, she smiled, she flirted, she laughed. As much as she hated to admit it, Annie had to concede the obvious—a chemistry had slowly blossomed between the hard-edged man and the little girl.

Annie's only hope was the DNA test. She'd scheduled an appointment—the first one she could get—with Bella's doctor for next week to discuss the details. Maybe her wild shot wouldn't be so wild after all. It was possible, wasn't it?

Annie was painting the living room and trying to calculate the odds when Maggie came in to help. Knowing there was one thing on Annie's mind, Maggie spoke. "Have you called Dr. Ellen to set up the DNA test?"

"Yes, I called and made an appointment." Dipping her brush into the bucket of pale yellow paint beside her, Annie shook her head. "I've never prayed for someone to be illegitimate before. Does it work when you pray for something like that?"

Her expression thoughtful, Maggie put down the roller she'd been filling with paint. "Is that really what you want?"

Annie carefully drew her brush down the side of the window, but the line she left behind was far from perfect. "I've never wanted anything more."

"That's not exactly fair, is it?"

"Fair?" Dropping her paintbrush to her side, Annie turned to her sister. "Who cares if it's fair or not?"

"You should." Maggie paused. "You always did in the past."

"Well, this is different. I'm fighting for Bella's sake, and I don't care if I fight fair or not."

"The guy's not that bad. You act like he's some kind of devil or something."

"He wants to take Bella away. If that test comes back positive, we may never see her again. Doesn't that bother you?"

"Of course it bothers me. But he's her father, Annie. Her father. He has rights."

"We're not sure he's her father," Annie said stubbornly, "but even if he is, he has no rights. He gave them up when he refused to believe Monica. To top things off, he came here under false pretenses. How can you possibly argue for a man like that?"

"I just don't think you're considering everything."

"Like what, Maggie? What makes him such a saint in your eyes?"

At Annie's tone, a troubled frown came over Maggie's forehead, but she forged ahead. "I'm not saying he's a saint. But I'd be willing to bet my next month's salary that you'd do the very same thing if your positions were reversed."

"What on earth are you talking about?"

"If he had Bella and *you* wanted to see what the deal was, you'd show up without advertising who you were. You wouldn't want to upset her—and that's *exactly* the reason he gave for not revealing who he was."

"That's ridiculous."

Maggie put her hands on her hips. "You know I'm telling the truth. Why are you being so stubborn? Why are you refusing to see the good side of this man?"

Annie threw down her paintbrush. "How can there be a good side to a man who wants to take Bella away? Think about it, Maggie. He could walk out of here tomorrow, with her in hand, and *we would never see her again*. Do you know what that means? *Never?* It means forever and ever and ever. She'd be gone." Annie's voice broke on the last word, but she repeated it anyway. "Gone."

"And have you thought that that might be the best thing for her? Have you considered *her* in this at all?" Maggie took a deep breath and faced Annie squarely. "Look, I know how much you want to be a mother, but this might not be the time...or the place...or the child. Have you considered that?''

The words went straight into Annie's gut, like a hard blow from a fist. Openmouthed, she stared at her sister, half of her wanting to cry, the other half wanting to lash out. ''How on earth could you possibly say something like that to me? You know I love that child like—''

Before Annie could finish, the door behind her squeaked open. She ignored it, staring at Maggie instead, heartsick that they were fighting, physically ill at the turn the argument had taken. Did Maggie really feel that way? Was she really questioning Annie's motives?

Gray's voice cut across the tension like a well-honed knife. ''Oh—I didn't know you were painting in here—I was going down to the river.''

Annie looked up and met his gaze. He was dressed casually, but his black eyes were as intense as ever. They took in everything at once—her, Maggie, the room. Annie couldn't help it; her heart stopped at his arrival and unbelievably, her breath turned tight and close in her chest. On top of everything else! How could this be happening still? How could he affect her like this when she should hate him with every bone in her body? It didn't make sense. When he'd been a stranger, she'd thought her attraction unexpected, but now—when she knew who he was—how in the world could it still exist?

Before Annie could speak, Bella shot into the room and stood beside him, grinning. She too had on shorts and tennis shoes, and her fishing pole clutched in her hand.

''We're going fishing!'' the little girl declared.

The frazzled ends of Annie's composure completely unraveled. She started forward, her heart zooming into panic. She hadn't wanted to let Bella out of her sight for days— and now this? She ignored the reality that she could see the river perfectly from where she stood. He wanted to take her fishing? No way!

"Why don't you go down to Rose's instead?" Annie's voice was warm as she spoke to Bella but her stare was like ice as she faced Gray. "It seems a little overcast to me to go fishing. The fish probably aren't biting anyway right now."

"There isn't a cloud in the sky," Gray replied evenly. "I think it's a perfect day to go fishing. In fact, I'd bet money the fish are biting."

Obviously confused, Bella stared at Gray and then at Annie, her head swinging back and forth. Finally, her gaze settled on Annie. "But Annie, I *want* to go. I was going to go before and then I had to go get my hair cut, but Gray said he'd wait and...and you said it was all right...and..." Her cheeks puffed out and she began to blink rapidly, her expression changing from excitement to uncertainty. "Why can't I—"

"Of course you can go." Maggie stepped forward and put her arm around Bella's shoulder, sending Annie a disbelieving look.

Almost desperately now, Annie glanced down at Bella and spoke. "But I...I just don't think it's a good idea, sweetheart. Gray doesn't have a lot of free time—he might want to be by himself."

Completely unaware of the fog-thick tension in the air, Bella looked up at Gray. "Is that true?"

He stared directly at Annie with a smoldering gaze and an expression to match. He'd tolerated one attempt to dissuade Bella, but a second one—forget it. They had a deal—or had she forgotten? his cold eyes seemed to ask.

"I wouldn't have agreed to go if I'd wanted to be alone," he answered.

Bella's face immediately changed, a wide grin coming over it. "See, Annie! He *wants* to go." She looked back up at the man standing beside her, then unbelievably, she slipped her small hand into his larger one, her fingers closing around his as naturally as if she'd done it a hundred times before.

Annie stood stock-still for two more seconds, then realized she had no choice in the matter. She had to give in, or the situation would only escalate, and Bella would be in the middle. "All right," Annie said quietly. "You…you can go, Bella. I'll watch from the windows here. Just be careful, and don't stay out too long. Wear your hat, too, and—"

"Yippee!" Bella yelled. "Let's go, let's go."

Gray allowed Bella to pull him forward. Then, too impatient to wait any longer, she slipped away from him and ran out the open French doors, tripping on her fishing pole and stopping short on the terrace, her giggles coming back into the room as she called to Maggie for help.

With disapproval in every line of her body, Maggie sent Annie one last look, then she stepped forward and went to Bella's aid. Gray crossed the space that was left between him and Annie and stopped at her side.

"Don't do this, Annie. Don't try to get in my way."

"Wh-what are you talking about?"

His black eyes glowed. "You know exactly what I'm talking about. We have an agreement. I get to be part of Bella's life. If you can't live up your part of that arrangement, then tell me now. I'll save us all a lot of grief and just make the cut a clean one. I'll take her and leave." He paused for effect. "Is that what you want?"

Her heart tripped against her chest and she felt her own eyes widen in fear. "You can't do that—"

"Watch me and see."

"But you promised…."

"And so did you. If you continue to make it hard on me…" His words died out but the threat was obvious.

"What? You'll make it even harder on me?"

"I could."

She had no doubt about that, but Annie had to fight. She couldn't just give in. He spoke again, his voice low and full of meaning.

"I simply think it'd be best if we kept our agreement. Otherwise, somebody's going to end up getting hurt. And I really don't want that to happen, especially when that someone could be Bella."

Staring into his eyes, Annie took a ragged breath, then slowly let the air out of her lungs. He was right, and even if he hadn't been, the warning was more than clear. He was a man who would do whatever it took to get his way. "All right," she said quietly. Turning away from him, she faced the glass. "Go ahead. Go fishing."

She heard his footsteps as he crossed the room.

Waiting for the door to open and close, Annie told herself she could stay composed until he left. Seconds passed—but the door didn't squeak. Instead, his footsteps sounded again—closer—and suddenly he appeared by her side.

"Would you like to go with us?" he asked.

It was the very last thing she expected him to say.

She stuttered in her surprise, an automatic excuse that sounded lame even to her ears coming to her lips. "I...I have to finish this painting and I have guests checking in at four."

"I can handle the check-in," Maggie said, walking back into the room. "And this painting isn't going to be finished for another two days at least. Why don't you go? It might be best...for all of us."

Still in shock over Gray's words, Annie let her eyes go to Maggie's face. Her answering stare was full of criticism and totally devoid of its usual good humor. Annie couldn't decide if she wanted to cry or yell. The last real fight they'd had was in high school when they both thought they wanted to date Stevie Earl Jones.

Annie turned to Gray. She didn't want to walk off with this man who was ruining her life, but she didn't want to stay and suffer her sister's rare criticism. It took her only a second to decide. "Let's go."

The day couldn't have been more beautiful. A slow breeze whispered in the leaves overhead and the green current of the river shimmered like a cooling mirage. Beside the path, the lantana Annie had planted earlier in the summer still blossomed, decorating the area with a riot of pink flowers. As Bella and Beau ran ahead, Annie wished she could appreciate it all. Instead she worried—about Bella, about the man walking beside her and his threats, and now about her sister. Why was she being so traitorous all of a sudden? How could she possibly think Bella should be with anyone but Annie? And that crack about Annie wanting to be a mother…that was mean. Downright mean.

If he'd overheard any of her and Maggie's conversation, Gray pretended not to notice. As soon as they'd stepped outside, he'd turned as relaxed and easygoing as he had been determined before. She wondered if it was an act, another way he had of controlling things, but he seemed genuinely at ease.

"Gorgeous day, huh?"

Annie nodded. She had nothing to say to this man. Why had she even agreed to come?

"Catch a lot of fish down here?"

She didn't answer.

He shifted his fishing pole from his right to his left. "I just bought this at Wal-Mart. Think it'll work?"

Annie stopped and looked at him directly. "Why did you ask me to come with you?"

He stopped and looked down at her, the filtered sunlight

making a dappled pattern across his face. "Until Bella gets to know me better, I think it's best if you're around while we're together. To her, I'm still a stranger." His dark eyes shifted. "Believe it or not, though, I don't want to make this situation any tougher than it already is. We don't have to be sworn enemies, you know."

Annie stiffened. "We have opposing goals. I don't think it's possible for us to be friends."

"Opposing goals? I think we both want the same thing—what's best for Bella."

"You have a strange way of accomplishing that. How can taking her away from the only family she's ever known be what's best for her?"

"I'm her father," he said simply.

"I can't see you in a fatherly role."

"Then you aren't really looking."

They reached the riverbank where Bella stood waiting. Beau was already in the water.

"We're going to have a tough time catching fish if that dog's in there stirring them up." His attitude completely different than it had been two seconds before, Gray looked down at Bella with a smile. "Don't you think you ought to call him out?"

"But it's hot," she said matter-of-factly. "If you had all that fur on you, you'd want to be in the water, too."

Gray nodded his head, the logic obviously overcoming any serious intentions he had of catching fish. "I see what you mean. In that case, maybe we should just let him swim, then?"

She grinned. "Yep."

He grinned back. "Okay."

Annie stood to one side and watched the interaction. It was as if the man and child had been together for years. Not only were they teasing and laughing, but both of them seemed totally comfortable with each other. She couldn't believe it. From Bella's point of view *or* Gray's. A twinge of something uncomfortably similar to jealousy made its way down between her shoulder blades. She'd never seen the little girl react so positively to anyone, man or woman.

As Bella threw a stick out to the dog, Gray kneeled down and pulled a small container from one of the pockets of his vest. "I bought these worms from a guy down the street. He said they're the best bait around."

Feeling like a fifth wheel but determined to stick it out all the same, Annie sat down in the grass beside him. She spoke in an undertone. "You'll have to bait her hook for her. She won't do it herself."

He looked up in surprise. "Why not?"

"She's a little girl," Annie explained, her voice patently patient. "Little girls don't like slimy worms." She glanced into the swirling center of the container and shuddered slightly.

His black eyes regarded her with amusement. "Looks to me like you're the one with the worm aversion."

Annie's voice came out defensively. "That's crazy. She doesn't like worms, that's all. You'll have to bait her hook for her."

He smiled again and Annie felt something turn inside of her. It was a feeling she didn't want to have, *couldn't* have, and she ignored it.

"Bella," he called out. "Bring your pole here. We have to bait your hook."

She nodded, then skipped to his side. "What are you using?"

He reached for his pole and spoke at the same time, nodding toward the container of worms. "Night crawlers." Without looking at her, he stretched his fingers into the bait and pulled out one of the reddish brown worms. In one fluid movement, he baited his hook, stood, then flicked the line into the water. He looked down at Bella. "Well? Aren't you going to fish?"

From the corner of her eye, Annie watched. Bella looked at the container of worms, then sent another glance—an uncertain one—toward Gray. Her feelings couldn't have been more clear if she'd written them out in the dirt beside her. She wanted to fish, and she wanted to fish badly. She also wanted to impress Gray.

What to do?

The mental debate continued a moment longer; then she screwed her face into an expression of disgust and thrust her hand into the container of worms, obviously moving fast so she wouldn't change her mind. Grabbing one and not even looking at it, she laid the squirming bug in the dirt by her feet, then stabbed her hook toward it. Two seconds later she was standing beside Gray and beaming, her line in the water, her little shoulders thrown back in a parody of his stance. Gray sent a smug look in Annie's direction, then turned to face the river once more.

They both hauled in catfish big enough for dinner.

As he cleaned the fish they'd caught and explained why they needed gills to breathe, Gray tried not to stare at the child beside him. It took all his effort not to give in to temptation. He wanted to examine her face, turn it this way and that, stare into her eyes. He'd had so little time with her that every minute counted.

Annie appeared at Bella's side. In the dwindling light of the evening, she looked tired and anxious. Her short brown hair curled around her face, and her eyes, usually the color of the Texas sky, seemed paler somehow, with dark shadows under them. She avoided his gaze and made her voice bright as she spoke to Bella. "Got those fish ready?" she said.

"Just about," Bella answered. "Got that fire ready?"

"Just about." Annie smiled. Beau came up and Bella reached down to wrap her arms around the dog. Annie finally looked up at Gray. "The grill *is* almost ready. Are you going to be much longer?"

"They're done."

Gray handed her the platter of cleaned fish and she walked back to the round black grill where the coals were already glowing, her tanned legs long and lean beneath her baggy white shorts. To a stranger's eyes, it would have looked perfect, Gray thought. A father, a mother, a child playing with a dog. The only thing missing—everything.

He picked up the garden hose and began to clean the slab of Texas limestone where he'd filleted the fish. Annie had made him angry earlier with her pointless attempts to keep him from Bella. Her fear was almost palpable—she was terrified she was going to lose her child. Then, when she'd looked up at him in the living room, with those blue eyes full of anguish, he'd found himself inviting her to go with them instead of walking out the door victoriously.

Why?

He had no answer. It had just seemed like the right thing to do at the time. It hardly mattered, though. In the end, one of them was going to lose, because they both wanted the same thing—Bella.

And the loser would not be him.

He finished cleaning the slab, then made his way to the table. They ate on the terrace, the Texas night balmy, the fish as flaky and tender as any he'd had in the fancy restaurants where he usually dined in Dallas. Alone.

When Bella asked permission to get up from the table, Annie said yes. Together they watched the little girl streak out into the darkness of the yard.

Despite the situation, Gray felt himself begin to relax. "It's so beautiful here," he said almost to himself. "The big yard, the river, the trees…" He turned and looked at

Annie. She'd placed three candles on the wooden table and their flickering light danced across her face. "I wish I'd had this kind of yard to grow up in."

It was obvious she didn't want to ask, but she *had* to know. "I thought you lacked for nothing as a child."

He raised his eyebrows. "Oh, really? What gave you that impression?"

She looked down at the table as if trying to decide what to say, then she raised her face. "Right after you and Monica married, she called me. From—Capetown?"

He nodded.

"She was so impressed with…everything. Said you were very wealthy."

He pushed back from the table and took his wineglass in hand. The candlelight made the crystal look as delicate as Annie's features. "Monica saw the surface of things," he said cautiously. "My family was quite wealthy, but…"

"But…" She repeated the word, obviously knowing there was more.

"But love was pretty scarce," he finished for her. "Love, affection, caring…things like that. My parents divorced when I was seven. The battle was hard, vigorous, and involved a lot of lawyers and mudslinging."

Her voice shifted, grew more understanding. "They both wanted you?"

"They both wanted the money." His laugh held no amusement. "*Neither* wanted me."

For a heartbeat, there was silence, then her voice—incredulous. "You're kidding, right?"

"No." He paused. "I'm not kidding."

In the silence that followed, Bella's voice drifted up from near the river. She was singing and chasing fireflies. He could see her slender form dancing around the trees like some kind of nighttime child-sylph.

"I'm sorry."

He glanced over the table, over the candles and met Annie's eyes. "Worse things happen," he said with a shrug.

The silence stretched longer this time. Then Annie broke it. "What happened? After their divorce, I mean."

"I went to boarding school, a military one in West Virginia. I stayed there until I finished high school, then I went to college in Austin. University of Texas. I never lived at home after I turned eight."

She shifted in her chair, leaned closer. "Never? Didn't you go home in the summer? For Christmas?"

"My mother got custody of me and she liked to travel in the summer, usually to Europe. If I left school at all— to join her—it was only for a few weeks, here and there. I usually met her wherever she was living at the time. London, Brussels, the Côte d'Azur—wherever." His voice was matter-of-fact and so was his manner. The pain had left a long time ago.

"What about your father?"

"I never saw him again after the divorce, but my mother said he remarried. Started a new family with a new wife, new kids. He lives in Boston now, I think."

"You think? You don't even know for sure where your father lives?"

He paused. "It's Boston."

She leaned back in her chair as if it was all too much to absorb. "What about you?" he asked, suddenly anxious to get the questions turned away from himself. "Somehow I get the impression you didn't grow up that way."

"No." She shook her head sharply. "I didn't, but..."

"Oh, no...another 'but.'"

She glanced over and took in his smile. Some of the stiffness seemed to seep out of her shoulders, and he found himself wishing he could just reach over and work the rest of it away with his fingers. The thought surprised him.

"I had a very different childhood," she replied. "I grew up here—in Timberley—and everything was absolutely perfect until I was in the fifth grade. My parents were very close, to each other and to us. Looking back at it sometimes, I wonder if it could really have been as great as I thought. I've asked Maggie, and she seems to agree with my memories, so I guess it was."

"But..." he prompted just as she had moments earlier.

"But my parents both died. In a car wreck." She reached over and took the wineglass from beside her empty plate, bringing the rim of it to her lips and sipping. "It was a freak thing, really. They were coming back from San Antonio where they'd gone to a concert. An eighteen-wheeler crossed the interstate and came into their lane of traffic. Their car was crushed. The driver of the truck had fallen asleep."

He had the sudden image of Annie in Bella's room. Kissing her good-night, telling her how much she loved her.

Who had told her that her parents weren't coming home to do the same for her that night?

"We moved in with our grandmother," she continued. "My mother's mother. She was a very strong woman, from South Dakota originally. She met my grandfather when he went up there on a cattle drive. They married and he brought her back to Texas." Annie glanced toward him. "She didn't have any problem raising two little girls alone."

"Alone?"

"My grandfather died the year before my mom and dad." She held the wineglass up and looked at the candles through it, then her gaze shifted to Gray's face. "It was just us girls after that...but we did fine, the three of us."

He stared, knowing full well what she was doing. "You didn't need a father?"

She met his gaze, level and without blinking. "My grandmother provided all the emotional support that Maggie and I could possibly have ever needed. She was everything to us, and if I say so myself, I think she did a pretty good job raising us. I felt no lack."

He leaned closer to her, his elbows resting on the edge of the table. "And you think you can do the same for Bella."

"I *know* I can do the same for her. Children need love and that's all." She mimicked his movement, came in closer to him. Close enough for him to see the darker rim of blue that ringed her irises, the flicker of freckles that bridged her nose, the flush on her cheeks that the wine had brought. "It doesn't matter if it comes from an old lady, a woman and a man, or the busy mother down the street who watches everyone's kids. Love is love, no matter where it comes from, and I've got more than enough for Bella."

Chapter 6

Dr. Ellen's office had the homespun appearance of an antique store rather than a medical facility. The waiting-room couches were upholstered in a soft plaid cotton, and the receptionist's rolltop desk was oak with a green-shaded lamp on top. The female physician had been Timberley's only pediatrician for the past ten years and everyone loved her, including Bella who'd been a patient since Day One. None of this mattered to Annie at the moment, though. She fidgeted on one of the couches, then jumped up in relief when the nurse finally came to the door and called her name.

The doctor walked into the examining room a few seconds later. A tall, silver-haired woman, Ellen Byers had beautiful, strong features and hazel eyes whose color matched the leaves of the weeping willow in Annie's garden. She spoke in a no-nonsense kind of voice as she entered the room and looked around. "Where's my patient? Hiding under the table?"

Annie smiled. "I'm afraid I'm it, Dr. Ellen. At least for the moment."

The physician peeled off her bright red glasses and began to polish them with the edge of her white jacket, sitting down at the same time on the stool beside the examining table. "Well, you're about twenty years older than most of my patients, but that might be nice for a change. Promise you won't bite or kick me if I examine you?"

"Actually, I'd like to kick or bite someone," Annie confessed. "Things aren't going too well." As simply and quickly as she could, she explained the entire situation to the doctor.

The physician nodded, a sympathetic expression crossing her face before she put on her professional demeanor. "Well, typically DNA tests like the one you need are done with a buccal swabbing. You use what looks like a long Q-Tip or sometimes a small nylon brush. You twirl it on the inside of the cheek to obtain mucosa cells, then you smear the sample on a slide. We do the same thing with the alleged father, and send the samples off to a lab in Houston. We can have the results back within seven to fourteen days if we have to."

"That fast?" Annie's voice held dismay. "I had no idea..."

"They've made big improvements in this kind of work. In the old days, we used hair follicles and the results would take about three weeks. Before that, we did blood tests, which could take four to six weeks."

"Do they still do them that way? With blood, I mean?"

"They can." The older woman pulled off her glasses and looked at Annie. "But most people are in a bigger hurry than that. They want to know the answer fast. You can rush any of the results, but I never advise it."

Annie glanced out the window at her side. Fast was the last thing she wanted.

Dr. Ellen's voice turned softer. "You believe he's the father?"

"Without a doubt."

"And you'd lose her?"

"Completely."

"Is he as bad as Monica said he was?"

Annie had never made a secret of what Monica had told her, so the doctor's question didn't surprise her. She started to answer, an automatic 'yes' on her lips. Then she thought again. About Maggie's arguments. About the conversation she and Gray had shared the night before. About the obvious lack of love he'd had in his own childhood. About the way she'd wanted to reach over and put her arms around him when he'd finished talking.

She tried to brush off the question. "I...I'm not sure. I know one thing, though. He'll take her away from me...and I just can't stand the thought. I...I'll die." She began to cry.

The doctor swiveled on her stool, found a box of tissues, then handed them to Annie. "You don't think you could work out some kind of arrangement?"

Annie shook her head. "I don't see how. He's some kind of high-powered oil consultant. Owns a company in Dallas. He wouldn't want to move here. I'm sure Timberley wouldn't be big enough for him." She sniffed, then looked up at the doctor. "Even if that weren't the case, Monica didn't want him anywhere near her child. She made that more than clear. Sharing Bella with Gray wouldn't work."

"It doesn't sound too good, does it?"

Annie shook her head. "At this point, Gray holds all the cards, and once that DNA test comes back, I'm sure he's going to do what he wants." She paused, then spoke again. "Can we do this test and not let Bella know what it's all about?"

"Sure." The doctor tapped Bella's chart. "She's due for her TB test. Bring her in for it, and I'll tell her the swab is a part of it. She doesn't have to have the full story. In fact, most kids don't even *want* to know the full story."

Annie hesitated, then plunged right in. "Could we do the blood test instead of the swab?"

The doctor's gaze was level. "It would take longer."

"I understand."

"Why drag it out?" she said softly.

"I...I'm hoping something will happen." Annie hated the desperate quality in her voice but she accepted it. There was nothing else she could do. "Maybe I'll think of something or...I don't know...maybe he'll change his mind?"

The doctor shook her head, her gray hair gleaming in the sunshine coming through the window. "The best thing is to be prepared. You may have to give her up." The hazel eyes filled with an expression Annie couldn't read. "Sometimes in life that happens, you know. You give something up...but you get something else in return. That may happen to you."

The breakfast rush was over and afternoon check-ins had yet to start. Annie loaded Bella into the car and the two of them headed for the outlet mall in San Marcos. Any other time it would have been an ordinary chore. Now, with everything hanging over her head, Annie felt it was a precious opportunity. Two hours later, they had most of Bella's school shopping done. She was so excited by the whole event, not to mention the prospect of school, that she could hardly sit still.

They pulled into the driveway of Riverside and Annie brought up the topic she'd been dreading all day. "We're going to have to go see Dr. Ellen next week, Bella. To get your TB test for school. It's a kind of shot and—"

"I know all about that," Bella replied. "Rose told me."

Annie turned in her seat to stare at Bella, her casual tone a surprise to Annie. "Rose told you, huh?"

"Yep." Bella licked the frozen yogurt cone they had to stop for at the Dairy Queen. "She's already had hers. And it's not a shot. It's called a…immuni…amuni…uh…"

"I think you're looking for the word 'immunization.' A TB test isn't exactly an immunization, but that's okay."

"Yeah…whatever. Rose said since we're big girls now and going to school we can't cry over stuff like shots anymore." She stopped licking and looked suddenly apprehensive. "But what if they hurt real bad? Would it be okay to cry then?"

Annie reached across the seat and squeezed Bella's arm. "It would be perfectly all right, but I don't think they'll hurt that bad." She paused for a second, then smiled. "I tell you what—what if we have a little party? To celebrate your going to school. Would that take your mind of the shots?"

"A party? Oh, boy! Could I invite Rose?"

"Of course. You can invite anyone you want to."

"Can Gray come?"

Annie's shoulders went tight, but she kept her smile.

"Well, he's got work to do, you know. He might not have the time," she hedged. "You…you really like him, don't you?"

"He's cool," Bella answered. "And he knows cool stuff."

"What kind of *cool* stuff?"

"Oh, you know…like how fish breathe. Stuff like that."

"I see. Important things."

Bella nodded, her expression serious. "Yeah."

Just then, Gray's Mercedes pulled into the parking lot beside them, and Annie watched as Bella jumped from the Jeep and ran over to him. Deliberately turning around in an effort to minimize the pain of seeing them together,

Annie climbed out of the Jeep herself and picked up the packages from between the seats. When she straightened up, Gray was at her side and reaching for the heavy bags she held, Bella chattering beside him the entire time, telling him about her day. Annie handed the sacks over to him, almost reluctant to acknowledge even this simple courtesy.

He took them from her hand, standing close to her, the sunshine warming his features, his eyes narrowed against the light. An errant breeze ruffled his hair, disheveling for a moment his usual perfect appearance. For some ridiculous reason, she wondered if his hair looked like that in the morning—when he'd just gotten out of bed—her bed, as it were. Annie's stomach did a funny little twirl as Bella's voice broke in.

"—and we're going to have a party. Annie just told me. A going-to-school party. I'm gonna invite Rose and Maggie, and Annie said you could come, too." Without taking a breath, Bella continued. "You can come, can't you? It's gonna be—" She stopped and looked at Annie. "When's it gonna be?"

Avoiding Gray's eyes, Annie looked down at the little girl. "I told you he might not be able to come, sweetheart. He's really busy and—"

"I have plenty of time." His black eyes suddenly seemed threatening to Annie in the bright sunlight. "I'd love to come."

She blinked and started to argue, then his words from the evening before echoed in her mind. *The harder you make it for me...* "Well...uh, great, then. How about next week? On Saturday evening?"

"On Saturday evening," Bella echoed, staring adoringly at the man beside her. "Perfect, right?"

"Perfect," Gray answered, his own smile answering the little girl's. "Can I do something to add to the festivities?"

"I...I can't think of anything at the moment," Annie said faintly.

"Let me know if you think of something."

"Of...of course."

The three of them started up the sidewalk, then Bella stopped abruptly, her green gaze going to Gray's face. "I have to go to the doctor next week, too," she said, her demeanor much more serious. "I've got to get my ammunitions."

Gray hid his sudden smile. "Oh, my gosh, that sounds terrible."

"It's not really," Bella said with authority. "Rose told me they didn't hurt."

"I'm sure they won't," he answered, "but maybe you'd like some company? Would you like me to come with you?"

Annie fought a wave of dismay. "I'm sure that's not necessary—"

He interrupted Annie before she could finish. "Oh, I think it is," he said with a pointed look. "I think I should be there for something as important as ammuniations." He turned and looked at Bella, his expression softening. "Maybe we could even stop for ice cream later. How does that sound?"

Bella grinned widely. "Yummy."

"Then it's settled. I'll go." He raised his eyes to Annie's face.

Annie knew her displeasure showed in her eyes, but having no other choice, she nodded tensely, more aware than ever of his dark eyes and generous mouth. He was paying her back for trying to cut him out of the party. *This,* his look said, *is how the game is played, so don't even try it.*

He surprised her once again, though, when he locked his gaze with hers.

"If you promise to be nice," he said in a serious tone, "I might even buy you an ice-cream cone, too."

From his usual spot in the garden, Gray waited for Annie to tell Bella good-night. All he could see was her silhouette against the lace curtains of the bedroom, but when the light went out, he knew the nightly ritual was finished. God, what he wouldn't give to be part of that himself! He wanted to stand by Annie's side and tuck Bella in, to kiss her brow, to reassure her that there weren't any monsters under the bed. That was a little too much to ask, though, and even he realized that. Even though their little battle today had proven his point, Gray found himself wanting to be reasonable about things....

Which surprised him as much as anything. Grayston Powers was not a man who generally cared what his enemies thought of him. In business, he was ruthless. In his personal life, what little he had, he wasn't much kinder. He hadn't expected an easy battle here, but things were turning out much, much more differently than he'd thought they would and primarily because of him.

He had never expected to love Bella. But he did.

He had never expected to like Timberley. But it was wonderful.

And he had never, ever, expected to be attracted to Annie. But he was.

Gray stuck his hands in the pockets of his jeans and leaned against a tree, watching the moonlight on the river. What was happening to him? What was going on? He'd come here prepared to fight a greedy woman and tell her there was no way he had a daughter, and instead he was finding himself upside down, every preconceived idea of his thrown to the wind. Something about Annie pulled him in and spoke to him. The blue eyes, the curly hair, the ready smile for everyone but him—she was the exact op-

posite of what he'd thought she would be. And the way
he was responding to her was exactly opposite as well.

Just like the other night. He'd never told anyone, including Monica, the whole truth about his childhood.
She'd thought it was perfect and had been content to hear
the stories about Paris and London without seeing the un-
derside. Something in Annie's dark blue gaze had made
him go on, though. She was the kind of woman who demanded the entire story, and he couldn't have told her
anything but the truth.

But there was only one way for this to end. When everything had been done and everything had been said, and
it was known that Bella was his, he'd leave and take her
with him. Annie would be crushed. He'd win and she'd
lose.

But someone had to, and he was as determined as ever
that it wouldn't be him. Because Bella *was* his daughter.
He didn't need a DNA test to prove anything. He knew
she was his as surely as he knew the sun would come up
tomorrow morning.

A sudden rustle sounded behind him, and he turned. It
was Annie. She hadn't yet seen him. She was walking
toward the water, her head down, obviously deep in
thought.

He spoke her name softly. "Annie?"

She jerked her head up, her eyes searching the darkness
until he spoke again. "Over here. By the dock."

"Gray?"

He stepped out into the silver light. "I didn't mean to
startle you."

She'd changed clothes. Out of the jeans and T-shirt she
usually wore to something soft and shimmery, a caftan
with wide, draping sleeves, the fabric shot with gold
threads that picked up the moonlight and moved when she
did. As she spoke, she lifted her hand and ran her fingers

through her hair, leaving the short strands curly and out of order against her cheeks. "I didn't think anyone came out here at night but me. I...I wasn't expecting to see anyone."

"Would you like me to leave?"

She hesitated a moment. Should she be polite or honest? He could see the struggle cross her delicate features.

"No," she said finally, almost reluctantly. "You don't have to leave...if you don't mind sharing the dock."

Unexpectedly pleased by her answer, he stepped aside and held out his hand. "You can have that end. I'll take this one."

Stepping closer, she passed him, then sat down on the built-in bench. He caught just a whiff of her perfume, something light and airy, unpredictably tantalizing. He sat down. On her side of the bench.

For quite a while, they said nothing. In the darkness, with the river softly murmuring nearby, Gray found the silence comfortable, something he'd never experienced before. With Annie, it seemed natural, right somehow.

After a while, though, as if she didn't feel the same way, she broke the quiet. "The doctor's visit Bella mentioned...I guess you know we'll do the DNA test then. If you're coming, Dr. Ellen might as well take your blood sample, too."

He lifted his eyebrows in surprise. "I thought we'd have to go to Dallas or Houston. You mean they do it here?"

"The sample is taken here, then it's shipped off to Houston for lab analysis."

Leaning forward, he spoke. "And how long till we get the results?"

Against the moonlight, Annie turned to face him, an expression he couldn't read shadowing her features. "A blood test takes four to six weeks."

"That long?"

Her voice was almost defiant. "Do you have a problem with that length of time?"

Something was off in the way she spoke. Her voice was filled with tension and deeper than usual. He answered carefully. "I'm anxious to move forward on this, but it doesn't matter, does it? If it takes that long, then it takes that long."

He waited for her to reply, but she said nothing else, and during that second, that heartbeat, he realized he wanted to kiss her. He wanted to pull her toward him, wrap his arms around her and kiss her. Maybe he wanted to ease the pain he was causing her or maybe he wanted to ease his own—he didn't know why he wanted to kiss her…he just did.

His words came out suddenly. "I didn't come here to tear up your life or ruin all your plans. You know that, don't you, Annie?"

She took so long to answer, he didn't think she would. Finally, she shifted against the seat, her dress shimmering in the moonlight, her skin almost glowing. "Then why did you come?" she asked softly, turning her eyes to his face. "Why didn't you just sign those papers and leave us alone?"

"If someone wrote you and told you you had a child, wouldn't you do what I did?"

"But you already knew there was a child! Monica told me just before she…" Annie stopped and took a deep breath, a breath he could hear. She started over. "Monica told me she told you she was pregnant and you said you didn't care. Why did my letter change your mind?"

"Your letter said there was a *child*. Monica—" He broke off abruptly now, too, suddenly reluctant to say more.

Annie's blue eyes, as dark and deep as the river in the moonlight, studied him. "Monica what?"

"It's not important," he lied.

"I don't believe you," she said, her gaze steady. "What were you going to say? What about Monica?"

He hesitated as long as he could, then gave in, the feeling strong once more that Annie would settle for nothing but the truth. "Before we married, Monica thought my mother would forbid a marriage between us unless she was carrying the Powers heir." He laughed lightly. "She didn't know at that time how little I thought of my mother's opinion. Monica told me she was pregnant and that's why we married in the first place."

Annie's stillness told him what he'd thought—she hadn't known Monica had tricked him. Her next, hesitant question told him even more—she didn't want to believe him, but she knew Monica too well to totally discount the scenario.

"But...she wasn't pregnant?"

"No. She wasn't pregnant. Neither was she ill when she tried to get me to stay at home and she wasn't suicidal because I had to travel." Suddenly it was important to him to make sure Annie understood. "I know I'm talking about someone you loved, but she wasn't the woman she seemed to be, Annie. Surely you knew that?"

"Then why did you stay with her so long?"

"I had to," he said quietly. "I was all she had and I thought I could make the world right for her. Her eyes...they were always searching, always wanting...I thought I could fix that for her. Not a good thing to base a relationship on, but I was young and ignorant...or at least that's my excuse."

She licked her lips and started to speak, then stopped.

"You know I'm telling you the truth, don't you?"

Annie looked down at her lap, her folded hands, then out to the river. Finally she let her eyes come to his. "Monica did have some...problems, I'll admit. She stretched the truth, sometimes, and she liked to exaggerate, liked to make things dramatic. It made her feel... important. Maybe that meant things weren't totally accurate, but I always felt she was a pretty good judge of character.''

"She was," he conceded, his voice rough. "She was an excellent judge of character."

"Then how can you defend yourself? How can you say you would make a good father for Bella? Monica said you were cold, unloving.''

"I was that way, but I changed," he said simply.

"Changed?" Her eyebrows lifted. "When did that happen?''

"It happened the day I looked into Bella's face. The day I saw my daughter for the very first time. I realized then what's really important in life.''

Her voice was skeptical. "And that is?''

"Family and love and caring. I...I never had it before, and even though I haven't had it yet—now I know I want it.''

She stood abruptly, with a flash of gold and silver, a scent of roses and jasmine. "I'm sorry, but I don't believe you. People don't change overnight. Real change is gradual.''

He stood as well. Inches separated them but they were a world apart. "And love?''

"Takes just as long," she said. "It's something you nurture, you bring along. You...you tend it like a rosebush, and if you're lucky, it blooms.''

"But it can happen quickly. Unexpectedly.''

"No." She shook her head and took half a step backwards. "I don't think so.''

He found himself moving toward her, and then somehow his hands were on her upper arms, holding them tight. Beneath the silky fabric of her gown, her skin was warm, more than warm. "Sometimes people just click. They don't expect it to happen...but it does."

She looked down at his fingers, then her eyes went to his face. "You said that once before, but I don't believe it. That kind of thing only happens in fairy tales. Not in real life."

"Then maybe it's not what you'd call love...but it's something, isn't it?" He tightened his grip. "You've never been attracted to a man suddenly? You've never wondered what it would be like to kiss him? To hold him? To climb in his bed while it was still warm?"

"N-no."

She spoke the denial, but something flickered in her eyes. Something dark and tantalizing. It pulled him in despite all the warning bells sounding in his head. "I don't believe you. Now you're the one who's lying."

"And what if I am?" she whispered. "What business is it of yours?"

He couldn't think of an answer. So he did the only thing he could.

He kissed her.

Chapter 7

His lips were not at all what she'd expected.

In the countless times she'd thought of this moment, in the infinite ways she'd imagined it happening, Annie had never dreamed his mouth would be this hard, this demanding. There was no hesitation. He took what he wanted.

She should have been terrified.

Even as the kiss was taking place, though, even as his hands went from her arms to her shoulders, then to her back to draw her close, she was feeling everything *but* terror. Part of her couldn't believe she was allowing him to kiss her and yet she found herself running her own hands over his shoulders and back. What was going through her mind? What was she thinking? Had she *lost* her mind?

She must have, because she wasn't thinking at all. She was feeling. The warmth of his breath against her neck, the stroke of his fingers across her back, the touch of his skin against her cheek. It seemed to Annie as though she'd never been kissed before, as if a man had never taken her into his arms and whispered against her ear.

She clung to him.

For countless moments, they seemed to be suspended. His mouth covered her lips and his tongue sought hers. Annie could do nothing but surrender to the sensations battering her. She was helpless to do anything else.

She didn't know which one of them pulled back first, but finally they separated as if a giant hand had flung them apart. One moment they were in each other's arms, and the next, they were apart, struggling for breath, looking at each other in disbelief. She stared at him, her breasts rising and falling, her pulse pounding so hard she felt as though her heart were about to leap from her chest. Covering her mouth with her fingers, she realized her lips were tender and swollen.

"This...this shouldn't have happened," was all she could get out.

His low voice throbbed against her senses as surely as his touch had a moment before. "But it did, didn't it?"

She stared at him. In the moonlight, his eyes looked even darker, even blacker, even deeper. She turned and fled.

On Thursday, the three of them headed for Dr. Ellen's office. Thinking it might make her feel better, Annie had put on a red silk dress she usually saved for church. When she came down the stairs and saw the look in Gray's eyes, she wondered exactly who she was trying to make feel better. The thought bothered her, but it was too late to change. Just like it was too late to take back the mistake of kissing him. She'd been over the whole episode in her mind a thousand times, and each time she came up with the same conclusion.

She was suffering from temporary insanity, brought on by unrelieved stress and anxiety.

They climbed into his Mercedes and took the five-minute drive to Dr. Ellen's office.

The waiting room was crowded and as they walked inside, Annie panicked. Timberley was a small town, very small.

How on earth would she explain Gray's presence if she saw someone she knew? Her gaze shot around the room, and she breathed a sigh of relief. One or two acquaintances, but of the nodding variety only. Thank God. Almost weak with relief, she started toward the front desk to check in, then stopped as Gray put his hand on her arm.

"Why don't you go over there and save us that place by the fish tank? I'll let them know we're here."

She looked toward the spot he indicated. The seats were the only ones in the room with a straight shot to the back and at the same time, slightly shielded from the view of everyone who walked in. Surprised by his perception, she nodded once, then headed for the chairs, Bella by her side.

Gray followed them a moment later and, sitting down by Annie's side, he began an earnest—and distracting—conversation with Bella regarding the difference between golden retrievers and Irish setters. Despite herself, Annie felt grateful. Bella had turned quieter and quieter the closer to the clinic they got. She didn't like needles—never had—and her anxiety was almost palpable. Annie understood this because she'd brought Bella to the doctor a hundred times. Gray understood…because he just did. The realization frightened Annie.

He glanced up at her and smiled. She looked at him and thought about their kiss.

Fifteen minutes later, they were in one of the waiting rooms. Dr. Ellen breezed in shortly thereafter. In between joking with Bella and removing the proper vials from the cabinet, the doctor's hazel eyes took in every detail of Gray. What did she think of him? Annie wondered. Did she approve? Did he look and act like the other daddies who came into these rooms, holding their daughters' hands?

With Annie's help, Bella climbed up on the table, then she slipped her fingers in hers. A second later, she looked at Gray and tilted her head, indicating she wanted him there as well. While Annie swallowed her protests, he moved to the table, and the three of them formed a ring, Gray on one side, Annie on the other, Bella in the middle. Annie found herself wondering what it would be like if it were a circle of love instead of what it really was—a tug-of-war.

The whole procedure took only a few seconds. In short order, the shots were given, the blood was taken, and stickers were awarded. Despite her initial anxiety, Bella handled the whole event perfectly and, obviously proud of herself for being such a big girl in front of Gray, she grinned once at him then jumped down from the table and ran back to the waiting room to check out the fish tank again.

As the little girl left the room, a sudden wave of weakness hit Annie. In a month—maybe a little more if she was lucky and the lab was busy—it could all be over. A knot the size of a baseball lodged itself in her throat, and she began to blink rapidly.

Misinterpreting the situation, Dr. Ellen's expression was concerned as she looked over at Annie. "You aren't going to faint on me, are you?"

"No, no." Now almost in tears, it was all Annie could do to answer. "I…I'm fine."

"Well, just sit down there for a minute and make sure."

The doctor glanced toward Gray and her attitude shifted. "Would you roll up your sleeve for me, please?"

Gray nodded and did as she instructed, his forearm thick and muscular as he neatly folded up his cotton sleeve. To distract herself from the reality of what was happening, Annie let her eyes go to his hands, remembering the day he'd checked in and what she'd thought of them then.

They were still as strong, as capable, as intriguing to her as they had been when he was a complete stranger. Only he wasn't a stranger any more. She knew who he was and what he wanted. And she'd actually felt those hands on her back. A ripple of unwanted feeling came over her.

Pulling another syringe from the nearby table, Dr. Ellen turned to Gray. ''Hold out your arm, please.''

He never flinched when the needle slipped in. A second later, two vials of dark red blood lay side by side on the table. Practically faint with tension, Annie looked down at them and her heart faltered.

They looked identical.

In just a few weeks, she'd know if they were.

They stopped to get ice cream, just as Gray had promised, but Annie barely touched hers. Her eyes were trained, instead, on the man and child beside her. It was as if the little girl already knew who he was, sensed, somehow, that he loved her and would take care of her. The anxiety that had begun in Dr. Ellen's office only seemed to grow and now, added to it, was such a sudden overwhelming sense of loss that Annie felt nauseated. She pushed the bowl of melting chocolate-vanilla swirl away from her. Gray's eyes met hers, and she turned away.

An eternity later, Bella finished her own ice cream and they all drove back home. As soon as he parked the car, Annie shot out of it as if it were on fire, ignoring the strange look from Gray. She had to get away from him and everything he represented. She ran into the house and headed for her study, telling Bella she had paperwork to handle.

Maggie came into the office a minute later, took one look at Annie, and sat down. It was the first time since their argument that she'd done more than pass through the room when they were together. Already upset and anxious, Annie stared at her sister warily. Another fight was the last thing she could handle right now.

"What's wrong with you?" Maggie asked bluntly before Annie could even speak. "You look like you're about to lose your lunch."

"Thanks for the compliment," Annie said. "Would you like to comment on my hair, too?"

Maggie shook her head and sighed, but she couldn't hide the sudden twinkle in her eyes. "I think it speaks for itself."

Relief swept over Annie and tears gathered in the back of her throat. She'd hated their estrangement. Not being able to talk to Maggie about everything had made the whole situation twice as bad. To make her own peace offering, Annie picked up the fudge-cookie bag she'd emptied the night before and held it out to her sister before she realized it was empty. "Well...I was going to give you a cookie, but..."

Maggie frowned. "No wonder you look sick. You've been a very bad girl."

Annie dropped the sack into the trash can. "You don't know the half of it." She swiveled her desk chair and looked out to the garden, her voice husky and tight.

The room behind her went quiet, then a second later Maggie was squatting in front of Annie, her hands on Annie's knees, a contrite expression on her face. "Look...I'm sorry I gave you a hard time the other day. I said some mean things, and I shouldn't have. They weren't true."

She paused, her eyes searching Annie's. "I'm on *your* side, Annie-Fannie. You know that, don't you?"

The name sounded as silly now as it had when they were kids and Maggie had teased Annie with it. Annie smiled down at her sister and patted her hand. "I know," she said softly. "And I'm grateful for it, believe me. I need as much support as I can get. I'm going to need even more when…"

"When he takes her?"

Struggling to gain control of herself, Annie finally found her voice and spoke. "I want to fight him, Maggie, but I don't know how. He's practically blackmailing me so he can spend time with her and there's nothing I can do about it. And what's the use anyway? That test is going to come back and the results are going to prove Gray is Bella's father. Then he's going to take her, and I'll have to sit here and watch. I feel so helpless!"

Maggie stood and walked to the French doors. Crossing her arms, she leaned against the white trim and looked out over the garden. "And they're very close, aren't they? Already?"

"Yes." Annie dropped her head and looked at her hands. They were clenched in her lap. "I know I should feel grateful for that, but I don't. I'm jealous and confused and mad and sad…and…and guilty, too. You name it. I'm feeling it."

"Guilty? That's about the dumbest thing I've ever heard! Mad, sad, confused—whatever—that's okay, but guilty?" Maggie shook her head, her hair swinging with the vigorous motion. "You need to save that feeling for important occasions—like drinking too much or gossiping real bad or kissing your best friend's boyfriend. Why in the world would you feel guilt—" Suddenly Maggie dropped her arms to her side and stood up straight, her eyes narrowing. "My God…that's it, isn't it? You're falling for Gray, aren't you?"

Annie's head jerked up. "Don't be ridiculous. I'm not—"

"No…no, that's it." Maggie moved closer to the desk, amazement filling her voice as all her words ran together. "On top of everything else, you're falling for this guy, and you feel guilty because he was married to Monica, and you guys were friends, not to mention the fact that she told you he was a rat and to stay away from him! God, I can't believe it."

Annie stood. She couldn't admit the truth to Maggie— whatever the truth really was—because it made the situation real and if it was real, then she'd have to deal with it. And she couldn't. Not now. "I'm not falling for anyone, Maggie, so just stop it. I've made my mistakes in the man department, and I don't intend to make any more."

Maggie shook her head. "Save it, Annie. I'm not buying."

"And I'm not selling!" Annie protested. Too loudly.

"Has he kissed you?"

"Maggie!"

"Well…has he?"

"Why would I let Grayston Powers kiss me?" Annie met her sister's look without so much as a flicker. "The man is—"

"As good-looking as James Bond, as rich as Donald Trump, and sexy as…as…as sexy as they come. Why on earth wouldn't you let him kiss you if he wanted to? *That's* the question."

Maggie was going to be relentless.

Annie sighed, looked out the window, and sighed again. Maybe it would be good to confess. Maybe it would take away the mystique, release the forbidden, lessen… whatever in the hell he had so much of.

She held out her hands. "All right! Yes. He kissed me, but that's all. I am definitely not 'falling' for him, as you put it. It's…hormonal, nothing else."

"I knew it." Maggie grinned hugely. "Tell me about it. Every little detail. I want to know where his hands went, where your hands went, how his mouth felt, where that tongue ended up. Tell me everything."

Annie couldn't help but laugh. "You're crazy!"

Maggie shook her head. "Not crazy. Deprived…or is it depraved? I always get those two confused."

"I'm not telling you a thing either way, so it doesn't matter."

Maggie mimed an exaggerated expression of sadness. "That's not fair." She pouted. "Why should you have all the fun?"

Annie's amusement fled. "It's not fun, Mags, and I shouldn't have done it. It was crazy. The man's trouble."

"They all are."

"Maybe…but this one is more so than others. Even if we didn't have this battle going on over Bella, I should know better than to go anywhere near him. Monica warned me about him. Not to trust him, not to have anything to do with him, not to let him near Bella. I've broken every promise I made to Monica. What kind of friend does that?"

"You were a great friend to Monica, Annie. You did everything you could for her. Don't be so hard on yourself now just because things are working out a little differently than you thought they would."

"This is not that simple." Refusing to meet Maggie's eyes and ignoring her words, Annie shook her head, a heavy weight pressing in against her. "It's not going to end well, Mags. I have a bad feeling about this…a very bad feeling."

* * *

Putting aside—at least for a few hours—the black cloud of limbo that hung over her head because of the DNA test, Annie surveyed the backyard with satisfaction. She'd used a schoolyard scheme to liven up Bella's party and the whole expanse of sloping lawn was covered with the makings of a mock classroom. Maggie had found an old blackboard in the attic and they'd placed it against the fence with a box of colored chalk. In one corner, a tall stool and a dunce's cap waited. At the other end of the grass, there was a miniature cafeteria complete with a homemade cake and cookies. The chug-chug of the electric ice cream maker filled the late afternoon air.

She wished she could have done more, but with the financial stress she was experiencing, Annie's resources had been limited. She was pretty sure Bella would like it, though. She hadn't stopped talking about school for days. Glancing down at her watch now, Annie turned and hurried toward the terrace for one last check of the grill and the waiting hot dogs.

Gray appeared suddenly at the edge of the porch, his black eyes as intense and unwavering as ever. A white short-sleeved shirt emphasized the tan he'd acquired since coming to Timberley, and pressed shorts revealed runner's legs. Annie told herself not to notice these things, but she seemed to have lost all sense of control in that department. He came toward her and stopped too close for comfort.

He stared at her for a moment, and her heart turned over. She was afraid he was going to say something about their kiss. Something awkward and uncomfortable. She didn't want to think about it, and she certainly didn't want to talk about it. And she *most* certainly didn't want to know what he thought about it.

"The place looks great," he said instead, indicating the party setting. "Very creative."

With relief, she moved toward the grill and opened it. "Thanks. I think the kids will have a good time."

He smiled rather mysteriously. "Oh, I bet they will. It's going to be a party they remember, I know that for sure."

"Well...thanks, but I didn't think it was that great a theme."

His smiled again, then the back gate squeaked, and suddenly a flood of people appeared. Without another word, he walked off. Putting the incident out of her mind for the next few hours, Annie mingled and tried to make sure that everyone was having fun—which was a simple task, as it turned out. The children loved all the games and silly school things, and the adults loved the margaritas Annie had mixed earlier in the day and left in the freezer. As the inviting smell of grilled hamburgers and hot dogs filled the early-evening air, she knew she had a successful party going.

She was in the kitchen getting more chips and guacamole when Rose's mother, Shelly, came into the kitchen. With her was Dana Villaret, who would be Bella's kindergarten teacher, and Nikki Moore, a neighbor from down the street. The three women crowded around Annie.

"Okay," Shelly said. "Give it up—tell us who he is."

She had her story ready, but Annie still felt a twinge of nervousness. Small towns and gossip—a lethal mix. If they knew who Gray really was, the talk would never stop. Annie hid her feelings as she laughed then spoke. "Who are you talking about, Shelly?"

"Who do you think?" Dana reached over and swirled one of the fresh chips through the dip. Holding it up, she eyed Annie with a grin. "The hunky guy who's probably sleeping in *your* bed!"

"The dish in the tan shorts." Nikki added, in case things weren't yet clear. "With the cute buns."

Annie held up her hands in defeat. "He's a guest. It seemed impolite not to include him."

Shelly reached for a chip, too. "And his name is…"

"His name is Grayston Powers. He owns Powerplay Engineering in Dallas. He's a consultant in the oil and gas business."

"Oh…good-looking *and* rich. How much better can it get?" Nikki rolled her eyes then asked the question they all really wanted to know. "So…is he married?"

Annie shook her head. "Divorced."

"What kind of woman would divorce a hunk like that?" Shelly asked. "Who cares what kind of bad habits he has? They couldn't be that bad!"

The three women laughed, Annie joining in with what she hoped was a genuine sound.

"How long's he going to be here?" Dana asked with a glance in Nikki's direction.

"I'm not sure," Annie answered, a curious twist tightening in her stomach. Nikki and Dana were close friends, and Nikki was divorced. She'd made no secret of the fact that she didn't like being without a man. Dana was obviously aiding and abetting. "He…he's here on business. He said it might take a while."

Dana nudged Nikki with her elbow. "You only have a little while…you'd better get to work."

They all laughed again, but this time, strangely enough, Annie's amusement was more forced than ever.

A few minutes later, she managed to get the still gossiping women back outside. Automatically, as she stepped off the porch, her eyes searched the crowd. She found Gray in the center of a group of men by the terrace. He looked up at the very same time and their gazes connected.

The jolt went down to her toes.

Gray felt the jolt all the way down to his toes.

His eyes locked on Annie's over the heads of her guests

and he remembered their kiss, something in her expression reminding him of that moment down by the river. It could have been the trusting openness of her blue eyes, or maybe it was the way she was tilting her head—he didn't know what it was, but it all came rushing back to him as if her lips had left his the moment before. He headed straight for her, then at the very last minute, he stopped, his eyes drawn to the sudden appearance of a huge truck and trailer that had pulled into the front drive.

He'd totally forgotten his surprise!

Changing direction, Gray started toward the gate with a big smile crossing his face. When he'd first heard about the party, he'd desperately searched his mind for a way to make it special for Bella. Finally he'd given up and called his office. "I don't care what it costs," he'd said. "I want to do something special…got any ideas?" Bill Kingsley, his assistant, had had the perfect suggestion. Ponies! Bill had even arranged it all, and as Gray rounded the corner of the house, he could see what a wonderful idea it had been. The children were already surrounding the trailer and crying out in delight over the five Shetland ponies waiting inside.

Gray crossed the driveway to where the horse trainer and Annie were talking.

"I'm sorry," she was saying, "but I think you're at the wrong house. I didn't call—"

"But I did," Gray interrupted with a grin. "Aren't they great? It's my little contribution to the party." He turned around and found Bella in the midst of all the children. "What do you think, Bella? You like the horses?"

At Gray's voice, the little girl turned around. Her green eyes were huge with delighted disbelief. "Did you do this? Just for my party?"

"I sure did," he said, pure happiness washing over him

at her expression. "Do you like them?"

"Oh, Gray," she breathed. "I can't believe it! They're s-o-o-o cool! Can we ride them?"

"You bet. All night long if you want to."

"Gray—"

He felt Annie's hand on his arm and, still smiling, he turned around and looked down at her. Her face wore a pleasant expression, but there was ice in her blue eyes. "I...I wish you'd told me you were going to do this."

"Well, if I'd told you, it wouldn't have been a surprise, now would it?"

She watched as the trainer walked back to the trailer and began to unload the pint-sized horses. "I don't like surprises," she said quietly. "Especially expensive ones like this."

Puzzled by her attitude, Gray spoke. "It's not that much, Annie. Don't worry about it."

She met his gaze with a level look. "I know exactly how much this sort of thing costs. I arranged for these same people to come to a party I did in Dallas once for a guest of the hotel. A man whose son was having a birthday." She shook her head, her hair gleaming in the evening light. "It cost a fortune then...I can't image what you had to pay them to come here."

"I wanted to do it...for Bella."

Annie glanced toward the children and adults crowding around the now unloaded animals. Several of the parents had run to get their video cameras and they were recording the event as the trainers saddled the horses and lifted the children onto the animals' backs. "Well, I can't let you," she said stiffly. "It's way too much money to spend on a simple little party. I...I insist on helping you with the bill."

"That's not necessary, Annie. I can handle it."

"I know you can handle it," she said, her voice growing slightly more frosty. "I know you can *more* than handle it. But until things are...resolved between us, Bella is still *my* responsibility and I can pay her way."

Gray stared Annie, his anger slowly mounting. "You're being unreasonable."

"I don't think so."

"She's my daughter, for God's sake. I can spend money on her if I want to."

Sparks of disapproval and indignation shot from Annie's gaze. "You don't know for sure she's your daughter, and even if she is, things like this are...are too extravagant for children."

"They're just horses! You're making too big a deal out of this."

"They aren't just horses! They're Shetland ponies with matching leather saddles that you've had trucked in over four hundred miles for a two-hour children's afternoon playtime. That's ridiculous, Gray."

"*You're* the one who's being ridiculous." He felt his eyes narrow. "If I can afford it and I want to do this, what right do you have to give me a hard time about it?"

"I have every right. She's *my* daughter, and in my opinion, it's wrong to throw money at kids." Annie's face flushed as she lifted one hand to push back a curl of brown hair. "You're trying to buy her affection, that's what you're doing, and it's wrong!"

He started to sputter. "B-buy her affection? You're crazy!"

"Am I?" She stepped closer to him, her hands now on her hips. "Did you even think twice about this? Did you wonder if she might be afraid of horses? Or even allergic to animals? Or did you just pick up the phone and order them—just like that?" She snapped her fingers.

"You're way out of line here, Annie."

"No—you're the one that's out of line." She tossed her head toward the animals. "You try to take charge of everything. Control everything! It doesn't work that way, Gray. Kids know when you're doing things out of love and when you're doing them because *you* think it's a good thing. If you'd been around all along, you might know that by now."

She stopped him cold. Not with her words, but the way she said them. Her voice was so disgusted she made it sound as if he'd committed a horrible crime.

He took a deep breath and let it out slowly. "I would have been around—*all along*—if I'd known Bella really existed. How many times do I have to tell you the truth before you'll believe me?" He stared into Annie's eyes and didn't blink. "Bella is *my* daughter, Annie, and I love her. I'm not going away, and nothing you can say will hurt me enough to run me off. You'd better begin to accept that."

Chapter 8

The end of summer always brought tons of guests to Riverside—families trying for one last getaway, couples who weren't quite ready to settle down, retirees looking for a calm spot before fall began in earnest. The week after Bella's party—the last week of August—was no exception, and Annie found herself swamped with more reservations than she could handle and more problems than she could solve.

And she was grateful for each and every one of them.

Because they kept her from thinking. Thinking about the way Gray looked when his eyes met hers. Thinking about the way he'd so easily spent all that money for the ponies. Thinking about the way he really could provide so many things for Bella that Annie would never be able to.

That was what had really bothered her about the whole party situation. The casual way he'd arranged for everything had more than sufficiently pointed out that Annie could never give Bella what Gray could. Ponies on demand, a private school, the finest college education without worrying about tuition bills. It tore Annie up.

Gray was going to win.

He was going to take Bella and leave, no matter what.

So all Annie could do was ignore the pain and confusion and terror…and pray.

There was one thing she couldn't ignore, though. Bella's first day of school. In just a few more days, she'd be walking out the door and getting on that yellow school bus. Every time Annie thought about that, she wanted to break into tears. She'd been dreading it before Gray had shown up. Now the day held even more significance.

It got so bad that Friday morning Maggie threw her out of the kitchen right after breakfast. "I can't stand to look at that long face of yours anymore," she announced. "Go out there and weed the garden. Work it off."

She'd been at it an hour when a long shadow fell over her. She looked up and straight into Gray's black eyes.

"Maggie told me you were out here," he said. His gaze was frosty. They hadn't even spoken since the party. "I'd like to talk to you about something."

She reached into the dirt and yanked out a tomato plant instead of a weed.

"It's about Monday," he said.

Her head jerked up. "Monday—as in Bella's-first-day-of-school-Monday?"

"That's right," he said. "I think—"

Before he could say anything else, she stood, her dirt-encrusted palms held out before her. "Oh, no. Don't even try it. There's no way I could explain that. You aren't going with us, and you certainly aren't taking her yourself. Forget it—"

His expression tightened. "I'm not an idiot, Annie. Even I know my appearance there would be awkward. It's just…"

"What?" she said guardedly.

"I don't want her to ride the bus that first day. I want you to take her to school yourself."

A flash of anger came over Annie at his presumptuousness. Here was something else he was trying to control—would it never end? Just as quickly, though, her irritation turned into wariness. His voice was still gruff and deep, but it held something else—something that sounded remarkably like concern, instead of intimidation. Was the change genuine, or was this some new technique to get her to lower her guard? She answered slowly, trying to figure out what was going on.

"I already asked Dana about this—she's Bella's teacher—and she was adamant. No driving them to school on the first day. According to the authorities, the children need to get on the bus and become accustomed to going that way. It's less painful for everyone and it makes the kids more indepen—"

"I don't give a damn what the school says," he answered, interrupting her. "I want to make sure she gets to the right classroom. *You* need go in with her."

He turned abruptly silent and said nothing else. She spoke again, even more slowly this time. "I've taken her down to the school already and showed her which room is hers. She knows the way."

She could tell by his stubborn expression that her words made no difference. His mind was made up. Once again, she felt powerless in the face of his determination and intensity. He was coming from a different place with this, but his tenacity was certainly familiar.

"It'll be different that first day. The halls will be crowded, there will be lots of other kids. She shouldn't be alone."

Before she could come up with another argument, he spoke again.

"This isn't open for negotiation, Annie. I came out here to tell you I want you to take her to school. If you disagree with me, I'll take her and *you* can worry about how to explain it. I don't give a damn how it bothers you. Either way—she is not going to find herself standing on the sidewalk out front wondering what the hell to do." He crossed his arms and glared at her. "Which is it going to be?"

Annie's spine stiffened. She'd never agreed with Dana and had been going to take Bella to school all along. In the back of her mind, Annie had known it might be one of the last times she'd ever get to do something so special with Bella. Now Gray was trying to control even this. Why? Why did he have to do this? A part of her sensed he had a reason, just as part of her had known he'd had secrets when he arrived. She told herself she didn't care, but then she noticed his hands. They were balled into fists, the knuckles white.

"What's it going to be?" he repeated.

Trying to read the complex emotions behind his eyes, she lifted her gaze and stared at him. She found the task impossible. "I'll take her," she finally answered.

He visibly relaxed, his shoulders losing their tension, the lines easing from his face. "I appreciate it," was all he said. A minute later, he turned and walked out of the garden, leaving Annie more puzzled and confused than ever.

Early the next morning, when they came out to leave for school, Gray was waiting for them, leaning against the Jeep, a gold-wrapped box in his hand. Bella ran up to him, her new book bag bouncing against her shoulders, her smile wide. Annie trailed behind the little girl, trying to act upbeat but feeling an emptiness already growing inside her for the loss about to occur. Bella's baby days were over the minute she walked into that classroom. Nothing would ever be the same.

"I'm going to school!" she cried as she reached his side. "It's my very first day!"

Gray nodded. "I know." His voice was serious and deep in the early morning quiet. He glanced toward Annie and something in his eyes caught inside of her. He was as nervous and upset as she was about Bella's first day. All at once she felt a curious mixture of understanding, sympathy and commiseration. As they shared a look that telegraphed these feelings, a strange sense of confusion came over Annie. Despite that devastating kiss the other day, they weren't supposed to have anything in common. What was this?

He broke their gaze and kneeled in front of Bella to hand her the box. "I have a little present for you."

Annie stepped to one side. A present? He hadn't said anything about a present. What was in that box? The moment of closeness they'd just shared evaporated. If he'd gotten Bella something outrageous and expensive... Like a pendulum swinging the other way, the warmth Annie had felt a moment before fled instantly, and was replaced by suspicion.

With a cry of delight, Bella tore into the gold box. Pulling back the top, she let her eyes go wide in surprise and sudden pleasure. "A watch!"

Annie leaned forward to see better. Expecting a gold Rolex at the very least, she was surprised but pleased by the simple digital face and leather band.

"That's right," Gray answered. "It's your very own watch and when it says three o'clock, Annie will be right in front of the school to pick you up. Right outside in the line where she's going to drop you off, okay?"

Annie looked down at him in surprise. He'd obviously called the school and found out when classes were over.

"Don't get in the car with anyone else, and wait right there for her. She'll be right on time."

Bella threw her arms around his shoulders and hugged him, her smile almost dazzling. "Oh, thank you, Gray. It's s-o-o-o cool!"

"I'm glad you like it." He stood up and looked at Annie. "Make sure she gets to the right room, and don't leave her anywhere else—"

"It'll be okay—" Annie put her hand on his arm before she even realized what she was doing. A second later, she snatched it back. "I...I'll make sure."

He nodded once, then he was gone.

Some things never change.

The minute Annie walked into Bella's classroom, she felt as if she were six years old again. The smell of chalk, the cries of the other children, the teacher's voice trying to override the confusion but failing...it all brought back so many memories. Annie could almost see herself and Monica huddled in the corner, Annie trying to calm some imaginary fear of Monica's, Monica clinging to Annie for reassurance.

It was a strange memory, bittersweet and heavy against her mind. Just like the incident before they'd left. Gray had seemed so worried, so concerned. She asked herself why she even cared, but deep down, Annie knew the answer.

"Oh, boy! This is it!" Bella cried.

"This is it," Annie said with a grin, putting aside her thoughts. "And look—there's Dana—Mrs. Villaret." Annie waved to the petite blonde at the front of the room. "Your teacher, remember?"

Bella nodded and smiled widely as the woman crossed the room towards them. She wore a denim pinafore with apples and blackboards and ABCs printed across the top, and her grin was as wide as Bella's.

"Bella—how great to see you! I put you right over there by the window. Why don't you go see if you can find your spot?" The little girl ran off, and Dana Villaret turned to Annie and smiled. "I see you didn't take my advice. I knew you wouldn't. No one ever does. They all have to bring the kids themselves."

Annie shrugged, her expression sheepish. "I thought it was better this way."

"It's okay," the teacher said. "I understand." She continued to speak, not even stopping for a breath as she glanced past Annie and spoke to the two children behind her. "Brittany—don't hit Gus like that. We're big people now—we don't hit each other." Turning back once more, she smiled apologetically. "Sorry, but I better start to calm the natives or they're going to bring down the house." She reached over and patted Annie on the arm. "Bella will be fine—don't worry about her, okay?"

Annie realized then she had tears in her eyes. Hiding them the best she could, she looked across the room at Bella and waved. The little girl came bounding across the room, obviously already thrilled with the entire situation.

"Did you see my table?" she asked Annie, her green eyes shining. "It's right over there—by the window! And that's Hannah—wave to her...she's sitting at my table too!"

Obligingly, Annie waved to the plump little girl sitting near the edge of the room. She waved back, then Annie turned to Bella, a big knot growing in her chest as she straightened the collar on the denim jacket Bella wore. "I want you to be a good girl, today, all right? And learn lots of neat things." Annie's throat tightened and suddenly she dropped down and wrapped her arms around the narrow shoulders. Breathing in the baby-shampoo smell, she fought back tears. "I'm proud of you, Bella, and I love you very much. You remember that."

Bella nodded seriously. "I will, Annie. And I'll be really good. I promise."

"I know you will, sweetheart. You always are."

They wrapped their arms around each other, then a painful burning started in Annie's throat. It edged its way deeper into her chest as the reality of the moment sank in.

In just a few short weeks, Gray was going to take Bella away. Annie would never get to see her again, never get to hug her, never get to put her to bed. Despite the moment they'd shared this morning, he would do exactly what he'd come to Timberley *to* do. He'd claim Bella and leave. And after that, he'd be the one taking her to school, tying her shoes, fixing her dinner. He'd be doing it all until she was big enough not to need him.

Until that moment, Annie hadn't *really* understood what the future held. She'd thought about it, agonized over it, considered it...but she'd never completely understood, deep down inside.

But now she did.

The comprehension came instantly with a blinding kind of clarity. It left her breathless and weak.

She was going to lose Bella.

She would be all alone.

With no one to love.

She was in the small square across the street from the school. From his parked car on the opposite side, Gray had watched her and Bella go inside. Then he'd waited until Annie had emerged alone. At that point, he'd been going to leave...to drive away and never even let her know he'd been there. Since the pony fiasco she'd been so distant and cold, he'd thought she wouldn't even talk to him anymore until he'd approached her yesterday. Part of him was still upset over her accusations, and the other part of him was wincing from the bit of truth her words had held. He *had* wanted to impress Bella, to make her happy, to win that smile that took his breath away.

But now, as he took one look at Annie's face, he knew leaving was impossible. It didn't make any sense at all, it scared him half to death, he wanted to just forget about it—but he could no more abandon Annie here than he could have left Bella once he'd found out she was his. That was just the way it was.

He got out of his car, crossed the street and entered the park.

She was sitting on one of the swings, tears running down her face. "Annie?" he said softly.

She jerked around, then her expression shifted as she recognized him. "Wh-what do you want?"

"To help," he said simply. Stepping up behind her, he took a chance and put his hands on her shoulders, squeezing them once with what he hoped was reassurance.

Obviously too miserable even to give him a hard time, Annie turned her back, saying nothing. After a few moments, he began to push her gently in the swing. The ropes creaked in the wind and the smell of late-summer roses drifted on the breeze. Every now and then, he caught snatches of sounds from the school across the street. The windows were open, and a babble of excited voices escaped, mixing with the noise of a barking dog a few streets over. Gray wondered if any of the voices belonged to Bella. Then he began to speak, softly, somehow hoping that his story might ease the pain radiating from Annie…the pain he knew he was causing.

"Before my boarding-school years began, I attended a small public school a lot like this one. My parents were still married at that point—still married but fighting like crazy—and neither one of them wanted to stop the arguing long enough to take me to school on my very first day. So the housekeeper drove me over." He paused for a few beats, then continued. "Drove me over, opened the car door, and told me to get out. I'd never even seen the place before. Had no idea what to do."

Beneath his fingers, Annie's shoulders tensed. He went on before she could say anything.

"I followed the rest of the kids inside. It seemed like at least a thousand of them were packed in the halls, in the rooms, everywhere I looked. Matter of perspective now, I guess." He laughed lightly at the memory. "I had utterly no idea of what to do, then all of a sudden, I saw someone I recognized. A kid whose mother helped clean our house sometimes when we needed extra help. I ran over to him and asked him where I ought to go." Gray paused, then went on. "He didn't have the foggiest idea, of course, so he did what any kid would do...he took me to the first-grade classroom where he had gone the year before. I went inside and sat down. About an hour later, when all the confusion sorted itself out, the teacher realized I didn't belong in her classroom. She sent me down the hall to the principal's office and I sat there for another hour. By the time they saw me and figured out who I was and where I ought to be, it was time to go home."

He had started the story to distract Annie, but now he was feeling something he hadn't felt in a very long time. Something he couldn't—wouldn't—put a name to.

"That...that's why you wanted to come today." A furrowed line crossed Annie's forehead.

He took his hands from her shoulders and held them out. "Guilty as charged."

She rose, her fingers gripping the worn ropes just under his own. They were only inches apart and he could almost feel the emotion hovering around her. It was heavy and burdensome, a problem she didn't seem to know how to deal with.

"How could they do that to you?" Her voice was husky with barely repressed anger. "How could two adults be so self-absorbed that something like that could happen?"

"They were too busy fighting." He paused. "And frankly...they just didn't give a damn."

"But they were your parents."

"It doesn't take a special emotional quality to give birth—only the right physical equipment."

She stared at him, silent, almost uncomprehending, her blue eyes even bluer in the morning sunlight, under the dappled shade. He leaned closer to her, close enough to catch her perfume, close enough to see the faint lines along the corner of her mouth.

"Do you understand why I'm telling you this, Annie?" He didn't wait for her answer. "I may not know what's appropriate for a children's party and I may not always hit exactly the right note, but I didn't have parents who even cared enough to do that! My mother was never there, emotionally speaking, and my father was way out of the picture. I was completely alone. I would *never* let that happen to Bella, I promise you. I know how important it is... I know what happens when nobody cares."

Her blue eyes filled and turned into liquid sapphires, shimmering with love and confusion and hurt. "I understand what you're saying, but it takes more than that. More than good intentions." She held her hands out, palms up. "You...you don't know anything about her. You don't know how she likes her clothes laid out, and you don't know how much sugar to put in her cocoa. You don't even know when her birthday is, for God's sake."

"I'll learn."

"How?" Her voice broke, cracked in two like a piece of delicate china. "Who's going to teach you?"

"You can."

She brought her hands up to her face and covered it; then a second later, she dropped them. "I can't do that, Gray. You're asking the impossible."

He refused to back down. "Then I guess she'll have to do it."

Her expression went into one of horror. "You can't do that to her...she's just a kid! Why should she have to tell her father who she is?"

"She shouldn't," he broke in harshly. "And I'll never forget that it's my fault she's in the place where she is." His fingers tightened on the rope until his knuckles turned white. "Have you got any idea how many times I've questioned myself? If I'd listened to Monica, none of this would even be happening. I was wrong, Annie, and I know it. I should have come back when Monica told me she was pregnant. Hell, I should never have left her in the first place. If I'd tried harder, listened to her better...paid more attention. Who knows what might have happened...." He paused and shook his head. "But I didn't, and now I have a second chance. I have to try and be the best father I can be for Bella. I...I think I can do that, too. I love her. I want to take her home, provide for her, give her the things I should have been giving her all these years."

"But giving her *things* isn't the answer," Annie said, a stubborn light shining from her eyes. "I can give her love—and that's what she needs."

"I can give her that, too. I have more than enough."

A breeze shook the oak tree overhead and a shower of golden leaves rained down. One landed on Annie's shoulder then lifted off on the very next breath of wind. Gray watched it sail away, then his eyes met hers once more.

"There's no doubt in anyone's mind that you've done a wonderful job." His voice was gentle, soft. "But I'm her father. And it's time for me to take over now."

* * *

Annie checked the clock on her office wall at least once every ten minutes, but the hands seemed to drag themselves around the dial. She'd never seen a day go by so slowly. Every few minutes she would find herself wondering what Bella was doing…if she was having fun…if she was missing Annie. In the very next second, Annie would tell herself to get used to it. If things went as Gray wanted them to, she could be spending the rest of her life doing the same thing. And she'd be doing it alone.

The thought drove her crazy. She'd tried to explain the emotion to Gray in the park, but it had been hopeless. He just didn't understand.

To keep some portion of her sanity intact, she returned to the half-painted living room and began to paint once more. As the afternoon progressed and she got more and more of the color of the walls, the room took on a honey-tinged glow that would be perfect for the upcoming wedding. Annie barely noticed, though. She'd been able to think of only one thing besides Bella for the last few hours, and the picture in her mind was haunting. She couldn't dislodge the image of a little boy, a lock of black hair falling over his forehead, his dark eyes confused and upset. How in the world could Gray's parents have been so selfish? Were people really like that? Did parents actually do that sort of thing?

She dipped her brush back into the bucket and told herself they did. The newspapers were full of stories about people who did that—and much much worse—but it was so sad! She remembered the look in his eyes when he'd handed Bella the watch. So earnest, so caring. With a start, she realized she was thinking about everything he'd done and said in the past few days. He *would* be a good father…and another piece of her heart broke off and shattered.

By a quarter till three, when Gray stuck his head inside

the living room and said, "It's time for you to go get Bella," Annie was a complete wreck. He didn't seem to notice, though, because he wasn't much better. The tie that was knotted at his neck was skewed to one side, and there were lines radiating like fans from the corners of his eyes. He held his briefcase in a death grip. Suddenly, incredibly, she found herself speaking.

"Would you like to go with me?" She regretted the words the instant they escaped, but it was too late to take them back.

Gray's eyes locked on hers, a flash of surprised gratefulness sparking in their depths before he hid it. "Yes— I'd like that very much."

Ten minutes later, just as Annie and Gray pulled up to the school, children poured out of the doors like a rush of water. Parking against the curb, both of them got out of the car. Before they could go forward, Bella spotted them and came running toward them. In her hands she clutched a sheet of wrinkled paper.

Kneeling down, her arms outstretched, Annie greeted Bella with a cry. "Hi, sweetheart! Oh, I missed you so much! How was your very first day?"

Bella sent a fleeting smile in Annie's direction, but she bypassed her and ran straight to Gray. Throwing herself around his knees, she hugged him tightly and looked up, her smile even bigger than it had been the second before. She finally released him, almost reluctantly, it seemed, and held out the puckered paper toward him. "I drew a picture," she said. "Wanna see?"

A stunning numbness descended over Annie as she realized what was happening. She couldn't move, she couldn't talk, she couldn't do anything but watch as Gray oohed and ahhed over Bella's drawing.

"I did it just for you," Bella said shyly. "You can keep it in your room."

Annie told herself it was only because he was new and different, a recent addition to Bella's world. Cursing her silliness, she struggled to hold back the tears burning in her throat. Just then, Gray looked up, his dark eyes meeting hers and reading in them everything she wanted to hide.

"Come look at this, Annie." He held out the paper toward her. "It's a wonderful picture. I think Bella's going to be a real artist, don't you?"

Rising slowly, she took the drawing. The image blurred and she couldn't even see what it was. "It...it's fantastic," she managed to get out. "Beautiful colors...and so...so nice!"

Bella beamed at Annie's praise, but she slipped her hand inside Gray's as she began to chatter once more.

The hole in Annie's heart grew larger.

The three of them climbed into Gray's car and he drove them home as Bella continued to talk excitedly. She loved her teacher, she "adored" her new best friend, and she'd hit a home run during recess. Even the food in the cafeteria was "outstanding." Annie tried to listen and nod her head at all the right times, but it was almost impossible. How much more could she take? Every day Bella was slipping away from her, inch by inch, and it felt as if the skin were being peeled off Annie's body each time it happened.

They pulled into the driveway a few minutes later and Maggie met them on the porch. She greeted Bella, then spoke over her head to Annie. "Am I glad to see you! We have a slight problem inside."

Annie fought the fog inside her. "What's wrong?"

"Mr. and Mrs. Hood are here. They have reservations for the Alamo Suite. The same suite they spent their honeymoon in last year."

"What's wrong with that?"

"Mr. and Mrs. Clark are here, too. Guess which suite you promised them?"

"Oh, God...don't tell me—"

"Okay, I won't tell you." Maggie held the door open. "But good luck and God bless..."

Swiping a hand across her eyes, Annie entered the dim coolness of the entryway and headed straight for her office. Behind her she could hear Bella begin her story all over again for Maggie, who was acting appropriately excited as well. Before Annie could reach the door to her office, a hand fell on her shoulder. She turned and found herself inches from Gray.

He was looking into her eyes, his hand warm and heavy, his gaze even more so. A circle of energy enclosed them, and even though Annie fought it, she knew it was an exercise in futility. Gray had some kind of power over her, some kind of undefined appeal that went beyond anything she'd ever experienced with a man. She tried to shrug off his hand, but he kept it where it was. "I'm sorry, but I have guests waiting—"

"I know," he said, his voice low and husky. "But I've been thinking about what you said this morning. I had a lot of time to think today while I was waiting for the school bell to ring." He smiled, then continued. "Would you go out to dinner with me tomorrow night?"

Her emotional roller coaster took another dive.

"Dinner?" What kind of trick was he planning now?

"You know—you go to a restaurant, order food, eat it? That sort of thing."

"I *know* what you mean, I just...well...I..."

He held up his hands, palms out. "No obligations. No strings."

She flashed on the kiss they'd shared. The kiss she'd told him would not, under any circumstances, be repeated. Was that what he meant by "no strings"? Part of her hoped so, while the other part felt a quiver of disappointment, as much as she hated to admit it. God, this was crazy!

"I don't know..." she wavered. "I have so much to do...."

"You have to eat, don't you?"

"Yes, but I..." *God, why couldn't she get the words out?*

"Here's the deal," he said finally. His voice had turned softer, but there was an edge to it as well. "I *do* have to know more about Bella. I realized that today after we talked. You're the only one who can help me, so please don't fight me on this, too."

She didn't know what to say.

"I heard about a little hole-in-the-wall place—"

"Tia's?" she asked automatically.

"Been there?"

"Not in a very long time, but it's good."

"Then you have no more excuses." Unexpectedly, he lifted his other hand to her face and trailed the back of one finger down her cheek. "Please? I really do need some help."

His touch radiated all the way down her body until it seemed as if she were vibrating. Her breath caught in her throat. Several answers hovered in her mind, but there was only one reply she could give him...the one she shouldn't have.

"What time do you want to leave?"

Chapter 9

"I really love Hannah," Bella announced as she watched Annie dress for dinner the following evening. "She has lots of brothers and sisters and they all live in a great big old house. Her daddy picked her up at school yesterday. Rose's daddy picked her up, too."

Annie was listening with half an ear. She'd given the Hoods the Alamo Suite, and the Clarks a gift certificate for fifty dollars, plus their choice of the rooms she'd had available. Then she'd picked up the phone half a dozen times to call Gray and take back her idiotic decision to go out with him. But her fingers froze over the dial each time. She didn't want to help him, but what choice did she have? Bella was more important than feeling comfortable, right? Like all the other dilemmas Annie had faced in the past month, her decision was also tinged with something else—the incredible pull she felt every time she was around Gray. The attraction hung over her like a storm cloud—waiting, threatening, inevitable in its ending.

She knew he felt it, too. Or at least she thought he did. The kiss they'd shared had made his interest seem genuine. A tiny part of her wondered about that, too, though. Was it all part of some elaborate scheme of his? Was this dinner and the kiss and the looks they were always exchanging a way of romancing her subtly in case he needed a backup plan to get Bella? She couldn't help but wonder.

Shaking her head and holding back a moan, Annie ripped another blouse off the hanger and jabbed her arms into the sleeves.

"—so I told her I'd ask you, but I was sure you'd say yes. I can go, can't I, Annie? You don't care?"

Annie buttoned the blouse and glanced toward the clock. Gray was probably waiting downstairs and she hadn't even combed her hair. Not that it would matter anyway. Her hair seemed to have a life of its own.

"Can I, Annie? Can I?"

Annie shoved the tail of the blouse into the waistband of her black skirt, then zipped it up and patted down the material. "Can you what, sweetie?"

"Aren't you listening?" Bella said indignantly.

Annie sat down on the bed and pulled the little girl toward her. "No. I wasn't listening. Try me again."

Bella grinned. It was a gap-toothed smile since she'd lost one of her front teeth the day before. "Hannah asked me to spend the night next weekend. I told her I had to ask you first. Can I go?"

"And what's Hannah's last name?"

"I dunno."

"And where does she live?"

"I dunno."

Annie already knew exactly who Hannah was. The resemblance was too strong for the little girl to be anyone but Mary Jo Martin's daughter. Mary Jo had sat beside Annie in the first grade, too. Mother and daughter had the same shape and the same sunny disposition. "You know you can't stay with friends until I talk first with their parents. Have Hannah's mother call me or get her phone number and I'll call her."

"A-a-l-l ri-ight." Bella drew the phrase out until it held four disgusted syllables. She reached up and touched one of the dangling gold earrings Annie had already taken off and put back on two times. "Where are you going?" she asked suddenly.

Annie thought for a second of fibbing, but she couldn't. Not to Bella. "Gray and I are going out to dinner," she said reluctantly.

Bella's eyes lit up like two green beacons. "A date?" she breathed. "You're going out with Gray on a date?"

Annie repeated the words she'd said yesterday to Maggie. "It's not a date. We're just going to Tia's for Mexican food, that's all. We have to...talk about some things."

"That's a date," Bella said seriously. "Is he going to sleep in your bed afterwards?"

Annie's mouth dropped open and she began to sputter. "I...I should hope not." *Liar.* "Only married people sleep together and we aren't married. What on earth makes you ask a question like that, anyway?"

"On Sally Maury Bovitch they talk about stuff like that all the time, and those people aren't married—at least not to each other." Bella's voice held great authority. "First it starts with kissing, then next they take off their clothes and—"

Horrified, Annie stood up and put her hands on her hips. "How many times have I told you not to watch those terrible shows? Where did you see that, anyway?"

Bella's bottom lip came out and quivered once, then she spoke. "I...I saw it at Rose's house. *Her* mommy doesn't care if we watch 'em."

"Well, I care," Annie said indignantly. "And I don't

want you doing that again. If you want to watch TV, it's
the Discovery Channel or nothing."

"A-a-l-l right."

Ten minutes later, Annie was closing Bella's door and
slipping outside, shaking her head at the conversation of a
moment before. Bella's voice stopped her before she could
step out into the hall.

"Annie?"

"Yes, sweetheart?"

"If you and Gray got married, *would* he sleep in your
bed?"

Annie closed her eyes. "Yes."

"Would he kiss you?"

"Probably."

A small silence, a small *waiting* silence, then a gush of
words. "If that happened, would he be my daddy? I'd
really, really like that, Annie. I'd like to have a daddy, and
Gray is really cool...."

Annie swallowed hard in the dark. It had been years
since Bella had said anything about wanting a daddy. Usually she seemed to accept the situation. Now this! Did she
have radar, for God's sake? Shaking her head, Annie finally interrupted the little girl's words. "Go to sleep, Bella.
We'll...talk about it later."

The tables inside were all full when Gray and Annie
walked into Tia's, the local Mexican restaurant. Which
was fine with Gray. The stretch of empty patio and its
tables under the spreading arms of the willow trees near
the river was much more appealing to him. It was prettier,
quieter and more private—something he would appreciate
because every time they got together, he ended up telling
Annie something about himself that he'd kept hidden for
a very long time.

She had that kind of effect on him.

Along with a few others, he was beginning to realize. Asking her to dinner tonight had been an impulse. He wanted to know more about Bella, of course, but he had also wanted more time with Annie. To study her, to hear her voice, to see if he could figure out why she was starting to bother him so much.

With his hand on the small of her back, they followed the hostess outside and selected a table near the edge of the river. The water gurgled softly as he pulled back Annie's chair. He sat down opposite her and they ordered a pitcher of margaritas.

From across the table, Gray studied Annie. She wore a blouse he'd never seen before, royal blue silk. The color made her eyes even bluer than usual and the soft fabric draped enticingly against the fullness of her breasts. Before they'd sat down he'd noticed her skirt as well—black and formfitting with a long slit up one side. She'd held it close to her body when he'd opened the car door for her, but a sudden gust of wind had defeated her purpose. The glimpse of soft, bare thigh had been tantalizing.

So he wouldn't think about that fact a minute longer, Gray spoke. "I really appreciate you coming with me this evening. There're so many things I wish I knew about Bella."

She looked uncomfortable but played along. "Like what?"

He crossed his arms and leaned his elbows on the table. "Well…for instance, how'd she get her name?"

Annie's eyes turned warm. "Bella was my grandmother's name."

He'd assumed Monica had named the baby. God—Annie really had done everything for this child, hadn't she? He hid his reaction and forged ahead. "When's her birthday?"

"July 21st."

"Was she a fussy baby?"

"Absolutely not." Annie's fingers twined around the vase sitting on the table. It held a single pink rose. "She had to stay at the hospital a little longer than usual because she had jaundice, but she recovered very quickly and after that, just the usual childhood things. She's always been very healthy—perfect, in fact."

The waitress returned, and after placing the pitcher of drinks on the table, along with two huge glasses, she took their orders, then disappeared. The patio stayed empty, the only conversation around them that of the leaves and the river. Annie lifted one delicate hand to corral a wayward curl, and spoke again. "She's very athletic now. Did you play a lot of sports when you were a kid?"

"Sure...track, basketball, baseball—whatever was in season."

"I thought so. Monica never did anything like that...." She trailed off. "But then I guess you know that, don't you?"

"Not really. She didn't talk much about her childhood. I always got the impression she was embarrassed about it somehow."

Annie looked down into the glass she held. For a moment she didn't speak, then she nodded. "She *was* embarrassed about it. She and her mother lived in a tiny little house right off the square. Her mother worked at the local hospital during the day, then cleaned offices at night. She did the best she could for them, but Monica was always ashamed by the fact that she worked, *how* she worked. Monica wanted a mom like everyone else had, she always said."

"Her father had already passed away by then?"

Annie's eyes were perplexed when she looked up. "Passed away?"

it was an act...if he was somehow trying to seduce her nd get her off guard. If that *was* his plan, she finally ecided, it was working.

By the time they drove back to Riverside, Annie felt as nough she were going to explode. She could hardly wait or Gray to open her car door so she could jump out of e Mercedes and run into her study to hide. If she didn't, he was afraid something drastic would happen. Something lose to the scenario Bella had described earlier. *First it tarts with kissing, then next they take off their clothes nd—*

He opened her door and she climbed out of the car, but nstead of stepping back, Gray stayed where he was. They tood so close together she could see the fine fan of lines t the corners of his eyes. Why didn't he move back? Why as he always so close to her?

As if reading her mind, he moved even closer. Then he fted one finger and put it lightly on her left eyebrow, on e scar she carried there. "How did you get that?" he id softly, his breath warm and seductive against her ieek.

Annie's own breath was trapped in her chest, making r feel tight and anxious. "Maggie gave it to me," she ally managed to get out. "We were fighting once when were kids and she threw a toy pistol at me. It hit me the head. I had two stitches and I was really proud of em. I didn't want the doctor to take them out."

He chuckled, a low, deep sound. "You two seem to ve a rocky relationship."

"Not really."

"But you were fighting the other day." His eyes rched her face. "I heard you before I walked into the ng room. What was all that about?"

'We were fighting about you."

'I'm sorry...who won?"

"He had a heart attack when she was fifteen, didn't he?"

This time she waited even longer before she spoke. "Monica's father never lived here. I...I didn't know him."

An uneasy feeling came over Gray. "I thought they all lived here. She told me he owned a small business and worked constantly."

"Her...her father was not in the picture, Gray. As far as I know, he abandoned them when Monica was five. If she told you anything about him, she must have made it up."

Gray leaned back in his chair, stunned and more than a little surprised. The panic that had been in Monica's eyes every time he left town, the anxiety in her expression when he came in late, the relentless fear she had of him leaving her... He suddenly understood, more than he ever had before. He swiped a hand over his face. "God...I had no idea."

In the summer darkness, the crickets began to chirp. A dove called out.

Annie's voice was soft, remembering, sad. "The first year she was here, the Friday before Father's Day, she hid on the playground at lunchtime. Afterwards, she skipped school completely. I found her when I was on the way home, rolled up in a little ball beside the corner of the school building. She told me she was sick." Annie took a sip of her drink, then looked over at him. "I didn't realize what was going on until later. All the kids got to invite their fathers to eat lunch with them in the cafeteria. Afterwards, we brought them back to our classes to see our artwork. She didn't have anyone to show anything to."

His chest tight, Gray looked through the darkness at Annie. "Oh, God..."

"The next year I asked her to sit with me and my dad, and after lunch, he looked at her pictures and then he looked at mine. Every year from then until he died, he'd do it that way."

She turned quiet and sipped her drink, but suddenly a lot more than just Monica's actions became clear to Gray. A myriad of things clicked into place, explanations and revelations. He'd expected Annie to be just like Monica, but the truth was she'd taken care of Monica…just as she took care of Maggie, and the old lady who sold cookies no one could eat, and the strangers that came through the door of Riverside. She liked to take care of people…just as she wanted to take care of Bella.

Annie was a woman who loved to love.

"Why aren't you married, Annie?" he said softly.

Her gaze came up. It was open and clear. "I was once. It didn't work out."

"Why?"

She shrugged. "It was a mistake. A five year mistake and I never intend to repeat it."

"But don't you want a family?"

She stared into her drink for a very long time, then finally she raised her eyes and met his gaze, her voice husky. "I thought I *did* have one."

Her words shot through him with painful accuracy. Gray didn't know what to say. Only the waitress's sudden appearance saved him. Putting the generous platters in front of them, she fussed about the table for a few minutes, then left. They both ignored their dinner.

Gathering his thoughts, Gray reached across the table and covered Annie's hand with his. "I know you find this hard to believe, but I genuinely don't want to hurt you, Annie. You've done a wonderful job with Bella. I don't know another person who has the ability to love and nurture like you do."

"Then why can't you leave her with me?" Annie whispered. "Why can't you just go away and leave us alone?"

"Because it's not that simple anymore. I can't ju out of her life now."

"But she doesn't know who you are yet."

"That's right. But I know who *she* is."

The air crackled between them and for a momen was sure Annie was going to jump up and run awa eyes turned blue-black and her jaw was a solid lin the edge of her delicate earlobe to the dimple in the of her chin. He tightened his grip on her hand.

"You know me now, Annie. You know the real n the Grayston Powers that Monica warned you abo you really think I could abandon my only child?"

Her eyes locked on his, then she slumped, her sho easing against the back of her chair. "No," she whis "I don't think you could…and that's what scares death."

She wanted to leave.

She wanted to jump up, run away and leave.

But she didn't. Annie stayed in her chair and ate bite of her dinner. Nodding politely, she listened small talk Gray was making and even managed to c ute some of her own. She felt as if she were spli two, though.

No matter what she said, no matter what she did, as determined as she was. He wanted Bella, and would change his mind.

So how in the world could Annie be sitting ac table from this man and be wondering which sid bed he slept on? And what he wore when he sle wore anything at all? And what his eyes looked l he first opened them in the morning? An and…the list went on and on. She couldn't believ she couldn't stop it. He was being charming and and attentive and all she could do wa

Annie's jaw tightened. "No one won...and no one *will* win."

Ignoring both the tone and meaning of her words, he lifted his hand again and traced the faint line of her scar.

A funny catch developed in Annie's throat. It took her a moment to speak. "Gray, this isn't—" she said.

He put his finger over her lips and stopped her from saying more. "Don't say it. I already know what you think." His eyes glittered in the faint light spilling from the windows of the house behind them. He was going to kiss her, and she knew it. By now she could read the signs—the huskiness that came into his voice, the darkness that intensified in his gaze. She wanted to stop him, but she couldn't.

So he pulled her into his arms and once again, Annie's world tilted.

Everything she felt, everything she knew, everything she believed in, shifted and reformed itself into another dimension. Wrong went right and up turned down.

How could one man do this to her?

His arms tightened around her shoulders and his hands slipped over the silk of her blouse, warming the skin underneath as though she wore nothing at all. His touch was gentle but insistent and when his fingers came around and cupped the fullness of her breast, Annie's legs felt as though they were made of reeds, too flimsy and insubstantial to hold up a bloom, much less her body. For what seemed like forever, his lips moved against hers, hard and demanding, then he slid his mouth away, down the side of her jaw to the edge of her ear. He took her earlobe into his mouth and sucked.

A light of desire went on inside of her, and everything she'd known about Gray, felt about him, been *told* about him, no longer mattered. A new image of him formed in her mind. He was a man who was very far from being cold, very removed from being heartless. He was just the opposite, in fact, and everything in his touch and his attitude—to her and to Bella—proved that. The light inside her shone even brighter.

And at that second, even despite this knowledge of what he wanted, Annie knew she was doomed. It was only a matter of time.

Fighting the awful realization, she jerked back suddenly, her eyes blazing, her whole body trembling with the knowledge that she wanted him, and he wanted her. "We *cannot* do this," she managed to get out. "It *can't* happen."

Her eruption was contagious. Gripping her arms with his fingers, Gray stared at her, his anger sparking and growing as well. "It's too late," he shot back, his voice ragged. "It's too *damned* late. It's already happened...and there's nothing you can do about it now."

Maggie poked her head into Annie's study the following day, took one look at Annie, then turned around and left.

And Annie knew why.

The woman who had looked back at Annie in the mirror that morning had appeared haggard and anxious. Dark shadows stained the skin under her eyes and her stare had held nothing but worry. Worry about Bella. Worry about Gray. Worry about herself. She'd never been in such a tight squeeze. Part of her wanted to give in to temptation and slip into Gray's bed. Throw caution to the winds. Live dangerously, for a change.

And the other part of her knew she absolutely couldn't allow that to happen. If she let him into her life, it would be even worse when the time came for him to leave. The pain of losing the little girl was something Annie couldn't even begin to think about. What would she do if she let herself fall in love with Grayston Powers at the same time?

To top it all off, a little part of her mind continued to hang onto Monica's admonitions. What if she'd been right? What if Gray really was the man Monica had known and not the one that Annie was seeing? The charming attitude, the interest he showed—it could all be an act, something to use against her later.

God, she was so confused!

She was almost grateful when the kitchen sink backed up into the downstairs powder room. The resulting mess took her mind off her problems, and the plumber's bill, when he left two hours later, practically made Loring's invoices look like greeting cards. An hour after that catastrophe, a honeymoon couple checked in. Seeing the looks they exchanged, the heated touches, the significant sighs...all it did was bring Annie full circle and make her think about the previous night all over again. By the end of the day, she was an even bigger wreck than she had been at the beginning. Maggie took a chance and stopped in one more time before leaving.

"God, you look like you're right on the edge! What in the world did that man do to you last night after he fed you enchiladas?"

Annie raised her head from her desk and gave her sister a ragged look. "Nothing," she said tensely. "He didn't do nothing."

"That's a double negative."

"Yeah...it was."

Maggie laughed and leaned against the doorjamb. "Boy, you've got it bad, haven't you?" She shook her head. "You're being ridiculous, you know. Why don't you just give in to your baser instincts like the rest of us do and jump his bones?"

"I can't do that, and you know it."

"I don't know any such thing."

"Maggie! I can't start a relationship with Grayston

Powers.'' Annie rose to her feet and glared at her sister. ''And I can't believe I'm even having this conversation with you.''

''No one said you had to marry the guy, Annie. Just sleep with him, for God's sake, and get it out of your system. Then go back to fighting with him over Bella. What difference does it make?''

''It makes a lot of difference...to me.''

Maggie said nothing. Her raised eyebrows communicated it all.

Annie turned so she wouldn't have to look her sister in the eye. ''I know you think I'm acting silly, but I don't care. I don't sleep with my enemies. It's dangerous.''

''What's dangerous?''

Both women turned at the same time to look at Gray as he stood in the door to the study. He held a package in his hands. It was wrapped and tied with a bright red bow. Obviously a gift. Annie's eyes went beyond the present to what he wore. The first cool front of fall had slipped in last night and dropped the temperatures to breezy, lower numbers. He'd dressed accordingly. Black slacks and a matching black turtleneck. Tailored to perfection and sexy as hell. She groaned inwardly. *What was dangerous? He had to ask?*

For once in her life, Maggie remained silent. She stared at Gray a little longer, then turned so he couldn't see her. Looking at Annie, she made a motion as if she was wiping her chin, then she grinned, turned around and left the room.

Annie and Gray were alone. Again.

He took two steps into her study and handed her the package, his eyes raking her face with an almost physical touch. ''This is for you,'' he said in the same arresting, low voice he'd used when she'd first met him.

She held out her hand to accept the package and their fingers brushed. The spark that leapt between them was as instant and powerful as the ones last night. "Wh-what is it?"

"A gift."

Annie frowned but began to remove the wrapping. A second later, her eyes filled with tears and the sudden tightness in her throat was so strong she couldn't speak around it.

In her hands, she held Bella's drawing, the one she'd given Gray after the first day of school. Gray had had it mounted in an elaborate gold frame so beautiful and expensive it could have featured a Monet instead of the childish stick figures of people, a house and a skinny little dog. Inside the frame, a double linen mat of pale pink and pale blue matched the crayon colors Bella had selected for the piece itself.

She pulled herself together and raised her eyes to his face. "Why? Why are you giving me this?"

"You sound suspicious. Can't I just give you a present?"

"I am suspicious," she said quietly. "Of everything you do and everything you say. I have good reason to be."

"Why?" His eyes burned into hers. "Because Monica told you bad things about me?"

"That's part of it," she admitted.

"And the rest..."

"Is because I know what kind of man you really are."

"No, you don't. You know nothing about me."

"You've been living here for more than a month. I think I can judge people for myself."

"And you have judged me, haven't you? The facts don't even matter anymore."

"The facts are exactly what matter. You made them more than clear to me again last night, just in case I might have forgotten." Annie took an angry breath and glared at

Gray. "You still want Bella. I still want Bella. Nothing else is important. We'll be fighting that to the very end."

His face took on a stony expression. "You don't know when to quit, do you?"

"That word isn't even in my vocabulary."

He stood silently a moment longer, then leaned closer to her. "Then maybe it's time to expand your stock of words." He spoke precisely, slowly. "I am going to be in Bella's life—one way or the other. Whether you like it or not. You can fight me all you want, but that one fact is not going to change, so you'd better learn to accept it." His gaze drilled hers. "Do you want to make it hard or easy on yourself?"

They were standing close together, so close she thought he should be able to hear the questions swirling in her mind. "I'll never give up." Her words were like rocks—hard, unyielding, impossible to ignore. "If that's what you expect me to do, then you're the one who's in for a hard time." She raised her hand and punched two of her fingers into the solid wall of his chest with each word that she spoke. "I will never give up."

He captured her hand so fast her fingers were locked inside his before she'd even realized he had moved. He looked down into her eyes, and something in his gaze flared and caught. The voice of reason screaming in her head, Annie knew she should have backed away right then.

But she didn't. She stood her ground and glared at him.

The air between them compressed and disappeared, and Annie felt herself tremble. A second later, he pulled her toward him, and they came together in a crazy kind of explosion—violently, surprisingly, forcibly—as if someone unaware had mixed two incendiary ingredients.

She couldn't believe it was happening, even as his hands roamed over her body, his touch going up and over her shoulders, her hair, her buttocks. She followed his lead and did the same, scrambling to bring him into her as if she wanted more than he could possibly ever provide. It was crazy and made no sense at all and she couldn't believe it was even happening.

He tore his mouth from hers and pressed his lips over her neck, biting and nibbling, teasing and tasting. His mouth was moist and warm and compelling, and she wanted—as she'd never wanted anything in her life—to taste more of him. Right now. Without reserve. His hand came up and cupped the heaviness of her breast and she twisted to give him more of the weight, to let him feel more of the warmth, to take over and above what he had already.

The rest of the world ceased to be. For Annie, there was the feeling again that nothing else existed but Gray—his smell, his touch, his taste. She wanted it all. And if his actions were telling the truth, he wanted the very same thing.

Chapter 10

She didn't know what brought her to her senses, but Annie finally pulled back. Out of his arms, away from his warmth. She felt the void instantly but ignored the empty yearning. He didn't move. His dark eyes fastened on hers, and she couldn't run away this time, couldn't disappear into the dark and pretend it hadn't happened. Her throat was too tight to speak, but somehow she did anyway. "Th-this has got to stop. It's crazy."

"Life is that way sometimes. Do you have to question everything?"

She stared at him, riveted by his voice, his eyes, the lingering feel of his hands. She suddenly knew how the snake felt when the charmer began to play his flute.

"Things as crazy as this—yes. Yes, I do have to question them."

"Why?"

"Why?" She almost laughed. "You have to ask me that?"

"It's a legitimate question."

"And the answer is obvious."

"Not to me, it isn't."

"Well, it is to me."

"Then explain it."

She stepped back, tried to get outside the circle of his power, but the extra space made no difference. The tension still sizzled between them.

"Tell me," he said, ignoring her movement and coming closer, taking her arm. "Tell me why it's so awful that I kissed you. You obviously wanted to kiss me back. I wasn't forcing you, was I?"

She pulled her arm away. "No—you weren't forcing me, but there are other reasons—good reasons—why we shouldn't get involved."

"They may be good to you—"

"They're good, period!" To avoid his eyes, she twirled around, her heart in her throat. "I can't believe this happened. Again!"

He walked around until he was standing in front of her. The lamp light from her desk turned his face into carved granite. "What is your problem? A kiss isn't a sin."

Annie paused for a fraction of a second, then she forced her voice to be level and calm—the exact opposite of how she felt. "You're right. It's not a sin...but there are... things...between us that we can't ignore. You were married to my best friend. Not only did I promise her I'd take care of her daughter, I promised her that I'd never let you near Bella. Now, you're more than near her, you may be taking her away. Should I be kissing you? Letting you touch me?" Annie shook her head. "I don't think so."

He lifted her chin and looked into her eyes. "You're fighting battles you aren't going to win. Why do you keep on?"

His eyes went over her face, searching for a reply, a

reaction, to his words, but she couldn't give him one. She didn't know what to say. She knew only one thing—Maggie had been wrong when she'd advised Annie to sleep with this man and "get it out of her system." It wasn't going to work that way. Not at all. There was a powerful pull between the two of them, a connection that went way beyond anything she'd ever felt for anyone else. And it had nothing to do with Bella. If the little girl hadn't even been a part of this, Annie knew instinctively that the same emotions would have been whirling between her and Gray at this very instant.

"There's nothing else I *can* do." Her voice was ragged. "I have an obligation."

"An obligation to ignore reality?" His eyes turned darker. "That's never a good idea, Annie. Things don't go away just because you pretend they aren't there."

He stared at her a little longer, then he lifted his hand and smoothed it over her hair. The motion brought with it a whiff of his cologne—light, airy, cool—a perfect counterpoint to the intensity that radiated from the rest of him. "Don't you know that by now?"

His stare was so mesmerizing. She wanted to fall into it and disappear. She let herself think about the possibilities for only a second, then she pulled herself back...away from the abyss.

"I'm not ignoring anything...in fact, I'm facing it square on. Someone in this room is going to lose." She shook her head. "I want Bella and so do you. We're enemies."

His forefinger went to the edge of her jaw and traced an electric path. "We don't have to be. When it ends, we'll figure something out."

"I don't think so...because that's part of the problem. It will end." She looked into his eyes and resisted the pull coming from their dark, deep depths. "It *will* end—as soon as that report comes back—and as soon as we know whether or not you're really Bella's father. Either way, we're going to be enemies. So *nothing* is exactly what's going to happen between us.''

He didn't understand it.

Not one bit.

Gray had no idea what was happening between himself and Annie. All he knew was that every time he was around her, all he could think about was pulling her into his arms and kissing her. She was in his thoughts constantly, and since their encounter the night before, she was there even more. Her image—and her words—had begun to haunt him.

That's part of the problem, isn't it? It will end—as soon as that report comes back—and as soon as we know whether or not you're really Bella's father. Either way, we're going to be enemies. So nothing is exactly what's going to happen between us.

Damn! Before this point, his life had been under control, managed, lived the way he wanted it. Even during the worst periods with Monica, Gray had always felt he could master the situation, but not this time. Not with Annie. Somehow she seemed more in control than him. At least she'd been able to step back from their kiss last night— he'd been unable to make even that move. And it wasn't going to improve. She was going to fight him forever. No matter how this turned out, Annie Burns was going to haunt him the rest of his life, even if he managed to get Bella and take her away.

All he could do was look out the window and shake his head.

On Wednesday, as if saving him, Bill called. He couldn't put off a group of investors any longer. Gray had to come to Dallas for a series of meetings. Gray found himself more than glad to oblige his assistant...for a change. Annie looked equally relieved when he told her he had to be gone for a couple of days. The look of disappointment on Bella's face, though—it almost changed his mind.

"Do you really hafta go?" she asked, twisting a strand of red hair around her finger. "I was hoping we could go fishing again."

"And we will," he promised, ignoring the frown Annie wore. "As soon as I get back."

He pulled into Dallas by noon and the meetings began. Bill had people stacked up like airplanes over Dallas-Fort Worth. Gray struggled to keep his mind on the issues at hand, but throughout the day, he found himself thinking about Annie and Bella. Had Annie managed to get the extra help she needed for the wedding this weekend? How had Bella's field trip gone? The kindergartners were going to the Timberley post office that afternoon. Had she had a good time?

By the end of the second day it was all Gray could do to keep from jumping up and running out of the office. He wanted to hear nothing about the bore size of wellheads and the projected tank requirements needed by the Rio Bravo Dome. Pipe size, drilling mud, cutoff valves? He couldn't have cared less. He squirmed his way through two more meetings, then stood up abruptly when one of the junior engineers launched into his second hour regarding the density of viscous fluids in the down hole. Ignoring the startled looks of the others in the room, Gray marched out and headed for his office. He was leaving.

He strode down the hall and passed Bill Kingsley's desk. Once in his own office, Gray grabbed his briefcase and started stuffing papers into it. Bill appeared in the doorway.

"Leaving already?"

"Yes," Gray said curtly. "I've sat still as long as I can. There's nothing going on here that I can't deal with from Timberley."

Bill nodded. The younger man's ability not to ask stupid questions was the primary reason Gray had hired him in the first place. Gray continued to shuffle papers as Bill looked down at the pad of paper in his hand and checked something off one of his endless lists. Finally the assistant looked up and uncharacteristically hesitated. "Have you..." His words trailed off into silence.

Gray glanced up, his mind already in Timberley. "Have I what?"

"Have you gotten the results yet? Of the DNA test?"

"No. It'll probably be a few more weeks. Those things take time."

Bill frowned, then spoke slowly. "I thought tests like that came back in a week. There was a show on TV just the other day about that sort of thing and the reporter said a week."

"A week?" Gray echoed the word while his mind filled with an image. An image of Annie standing by the dock the night they'd talked about the test. She'd seemed so tense that night, so wary. Afterwards they'd kissed for the very first time. Had she sensed that was coming or had she been worried about something else...something like the DNA test?

A sudden uneasiness swept over him, but he immediately dismissed it. Annie would never lie about something that important. She wasn't that kind of woman. She wanted to win Bella, sure, but she wouldn't deliberately lie about anything. Right?

A knot of tension developing instantly between his shoulders, Gray met his assistant's hesitant gaze. "There can't be that many labs in Houston that do this sort of test.

Get them on the line." Gray slammed his briefcase shut. "We'll straighten this out right now."

Everything looked perfect.

A haze of purple clouds threaded with ribbons of peach hung over the riverbank like an artist's backdrop. Luminarias—paper bags with glowing candles inside—lined the terrace, then led the way down to the dock where more rested around the perimeter of the cedar steps and benches. A series of round tables decorated the sloping lawn and on the top of each, more candles flickered in the dusky twilight. White cushions made the chairs inviting, and silver ribbons tied on the back of each one added to the festive, elegant look. With a great sense of satisfaction, Annie stood by the back door and surveyed it all, one remaining bow clutched in her hands.

In a few short hours, the Chavez wedding would be the talk of Timberley. It had to be. Annie had devoted too much time and effort to the preparations for it to be anything else.

She stepped out onto the grass, her heels sinking down slightly. Mr. and Mrs. Lawton were going to be guests tonight and their daughter, Laura, was engaged. Annie would make sure they were impressed—more than impressed—and then she might get even more business. In the back of her mind, she was still hoping there might be a way for the adoption to go through—and she'd need money for that.

Attaching the final bow to the chair that had needed it, Annie looked up as the gate creaked. Mrs. Chavez and Yolanda stood at the entrance. The older woman was staring at the garden, a look of utter awe and disbelief on her face. She lifted one hand, covered in diamond rings, and placed it on her generous, quivering bosom. "Oh, *Dios mio*," she cried. "*Que bonito, que lindo!*" Then she burst into tears.

Yolanda immediately dropped the bags she'd been holding and wrapped her arms around her mother. "Oh, Mama! Don't cry—please! Please, don't cry."

Annie might have been alarmed if she hadn't seen the pleased expression on the woman's face as she stared at the garden. Understanding instantly, she crossed the patio and came up to the older woman's side, patting her on the shoulder. "Mrs. Chavez! This is supposed to be a happy day for you. So many tears…"

The woman sniffed and pulled a lace handkerchief from her sleeve. Touching it to the corner of each eye, she spoke tearfully. "I know, I know, and you've made everything look absolutely perfect. But I just can't believe my baby's actually getting married. She's leaving me and…and…" The tears started once more. Yolanda wrapped her arms around her mother, then she started to bawl as well.

Annie looked at the two of them and her own eyes welled up. Would she ever get to share that kind of emotion with Bella? She was so glad now that she'd sent the little girl to Rose's for the night. She'd be tempted to sweep Bella into her arms and never, ever let go. Pushing all these thoughts aside, Annie swiped a finger under one eye and spoke in what she hoped was a cheerful voice. "Okay, ladies…let's go into the house," she said, turning the two women toward the door. "We need to get you two dressed."

An hour later, Annie had managed to get both women dry-eyed and dressed, along with the five attendants, the flower girl and the ring boy. Now, as she peeked over the balcony and down the stairs, she prayed that everything else would go as smoothly as it had so far. It was looking like it would. The murmurs of the crowd in the living room died as the music began to swell, and at the bottom of the stairs, Maggie gave Annie the high sign—it was time to send the first one down.

One by one, the women and the little boy, walked solemnly down the white velvet runner Annie had rented to cover the hallway stairs. They entered the living room just as the evening sun warmed the newly painted walls to a honey glow. A second later, the bride glided in, the pearls on her gown gleaming as brightly as her eyes when she spotted her groom waiting by the front of the room beside the judge.

Before she could start to cry again, Annie slipped away. There were details in the kitchen she had to see to…and she didn't want to think about Bella in a wedding gown.

The next hour was a blur for Annie. Before she knew it, the ceremony was over, and she had fifty people mingling outside on the terrace. Directing the extra help she'd hired for the event, she managed to get out the starters and champagne while Yolanda and her new husband, along with the wedding party, all posed for photographs. In no time at all, everyone was seated, and Annie had begun serving the main course—salmon mousse, topped with caviar and dollops of cream—the "extravagant" option Mrs. Chavez had had to call Annie and remind her about.

Annie looked down at one of the plates as she passed it on the server. She'd been so distracted the day of their initial conversation that she'd had no idea what Mrs. Chavez had been talking about until she'd called back and told Annie. And all because of Gray. Pressing the plate into the waitress's hand, Annie closed her mind to the image of Gray. He had no place there and he never would. She'd been glad when he'd gone to Dallas for a few days. She'd needed the breathing room.

The time finally came for the wedding cake. Annie glanced in the mirror beside the kitchen door. Her face was flushed from the heat of the kitchen and her hair curled around her face. Putting on a smile, she pushed the serving cart through the kitchen door and onto the terrace.

The bride and groom rose and came to meet her, each of them clapping their hands in delight over the gorgeous confection. Annie had spent hours on it and it showed.

Three layers of fluffy white cake with coconut filling in between. Lavender pansies of sugared icing and tiny green leaves that matched. An intricate latticed pattern across the top. It was a work of art...and an hour later, it was decimated.

But everyone loved it. The cake, and the wedding, were both more than a success.

Hours later, Annie helped Yolanda change into a pale pink suit to get ready to leave. "I really appreciate everything you did," the young girl said. "You made my wedding something I'll always remember, Annie."

"I'm glad you were pleased," Annie answered, smiling. "I think your mother felt the same way, too."

The dark-haired girl smiled as she slipped her feet into a pair of pale ivory pumps then straightened up. "She did! But this wedding was very important to her. She and my father eloped, so I think she planned it as much for herself as she did for me." She glanced into the mirror and fluffed her hair. "I don't care, though. I'm just happy she's happy. And now—it's over, thank God. We can all get back to a normal life." She reached over and kissed Annie on the cheek. "Thanks for making it so perfect."

Annie closed the door on the final guest, sent the extra staff home, and took off her shoes with a sigh of relief. She was exhausted, emotionally and physically, but one thing was clear all at once: the big old house seemed strangely deserted. Wandering back toward the kitchen, she realized suddenly the feeling of emptiness had as much to do with Bella's absence as anything else. For just a second, Annie thought about calling Rose's house, but the clock on the kitchen wall showed it was past midnight. She couldn't call now—it was simply too late.

She sat down abruptly in the nearest kitchen chair and tried to tell herself the worst wasn't going to happen. That she wouldn't lose her child, that she wouldn't be alone, that she wouldn't be sitting in an empty house just like this when everything was said and done. But the words just wouldn't come. She couldn't make herself believe what she knew wasn't the truth. All at once, it seemed everyone in the world had a family, a husband, love that was steady and true—everyone but Annie. She was never going to have any of those things. Without thinking further, she dropped her head into her hands and began to cry—great sobbing gulps that racked her shoulders and made her tremble. Sobs that she'd been holding in since she'd realized who Gray really was and had understood the terrible power he held over her life. She didn't even know he'd entered the room until he spoke.

He'd never seen Annie cry. Throughout their whole ordeal, he'd seen her mad, sad, upset, and agitated...but he'd never seen her cry. The heart-wrenching sobs twisted something deep inside of Gray, but he immediately suppressed the feeling and let his anger return. The anger that had fueled him all the way from Dallas to Timberley. The anger that had made him realize Annie would never stop fighting him. The anger that had come to him after talking to the people at the DNA lab in Houston.

He stepped into the kitchen and Annie jerked her head up. Immediately she wiped at her eyes and tried to cover up the fact that she'd been crying. "Wh-what are you doing here?" she said. "I...I thought you had business in Dallas."

"I took care of it," he answered. "Along with a few other things."

His icy tone hung in the warmth of the kitchen, obvious and out of place. Her eyes turned wary, but she didn't say a word.

He walked closer and deposited his briefcase on the table, then he moved toward the coffeepot. Filling up a cup, he thought about what he was going to say. The words were ready; he'd carefully planned each and every one of them on the trip back to Timberley. Angry disbelief had provided fertile ground. In a dim corner of his mind, a voice asked him if he knew the *real* reason behind what he was about to do, but he shook the query off.

This was the only way.

He turned around from the coffeepot and met Annie's gaze. "I know what you did," he said calmly. "You can quit pretending."

Her face framed by chestnut curls, her blue eyes so innocent...he couldn't believe it.

"What are you talking about?" she asked.

He could barely get the words out over the anger boiling inside him. "The DNA test. I know you had the results delayed."

She blinked once, then twice. For a moment, there was silence between them. Then the blue turned into ice, as did her voice. "I can't control the lab."

"But you could have controlled the sample. You selected the slowest possible way, when you knew I wanted it done as quickly as possible." He spoke between gritted teeth. "Why, Annie? Why did you do this to me?"

Something crossed her face. It looked like a flicker of guilt but it was so quickly replaced by defiance he wasn't sure. "I thought it was—"

"Don't bother," he said, holding up his hand to stop her excuse. "There's nothing you can say that could justify what you did. Nothing. We had an agreement, or did you forget?''

She stood up. Her silk suit was rumpled and mussed but she still managed to look beautiful, to look dignified. He wondered briefly how she did that, but her words distracted him. ''Our agreement was that you could be part of Bella's life while we were waiting for those test results. I've honored that agreement.''

''Only because I forced you to every time I turned around.''

''But you've been involved with everything! What more did you want?''

''A little cooperation would have been nice! Instead, you fought me every step of the way,'' he said tightly. ''You tried to make it impossible for me to get to know her and impossible for her to spend any time with me. I've had to fight you constantly and I'm sick of it.'' His expression hardened. ''It's going to stop right now, Annie.''

Her look was openly rebellious, but it couldn't hide the fear behind her eyes. ''I'm Bella's legal guardian until this whole thing is resolved. You can't take her, so don't throw that at me again.''

''I don't intend to take her,'' he said quietly. ''My plans have changed.''

''Changed?'' Her hand went to her throat, a gesture of uneasiness. ''Wha-what are you saying?''

''I have a solution for our problem. I should have thought of it earlier, but at that point I was still trying to figure out what was actually going on. If Bella *was* my daughter or not, what I should do...everything about this whole situation.''

As he spoke, her eyes were huge with a mixture of fear, skepticism and wariness. He stared at her, a flicker of hesitation brushing over him that he immediately ignored. This was the right thing, the only answer, the most effective way. She would fight him for the rest of his life, regardless of how this ended. He *had* to control Annie and he *had* to control the situation. Otherwise, the court reporter would know them by name, the lawyers would take all their money, and the judge would get bored. Gray knew. He'd seen this before in his childhood. He'd be damned if he did it to his kid like his parents had done it to him. He looked Annie right in the eye.

"There's only one solution to this problem, and whether we like it or not, it's the step we have to take. I've thought about it long and hard, and it's the only way. You have to marry me, Annie. Right now."

"Marry you?" Annie didn't even know she'd spoken until the word sounded in the tension-filled kitchen. "You and me? Married?"

"That's right." Gray's expression was grim. Grim and determined. "I thought out all the details on the way back from Dallas. I have it worked out. If you want to see Bella grow up, you'll say yes."

Her mouth worked but no words came out. Marry Gray? It was the last thing in the world she'd expected him to say. The very last thing.

"I told you all along that I wasn't going to ruin your life. But you insisted on making things difficult. Fighting me all the way." He shook his head, one dark lock of hair falling over his high forehead. "I won't put up with it anymore and I'm certainly not going to put up with it for the rest of my life. We'll marry, we'll live together—here at Riverside—and when Bella's grown, we'll go our separate ways. It's the only solution that makes any kind of sense, and I'm sure you'll agree once you think about it."

"The only solution that makes sense?" Annie stared at him in amazement. "I...I'm not so sure I agree with that assessment."

"Do you want to watch her grow up?"

Annie's heart flipped over. "Of course I do."

"Do you want to be there for her when she needs you?"

Her look answered the question.

"Then agree to this," he ordered. "Otherwise, the minute those test results come in, I'm taking her and leaving."

"That's what you were going to do anyway."

"No." He shook his head. "That was never my intention, and I tried to explain that to you. You never listened, though. You were too busy fighting me. I would have worked something out. We could have eased Bella into the change, but you've shown me that scenario would never work. You'd fight me—just like you've fought me on everything—and every time I turned around you'd be pulling some stunt like you did with this test. It'd be one battle after another and we'd spend the rest of our lives in court. I can't let that happen. I *refuse* to let that happen."

Taking a step backward from the barrage of words, Annie started to deny his accusation, then knew she couldn't. He was telling the truth. She'd never give in, never let him take her child. No matter what the damned DNA test said, she'd known all along she'd fight Gray to the bitter end. Only hours before, she'd been trying to get more business, so she'd have more money she could fight him longer. He was right. Totally and completely right.

But marry him?

She turned around to get away from his gaze, that hot, black gaze that had pinned her down since the moment he'd walked into Riverside.

Marry him?

Her mind clicked through a variety of perfectly valid reasons why it would never work, but only one reason why it would. And that reason was more important that anything in the world. Bella. Annie had always done what was best for Bella. Still…this was an awfully big step. She kept her back to him.

"And what would we tell Bella?"

"We'd tell her I'm her father. That *is* why I came here, if you'll recall."

Annie turned around slowly. Met his angry gaze. "I mean about the marriage."

"We'd tell her we're in love. She doesn't need to know differently."

She remembered their kisses, remembered his touch on her skin, then instantly dismissed the images. Attraction was one thing…love was something else. She was shaking her head before he even finished the words. "That's ridiculous. I can't do that—"

"You can do whatever you have to for her. No one needs to know differently." His gaze was level and straight. "We're going to be making a home for Bella. A home includes love."

Annie couldn't help herself. The words came out before she could stop them. "How would you know?"

He tilted his head. *Touché*, the movement seemed to say. "That's what I've been told," he answered. "By a very good source."

She blushed, remembering their conversation. "Love isn't something you can fake."

"I think your powers as an actress will improve vastly when you consider the other choices."

The threat filled the room, and for the very first time, Annie realized how serious he was. The choice was hers. She could lose Bella immediately…or she could watch her daughter grow up. All Annie had to do was marry this man. She'd known he was a determined person, but this…this went beyond determination.

"You really mean it, don't you?" she said quietly.

"I don't say things I don't mean. You should know that by now."

She studied him for one long moment. Shadows filled the area beneath his eyes and there was a tight slump to his shoulders that she just now noticed. "Why?" she asked. "What's in this for you?"

He took a moment to answer. "Peace of mind. I'll know you won't be fighting me."

"But there's more," she said, her intuitive warning bells going off. "Isn't there?"

He looked surprised for a moment, then his gaze grew sharp. "Yes. There's more."

"And that is—"

"She needs a mother. You know her, you've raised her, you're comforting to her. After our meal the other night, I realized there was too much I didn't know about her. I would hate to think that this upheaval hurt her somehow. Despite what you think of me, I've never wanted to totally disrupt her life…or yours."

She couldn't hold back her incredulity. "Marriage isn't a disruption?"

"Bella is more important than either one of us. She'll be happy. That's all I care about."

For the second time that night, Annie realized he was telling the truth. Which meant only one thing. Dictated only one answer. She wasn't ready to give it to him yet, though. There might be another way. Then she realized what she was doing the instant she had the thought. She was delaying things—just as she'd done before. Even so, the words came out. "I…I'd like some time to think about it."

He said exactly what she thought he would.

"I'm sure you would, but you're not getting it. This is a one-time offer, as they say on the radio." His fingers tightened around the coffee mug he'd held throughout the conversation. "Say yes right now, or I'm leaving the minute those test results come in. I'm leaving, I'll take her with me and you'll never see her again."

Never see her again. The words sliced through Annie, straight into her heart. "I'd fight you."

"Which is exactly my point. It'd drag out forever, but I've got more money and better lawyers. By the time the whole thing was finished, we'd all be devastated and the final results would be the same, only worse. You'd lose everything, not just Bella. Riverside would be gone, and even if you somehow, by a remote chance, managed to get partial custody, you'd have no way to support yourself or Bella." His attitude was grimly resolute. "I'd ruin you, Annie."

She wanted to argue, but her heart thumped with every painful word he'd spoken. He was right. Again. Her hope deflated, but she had to give it one last try. "And if she's not your daughter?" she said desperately.

"I don't have to worry about that," he shot back. "She is my daughter. If she wasn't, though, of course I wouldn't hold you to this." His mouth went into a line that brooked no argument. She knew her time was up. "What's it going to be, Annie? Do you want to be there for Bella or not?"

Annie looked into his waiting eyes, but she didn't see Gray. Instead, she saw two futures, like the branches of a dividing tree. One was an image of her and Bella...and Gray. The three of them together, laughing, playing, at least *acting like* a normal family. The other image was of Annie.

Alone.

She crossed her arms as if for protection, then she lifted her gaze to his face, and gave him the answer she'd known she was going to give all along. "All right," she said quietly. "If the test comes back and says she's your daughter...then I'll marry you."

*   *   *

Annie didn't even try to work the rest of the day. She instructed Maggie to take care of the check-ins and left Mari to clean up the rooms, then she got in the Jeep and took off. She didn't know where she was going—but she had to leave so she could think about what she'd just agreed to do.

Three hours later, when she pulled back into her parking spot at Riverside, Annie was as confused and crazy as she had been when she'd left. One fact remained the same, though. She'd get to keep Bella. What else mattered? She killed the engine and climbed out of the Jeep.

Her hands twisted in a dish towel, her hair disheveled, Maggie met Annie before she could come up the porch steps. "I've been worried about you. Where have you—"

Annie brushed past her and walked into the dim hallway of the house. "I'm fine," she answered. "You worried for nothing." Taking off the cap she'd stuffed down on her head, Annie shook her curls loose and looked around. "Where's Bella?"

"She's still at Rose's. She called and begged for more time, and it seemed like a good thing to let her stay." As Annie stopped in front of the antique mirror in the hall, Maggie leaned against the doorframe of the study and watched. When she spoke, her words were casual as always, but her body held a tension that denied her offhandedness. "Gray lit out of here this morning like a scalded cat. You disappeared for three hours…are you going to tell me what happened or do I get to make up the lurid details myself?"

Annie's voice was as flat as the mirror she was staring into. "Gray thinks I'm always going to be fighting him over Bella so he asked me to marry him. And I said yes."

Maggie's hand automatically came up her throat, and her eyes were wide in obvious shock. Her mouth opened, then closed. A second later, she shook her head in confusion. "I...I think I'd rather have the extended-play version of that song, please. Sounds like you're leaving some details out."

"I am." In the mirror, Annie's eyes were two hollowed-out coals, and deep grooves she'd never noticed before now had etched on both sides of her mouth. "But they aren't important. The only thing that matters is Bella. I have to do what's best for her...and this is it."

Behind Annie, Maggie appeared in the mirror's reflection. Her hazel eyes were huge with disbelief. "I can't believe this. You're serious? You're really going to marry Gray?"

Turning around, Annie stared into her sister's eyes. "It's the only way, Mags. The only way I can..." The words died slowly and suddenly Annie couldn't stand it a minute longer. Her world was crashing around her and there was absolutely nothing she could do to stop it. She began to cry, her shoulders shaking with deep, wrenching sobs that seemed to have no end. Without a word, Maggie wrapped her arms around Annie and began to pat her back, love and support obvious in her touch. They stayed that way for several minutes. Then very gently, as if she were guiding a child, Maggie led Annie into the study and closed the doors behind them.

Annie sank down to the couch, her fingers reaching blindly for the box of tissues that Maggie held out. For several more minutes, the tears continued, then finally Annie hiccuped into an upset silence.

"Start from the beginning," Maggie said. "Tell me everything."

In an uneven voice, Annie began. The wedding, the emotions, the letdown afterwards. "He...he found me in the kitchen, crying," she said. "You...you know I don't cry that much and—"

"Except that once you get started, you don't seem to stop."

Annie nodded. "He came in and said he'd found out that—" She stopped abruptly.

"Found out what?"

Annie looked out the French doors and let the silence build. Gray had made it sound as if she'd killed someone. A small twinge of guilt rippled over her, but she refused to think she'd done anything that bad. She'd been protecting Bella—that's all. "He'd found out that I delayed the DNA test results. There are faster ways, but I...I picked the one that would take the longest."

Silence reigned for only a moment, then Maggie's breath came out in a whoosh of disapproval. "Oh, God, Annie...why on earth did you do that? You should know better...."

Annie couldn't keep the defensive note from her voice. "I was doing what I thought was best. I wanted to buy some time so I could think of something...think of some way to work it all out."

"Oh, good grief." In a gesture of frustrated irritation, Maggie threaded her hands through her hair, leaving the ends standing straight up. "I can't believe this! Did you really think you'd get away with something so obvious?"

"I wasn't even sure Bella was really his daughter at that point! I had to do something—"

Maggie dropped her hands from her hair and held them out. "Not sure! How on God's green earth could you not be sure?"

"I just wasn't!" Annie shot back. "Call it denial if you want to, but I believed it, okay? Then things got...complicated. I couldn't exactly go back and ask him for another sample by that point."

Maggie paused. "'By that point'...you mean by the time you'd fallen in love with him?"

"I am *not* in love with Grayston Powers. And he's definitely not in love with me." Annie took a deep breath and remembered her thoughts when he'd told her they'd have to act as though they were in love. Remembered his words after that... *Of course, if she's not my daughter, I wouldn't hold you to this.* No...he definitely had no real feelings for her.

"If you're not in love with him, then what did you mean?"

"I meant that by that point, I'd seen what kind of father he'd really be. Even though I would have continued to fight him, I'd realized how bad his own childhood had been, and I'd come to understand how wrong Monica had been to do what she'd done. How wrong *I'd* been to make the promise I did to keep him away from his daughter."

Maggie stood still a second longer then she kneeled in front of Annie and covered her hands with her own. She spoke as if Annie hadn't said a word. "Tell him, Annie. Tell him you love him and tell him you made a mistake. It's not too late. The three of you could be a real family."

"I don't love him, Maggie. How many times do I have to tell you that?"

"You feel *something* for the man and it's a pretty damn strong something. Are you going to deny that?"

"But it's not love. It's just some kind of crazy attraction or magnetism—whatever." Annie felt her jaw tighten. "Even if it was love—and it's not—a real relationship would never work between Gray and me. He isn't the kind of man who loves. He controls people, he doesn't love them."

"How can you say that?" Maggie stood, her hands on her hips. "He obviously loves Bella. That's love—"

"It's safe to love Bella. She already adores him. I'm talking about a different kind of love, and you know it."

"Love is love."

"No. This is different." Annie shook her head violently. "He's doesn't understand real feelings, real emotions. He grew up where they didn't exist and it's too late for him to learn them now, even if he wanted to." She wrapped her arms around her chest and shook her head again.

"It'd be a disaster, Maggie. Another disaster."

Maggie stared at Annie in measured silence, then finally she spoke. "So you're just going to marry the man. You're just going to pretend to be in love with him."

Annie swallowed. "That's right. We'll just pretend." She took a deep breath and felt her heart racing inside her chest with the enormity of what she was about to do. "We'll pretend for Bella's sake."

Chapter 11

For the following week, Annie felt nothing but numbness. She existed inside a wall of cotton. Nothing penetrated the shield—noise, feelings, emotions—and she was grateful for the protection. It kept her from thinking about Gray and how she felt toward him. Kept her from thinking of the kiss they'd shared. Kept her from thinking about all the ramifications of the action she was about to take.

Only one thing got past the barrier, and that was Bella. Her voice, her antics, her sweet little hugs pierced Annie's walls as nothing else could, sharply and painfully. Every moment they spent together was wonderful and, at the same time, agonizing when Annie let herself think of what would happen if she wasn't able to carry through with Gray's plan. Second thoughts were plaguing her, but when she had them, she told herself there was no other way. She wanted to see Bella grow up, she wanted to be there for her. The niggling doubts that came along, doubts about herself and her feelings—her *real* feelings—about Gray, she simply tried to ignore. Maggie had been wrong, terribly wrong. Annie didn't love Gray and she never would. She wanted a man who was warm, loving, understanding...not a man who forced people into doing things they didn't want to do. And certainly not a man who didn't have feelings for her.

Still, she'd agreed to talk to Gray that afternoon about their wedding plans. With a sense of disbelief, she realized she'd soon be doing everything for herself that she'd just finished doing for Yolanda. To escape the reality of what that meant, Annie headed for the garden.

Once there, her thoughts grew even more tangled than the weeds in her hands. While the bees buzzed in the nearby trellis roses, she kept thinking about Gray, and their kisses. The touch of his hands, the warmth of his body, the scent of his skin—the sensations haunted her like unrelenting ghosts in the bright sunshine. Finally, in disgust, she stood up, threw down her gloves and headed for the house, more confused and anxious than when she'd started out that morning.

It took a moment for her eyes to adjust to the dim, cool light of the hallway after she walked inside. Once they had, she immediately saw Maggie standing near the console, her hair more mussed than usual, anxiety filling her hazel eyes.

She held out an envelope. "It's from the lab."

Annie's heart stopped. She closed her eyes and heard the echo of her pulse roaring in her ears. She couldn't speak. This was the final point. If, by some miracle, Bella wasn't Gray's, then Annie wouldn't have to marry him. If she was... To prepare for the pain she knew was coming, Annie took a deep breath and released it slowly. "You...you open it."

As if from a long way away, Maggie's voice floated back to Annie, disembodied and faint. "Are you sure?"

No. She wasn't sure of anything anymore. No part of her life made sense. The minute Grayston Powers had walked into Riverside and stood where she was standing now, life for Annie had been shattered.

But she nodded anyway, and a second later, the jagged sound of tearing paper filled the anxious silence. She felt as though it were her heart being ripped open. She waited, her breath catching in her chest in a painful squeeze.

There was silence. And more silence.

Finally she couldn't take it any longer. Annie opened her eyes and stared at her sister's face. In the cool, quiet hall, Maggie's expression was as white and ragged as the envelope in her hand. An icy wave of dread washed over Annie.

"No," she whispered. "No..."

Maggie shook her head, and in a blur, Annie snatched the report from her sister's hands. In her own fingers, the paper shook violently, the words and numbers running together, except for one important one that stood out as if it were underlined in red and written in capital letters. "Giving consideration to factors present, the samples appear to *match* within given tolerances for..."

Annie closed her eyes and swayed, her throat tightening with crushing disappointment.

Grayston Powers *was* Bella's father.

If she didn't want to lose her daughter, there was only one thing she could do. She had to marry him. A man who didn't love her. A man she was wildly attracted to despite the enmity between them. A man who would control the rest of her life.

Annie turned and ran out the front door.

Gray pulled into the driveway at Riverside, parked, and cut off the engine of the Mercedes. Silence enveloped him completely, but it couldn't quiet the anger still sounding inside him from the week before. He wanted to pound the steering wheel, curse to high heaven, get drunk. Do all three at once. Instead, he took a deep breath and stared at the stately home waiting patiently at the end of the red-brick sidewalk in front of his car.

He was practically back to square one. He should have taken Bella and left ten minutes after he'd gotten there.

He had wanted to do the right thing, though. Had wanted to make sure she wasn't hurt in any way, that Annie wasn't hurt. Now it'd come to this. His entire life was at a confused standstill because of Annie Burns. She'd taken his world and turned it upside down. *He'd known this was going to happen.*

The minute that test came in, they were getting married and that was that. He'd be able to watch his child grow up and not have to worry about Annie making more trouble for him.

The desire that refused to be quelled between the two of them had nothing to do with his offer.

Nothing.

Stepping from the car, Gray glanced up as the front door of the house opened and Maggie came out. Something about the way she held her body alerted him. Wearing an expression that was tense and upset, she was pale beneath her tan, her hands clenched at her sides. By the time he reached the porch, his alarm bells were ringing loudly.

"What is it?" he asked immediately, one foot poised on the first level of the wide, covered breezeway, the other on the sidewalk.

"The results came in," she said quietly. "The results from the lab."

His mouth suddenly dry, he took a step up, toward her. "Where are they? What did the report say?"

"I think Annie should answer that. She's down by the river."

He dropped his briefcase on the porch and turned to go to the side of the house.

"Gray?"

At the sound of Maggie's voice, he swirled, impatient and anxious. "Yes?"

"Whatever you do—please remember one thing." She paused, as if searching for the right words before speaking again. "That child has been Annie's life. She's...she's all Annie has."

He kept his expression neutral but he knew instantly what the report contained. If nothing else, he could hear the loss in Maggie's voice. Something turned over in his chest, something close to disbelief, something even closer to joy. In the middle of the night, when he couldn't sleep, he'd had his doubts, he could confess now, but his heart had always known.

Bella was his daughter.

For the first time in years, he issued a silent prayer.

"Do you understand what I'm saying?" Maggie asked, her voice cutting through the afternoon heat and this incredible revelation. "Annie's ability to love—it's what defines her. It's what makes her *her*. Please don't take that from her."

He met Maggie's gaze square on. "I don't plan on taking anything from her, Maggie. Bella will be staying right here."

"I know that," she said. "I know the whole plan. But I'm not sure you've given it the thought this step deserves." She stared at him, her hazel eyes taking on a greenish, protective cast. "Do you understand what I'm saying? Annie isn't the kind of woman who can live without love. Not forever...are you prepared for that?"

Impatient to see the report for himself, he'd already turned and started down the walk.

"Gray? Did you hear me?"

He slowed and spoke over his shoulder. "I'll work it out. Somehow."

"For everyone's sake...I certainly hope so."

She heard him coming down the path. By the time he reached her side, Annie had managed to compose herself. Wordlessly, she handed Gray the report, but she knew by his expression that it wasn't a surprise. Maggie had obviously told him something, and Annie found herself grateful that her sister had saved her from seeing his initial reaction. Even as it was, he read the page with greedy eyes and there was no way he could hide the joy that lit up his face as the reality sunk in.

"My God," he breathed. "It's true. She's really mine." He closed his eyes for just a second, then opened them again and took in Annie's face. "She's really mine. Bella is *my* daughter."

On the inside, Annie was dying. Bella was *her* daughter, she wanted to scream...but what good would that do now? She forced her voice to reflect a level of calmness she wasn't even close to feeling. "I didn't think you doubted it."

"I didn't," he said quickly. "Not really. But to have the proof in black and white. It makes it more...real somehow."

Her throat closed but she managed to speak. "I see."

As if he wanted to confirm the findings, he read the report again. When he finished, he looked up. "Did you tell her?"

"Of course not. I...I think you should do that." The words—and the realization—were as painful as anything had been in this whole horrible nightmare. It felt like her first abdication of responsibility and the sensation was so strange and painful it stole her breath. She told herself to get used to it and forged ahead, her voice ragged. "I think it would be best for you to do that. After all…you're her father."

The words hung between them in the heat of the fall afternoon. A frog on the other bank of the river croaked hoarsely. A pair of mourning doves called to each other.

Gray lifted his face to Annie's.

"Her father…" He said the words with wonder, as if he'd never expected the description to fit him. A moment passed while he seemed to struggle for control, his emotions going off without him. Finally, when he did speak, his voice was as strong and domineering as usual, making Annie think she'd imagined the second before.

"I'd appreciate it if you would come with me when I do tell her," he said. "I think she'd do better with you there."

This time, his eyes gave him away, and she realized she hadn't imagined a thing. There was just a hint of anxiousness in their depths. Annie felt something twist inside her at this unexpected glimpse of how he really cared. If he could only allow himself to be that way all the time.

"I'll be there," she answered, "but just tell her the truth. Tell her you're her father. Tell her that you…" Her voice grew thick and she had to swallow. "That you love her. She'll be thrilled to have a daddy—*her* daddy."

The anxiousness disappeared and his eyes lightened at once with a kind of happiness, a level of openness, that she'd never before seen in his gaze.

And it was heart-wrenching for Annie to witness. Even though she wouldn't have wanted it any other way.

A second later, it was gone.

"We'll tell her then we're getting married, also."

"All right." Her throat ached with the effort of sounding calm, and she closed her eyes briefly in an effort to hold on to her composure.

A second later, she opened her eyes when she felt his

touch on her cheek. He was turning her face to his, and for one crazy minute she thought he was going to kiss her.

And for one crazy minute, she was going to let him.

Then she realized his intent was something else. His eyes were searching hers for understanding. "This is the only way. You understand that, don't you?"

She stepped away from him, out of the range of his touch, at arm's length from his words. Ignoring his question, she spoke abruptly, her eyes avoiding his. "I'll see that Bella's back early so you can talk to her."

Gray watched Annie disappear up the path toward the house, the report still clutched in his hand. When she stepped out of view, he looked down and realized he'd crumpled up the most important piece of paper he'd ever received. Carefully, slowly, he flattened it out across his knee, then sat down on the bench beside the water and reread the whole thing.

He couldn't believe it.

Bella really was his daughter.

He allowed himself to imagine what he'd been afraid to think of before. Scenes popped into his mind. Tossing her a baseball, watching her swing the bat. Taking her to the movies, bringing her popcorn to eat. Tucking her into bed at night, telling her that he loved her.

The images were heartwarming, but something essential seemed to be missing. He puzzled over it for a while, then when he unconsciously added to the picture and completed it in his mind, Gray was shocked to see the results.

There were three people in the mental photo; him, Bella *and* Annie. Without Annie, it just didn't seem right.

Almost immediately he shook his head angrily, sending the image fleeing and his questions with it. He was being ridiculous. The emotions of the moment were overwhelming him. *Get a grip, Powers. There's only one reason*

*you're doing this—so you can control the situation. That's
it.*

What he needed to concentrate on was how to tell Bella
everything. He wanted to choose his words carefully, and
despite what Annie had said, Gray knew there was a right
way—and a wrong way—to tell the little girl the truth.

By the time Bella finally came home from Rose's, Gray
was still not ready. Bella's footsteps, ringing down the
wooden floor of the hallway, brought him to his feet from
the living-room sofa where he'd been waiting with paperwork he'd never read.

"Hey, Gray!" She bounded into the sunny room with
all the energy of a wild tornado. "You'll never guess what
Rose and I did today. We built a playhouse in Rose's dining room—under the table with a blanket and everything.
We even took her puppy under it. It was way cool. You
should have seen it. Maybe I can build one here, too—"

Standing beside Bella, the shadow of pain still more
than visible in her blue eyes, Annie interrupted the flow
of words. "Bella, Gray and I have something we need to
talk to you about. I want you to sit down and listen to us
very carefully, okay? It's important."

Bella's eyes immediately grew round at Annie's serious
tone. "If it's about that vase in the hall, I didn't mean
to—"

Annie held up her hand patiently, but Gray could see it
was trembling slightly. "It's not about that. This is more
important than any piece of crystal."

He couldn't help but admire her calmness. He knew she
was torn up inside, but on the outside she was the picture
of a perfect mother—poised, understanding, levelheaded
above all.

Bella grew quiet and so did the room. Belatedly, Gray
realized Annie had turned to him. It was his turn now.

Bella took her cue from Annie, and her huge green eyes focused on him as well.

"Why don't you come over here?" he said to the little girl.

She crossed the room and stood before him.

He kneeled down and took one of Bella's hands in his. It was the first time he'd ever touched her, knowing she was really his, and a lump came into his throat. A fierce protective lump. He looked into her eyes.

"Annie and I have some news, Bella, and we want to share it with you because it *is* so important. We—I—hope it's news that makes you happy, too."

"Okay." Her voice held a questioning note, a wary look coming instinctively into her gaze.

He wanted to just come right out and say it. *I'm your father, Bella. Your natural father, and I love you more than anything in the whole wide world.* The words were on the tip of his tongue, but he couldn't seem to make them go any further.

Silence took over, then Bella looked from Annie back to Gray. "Well?" she said. "What is it?"

"We're getting married," he said without thinking. "Annie and I are getting married...."

The green eyes grew huge, then excitement lit her face with a delighted glow. "You and Annie are getting married? Oh, wow!" She turned to Annie and grinned. "So that means you love each other and you'll be kissing and—"

From the sidelines, for the first time, Annie spoke up, so quickly she almost stumbled over the words. "Yes...yes, that's true, sweetheart, but getting married means lots of things...."

"That's right!" Bella answered with a beaming smile. "It means Gray will be my daddy. I'll have a daddy!"

Gray smiled back, his heart clutching. "That's right,

Bella. In fact…I really am your daddy. I know it's hard for you to understand, but a long time ago, I used to be married to Monica, your mother. Do you understand what I'm saying?''

"You're my *real* daddy?" The green eyes went back to his face. This time they were confused, uncertain, the smile fading. "I…I don't think…"

"I know it's complicated but I was married to your…your *other* mother before she died. I didn't know about you or we would have been together all this time. I only found out that you were my daughter when Annie started to adopt you. Now, Annie has decided to marry me. So we're going to be a family. All three of us.''

For a change, Bella took the information in slowly, carefully. He could almost see the wheels clicking inside her brain as she worked through the information. She stared at him a little longer, then turned to Annie. "I thought we already were a family.''

Annie rose from the sofa where she'd been sitting and came toward the little girl, taking a seat beside Gray without meeting his eyes. "We are. But now we're going to be a bigger family. It's growing, that's all. Remember when Rose's mom came home from the hospital with Alex? This is kind of like that…our family is growing because Gray is joining it.''

Bella frowned. "But he was my daddy already?''

"Yes. Remember our conversation about daddies and mommies and guardians? Well, what Gray is saying is that he's your *real* daddy, just like my friend, Monica, was your *real* mommy. You remember her—we've talked about her a lot.''

"I *do* remember, but if he's my daddy and my mommy's gone, then…what are you, Annie? I thought *you* were going to be my mommy.''

The pain radiating off Annie came to Gray in a wave

the minute Bella spoke. He could have felt it a mile away. As it was, with her sitting beside him, it was all he could do not to turn and put his arms around her. He knew how she'd react to that, though, so instead he squeezed Bella's hand encouragingly. She turned to him again. "Annie *is* going to be your mommy, Bella. As soon as we get married."

Her little forehead cleared slowly as the complicated situation seemed to soak in. She looked at him warily, though. "Well, what do I call you?"

His heart thumped painfully. "You...you can call me Daddy, if that's what you want to do."

Again, the green eyes turned to dark jade while she mulled over all the information. In the meantime, Gray's heart seemed to pause, to wait to beat until she spoke again. He hadn't realized until now how much he wanted this little girl's approval. It was silly. She was a six-year-old kid, for God's sake.

But she was *his* six-year-old kid.

Finally, she broke the silence. "Okay," she said perkily. "That's hunky-dory with me." Turning to Annie, she spoke once more. "Can I go outside and play now?"

Chapter 12

If she hadn't been so upset, Annie would have laughed out loud at the look on Gray's face. He looked absolutely dumbfounded as Bella disappeared down the hall.

"That's it?" he said. "All this big news and she just turns around and leaves?"

"She's only six. What did you expect?"

"Well...not that," he answered.

"Children are very accepting." Annie crossed the room and absentmindedly adjusted a row of magazines that were spread across the sofa table. "She likes you, she's asked me before if I would marry any time.... Nothing's about to change. Her life will stay the same, so she doesn't see any problems. Why should she get upset?"

Gray seemed to mull the question over, then he rose and moved around the couch. He stood beside Annie, his dark eyes intense again. "And that's why we're doing what we're doing, right? We wanted that for Bella. For her life to stay the same."

He was asking her for confirmation—of her decision and of what they were about to do. Annie felt her mouth go dry. A part of her had been thinking, as always, that at the very last minute, Gray might change his mind, might decide marriage was too drastic.

And another part of her—shockingly—had hoped he wouldn't.

She finally spoke. "Tha-that's right," she managed to get out. "It is the best thing to do…for Bella."

"Then we need to arrange the ceremony. Is there anything special you want?"

She shook her head. "I know all the judges here in Timberley. I can call one and find out what we need to do."

He reached out unexpectedly and took her chin between his thumb and forefinger. Lifting it up, he stared, his eyes going over her face with that old familiar intensity. "This isn't how you thought it'd be, is it?"

He'd fanned the rest of his fingers down her neck. The heat of the touch was almost too much to bear. "Wh-what are you talking about?"

"I'm sure you had better plans for your own wedding than calling a judge and going to the courthouse." His voice was harsh.

"It doesn't matter. Anyway, a big event would be like we were—"

"Lying?" Dropping his hand from her neck, he continued to stare at her. "Is that what you were about to say?"

"Yes," she answered almost defiantly, almost as if she were testing him. "We're not in love. Most weddings are celebrations, an occasion to mark something special. What we're doing isn't like that at all."

"But no one's supposed to know that."

"Well, *I* know it."

His dark eyes glittered, and once again he was the man

in charge, the man who had to be in control. "Then you'd better go about forgetting it. Part of the deal was that we act as if we love each other. I don't expect that act to end when the audience isn't around."

Her pulse jolted into a faster gear. "Are you saying you expect me to sleep with you?"

"Yes. That's exactly what I'm saying. Did you think I was going to stay celibate for the next fifteen years or so? Did you expect that for *yourself?*"

"I...I don't know what I expected," she said faintly. *Liar.*

"Well, I can't speak for you, but abstinence is not something I enjoy. Sex is part of life, and I don't intend to give up my life just because I've become a parent. I don't think that's how it works."

Annie looked up at him. "Then...what are you proposing?"

"I'm proposing that we live a normal life. That we live together, eat together...and sleep together. I assumed you understood that when I told you what I wanted."

She licked her dry lips. "Then our wedding night..."

"Will be a normal wedding night," he said quietly. "I'll be prepared for that circumstance, unless you'd like to take care of it."

She realized what he was talking about. "I...I'll take care of it," she answered.

"All right." He moved away from her and stepped toward the window. Locking his hands behind his back, he rocked slightly on his heels and looked out the window, his thoughts lost in silence while hers churned in turmoil.

Hadn't she known all along? Who was she trying to kid? From the minute he'd said "marriage" Annie had known exactly what that meant. Of course, he'd expect her to sleep with him.

And vice versa.

Behind his back, she shook her head at her own thoughts. What was she doing? Had she lost her mind?

"I suggest we set the ceremony for next week," he said, interrupting the confusion of thoughts exploding inside her. "I'd like to wrap this up."

She said the only thing she could. "I'll get right on it."

It came together quickly. Before Annie knew what was happening, she was standing in front of the judge, her trembling left hand locked inside Gray's, a wide gold band covered in diamonds twinkling on the third finger. She couldn't believe it.

She'd organized the wedding in a daze, ordering flowers, renting tables, finding a photographer. Thank God for Yolanda! Planning the girl's wedding a few weeks before had made Annie's plans take form like a well-thought-out quilt. She didn't know how she would have accomplished the whole event if she hadn't just done the very same thing for someone else. She'd told herself that the experience had made it easier, as she'd run from one place to the next, making plans and taking care of everything, telling everyone she saw in the process that they were invited, but part of her had wondered. It had all gone exceedingly smoothly, almost as if it was destined. That possibility gave her goose bumps when she let herself think about it.

Strangest of all, though, no one had seemed surprised.

Bella had announced the news of the wedding at Show-And-Tell. When Annie had seen Dana at the Wal-Mart later that afternoon, the teacher had just grinned and shook her head. Shelly, Rose's mother, had seemed thrilled but certainly not shocked. The only person to express anything other than pleasure had been Nikki...and Annie understood that.

Oh, yes, she understood. Late the previous afternoon, a package had arrived. Gray had opened it and tugged back the tissue to reveal a custom-made tuxedo, pressed to perfection. He'd looked at her calmly and told her he kept it for corporate events. Glancing over at him now as the judge droned on, Annie took in the width of his shoulders and the way the crisp blackness made his features even more intense. Oh, yes...she understood Nikki's reaction completely.

Immediately after Gray's tuxedo had arrived, though, Annie had panicked. Running upstairs, she'd torn through her closet in search of something to wear. She hadn't even thought about it until then. Without hesitation, her hands went directly to a pale blue silk-shantung suit. She'd bought the beautiful outfit on a whim at Neiman-Marcus two years before and the tags still dangled from the sleeve. For some reason, she'd even gotten shoes to match— they'd cost almost as much as the suit. All in all, it had been a wild extravagance, but one she hadn't been able to resist when she'd tried it on and seen how blue it made her eyes. Pulling the suit out, she'd slipped on the jacket and skirt and prayed it still fit.

Thank God for small favors.

Now, with her right hand pressed against the side of the skirt, Annie glanced through her lashes at Gray. His expression, when she'd come down the stairs, had revealed what he thought of the outfit, his heavy gaze going to the slim, snug skirt, then traveling up to the dipping neckline to stay for a moment too long. When his eyes had finally reached her face, his stare had held more than approval. The thrill she'd felt then—a thrill of something she didn't want to define—was still with her.

She straightened her back and stared at the judge. That thrill, though, that feeling, wasn't why she was standing here. Bella was. Nothing else mattered. Looking down to her left, Annie felt a wave of love come over her as she saw Bella's halo of red hair peeking out from beneath the hat she'd insisted on wearing. *She* was the only reason they were all there. Annie's daughter. Decked out in a pale ivory dress trimmed in lace and tucked across the front into a thousand tiny pleats, she looked like a miniature bride herself. Perfectly beautiful.

Annie's heart turned over and despite everything, she felt a flash of affirmation. They'd be together. That was the only important thing. She wouldn't lose her daughter. If she had to marry a man who didn't love her in order to avoid that, it seemed like a small price.

The judge's deep voice broke into Annie's troubled thoughts. "You may now kiss the bride," he concluded, a wide, expectant smile across his face as he shot a glance toward Gray.

Behind her, the small gathering waited. Beside her, Gray waited. The music swelled. With her heart in her throat, feeling like a fraud, Annie finally lifted her face and met Gray's eyes. There was nothing deceitful about the expression he wore.

He wanted to kiss her.

There was no hesitation, no confusion.

Cupping her face in his hands, he lowered his head to meet hers. His breath was warm against her cheek as he first brushed his lips there. Thinking he would stop at that point, Annie felt a wave of relief, mingled with disappointment. That feeling fled an instant later as his lips moved again and captured her mouth, taking away any notion she might have had that he hadn't been serious about their upcoming wedding night. His lips were hard, demanding, and delivered a message that zinged over her entire body, leaving no doubt at all about where he stood.

You're mine, the kiss seemed to say. *You're mine and will be forever. Even if I don't love you, even if you're doing this for your daughter, you will always belong to me, and nothing will ever change that.*

While this astonishing thought took form in her mind, Annie's hands tensed. Gray responded instantly, obviously thinking she was trying to end the kiss. His caress deepened, his tongue going into her mouth, an automatic moan escaping from hers. For one long moment, Annie lost herself in the feeling and let herself act as if it were real. Then, finally, she pulled back.

But not before he'd looked into her eyes and confirmed everything his kiss had just told her.

Gray looked around the crowded room at the mingled guests and prayed for patience. Was this damned reception ever going to end?

There were people everywhere, dressed to the nines and laughing and having a good time. He told himself to enjoy the moment but he couldn't…because he wanted nothing as much as he wanted to sweep Annie into his arms and carry her up the wide, generous staircase and into his room. Their kiss had sparked a fire deep inside him and nothing would put that out but having her. He wanted to run his fingers through her chestnut curls, trail his mouth over her face, then peel the blue silk from her shoulders, and mold his body to hers. The passion he'd been holding back had exploded and now he could no more contain it than he could have held back a hurricane.

But the congratulations continued. Standing beside him in the cool blue suit that matched her eyes, Annie patiently introduced him to what seemed like all of Timberley. From little old ladies in fussy flowered dresses to friends of Bella's in denim and lace, she repeated their names, accepted their kisses, and smiled graciously. She looked cool, calm and definitely collected.

Completely the opposite of him. He struggled not to stare at the sweeping expanse of creamy skin revealed above the curve of her neckline and fought to keep his mouth away from hers. It was almost impossible, but he finally managed to settle for the simple pleasure of placing his arm around her waist and resting his hand lightly on the sweet swell of hip beneath his fingers. Just as he got used to that, though, she would move slightly, and the torture would begin all over again, his awareness of her jolting him back into a state of unbearable neediness.

They cut the cake and took the first sip of champagne. All Gray could do was watch her mouth.

They sat down for a second and she crossed her legs. The silky whisper called out to him.

When they posed for the photographer and Gray took her into his arms, he'd had enough. He simply didn't let go.

She looked up at him, the dappled sunshine caressing her face, the lacy pattern of the pin-oak leaves moving with the breeze. "I...I think the picture's done. I heard the camera click."

"No, you didn't," he said, his voice a husky whisper. "That was something else. We have to stay this way."

She squirmed slightly, her breasts moving against his chest. "No...I think you're wrong, Gray. He's—"

She started to turn her head to look, but Gray reached down and stopped her, putting his hand against her cheek. Her skin was warm and flushed. "He told me to kiss you next," Gray said seriously. "That's what he wanted to get."

Her eyes turned a shade darker. "He did? I didn't hear him say anything like that. Are you sure—"

Gray nodded. "I'm positive...and besides, everyone's watching. You don't want them to think you don't want to kiss your new husband, do you?"

She finally realized what he was doing, her eyes turning wary, her body going stiff in his arms. "No one's looking at us," she said. "They're all eating cake and drinking champagne." She started to pull back.

He tightened his arms.

Their stares locked. The force of hers held no less strength than he knew his did. "Kiss me," he said hoarsely, suddenly, his need overcoming his caution. "Kiss me just once like you really mean it, Annie. Kiss me like you did down at the river that night. Kiss me as if you really love me."

"Why?" The word escaped her lips as though it pained her. "Why do you want me to do that?"

"I want to know what it feels like. Just for once. I want to know how it would feel for you to kiss me, not because you have to and not because you've been carried away, but because you love me."

For a moment, he thought she'd refuse. Her expression seemed to close, to fold within itself so that he couldn't tell what she was really thinking. Then, slowly, she appeared to make up her mind. She put her arms around him and drew him close.

"Are you sure you really want this?" Her voice was seductive, provocative. She wasn't trying to make it that way, it just was. Just like the rest of her was. His gut tightened.

"I wouldn't have asked for it if I didn't." His voice turned serious. "I make sure I know what I want...because I always get it."

A speculative gleam came into her eyes. "That's a pretty presumptuous thing to say."

"It wouldn't be the first time I've been described that way. I can live with it."

"Then perhaps I shouldn't do this," she said. "It might be better to show you what it feels like not to get your way...for a change."

He stared into her eyes and thought she was probably

right. It might be good for him…but he didn't want what was good for him. All he wanted right now was Annie. And he wanted to think she wanted him, too.

"Just kiss me," he said. "We'll work on my character later."

By the time the last guest had left, a huge fall moon dominated the midnight sky. Annie waved goodbye to the departing car, then turned to find Gray at her side. He'd slipped up behind her on silent feet, just as he had the first time they'd talked in the kitchen about Bella and her father…and how children needed their own parents nearby. Annie remembered every word of the conversation.

"Are you tired?" he asked, one dark eyebrow going upwards. "You've had a pretty busy day."

She started to say yes, then realized she wasn't. An electric sense of energy hummed around her. She felt like a wire someone had stretched to the very limit of its strength. Ever since the moment he'd kissed her—at the ceremony and then later—she'd felt this way. Expectant. Excited. Impatient. She hated to admit to the emotions, but she couldn't deny them, either. Before Annie could answer, Bella's voice floated outside from somewhere in the house.

"We're leaving now…Annie…where are yo-o-o-u-u-u-u?"

She and Gray both turned at the same time and started toward the voice. "We're here," Annie called as they walked toward the house. "Out on the terrace."

Bella's face appeared at the back door. Maggie stood beside her, a small overnight bag in her hand. Each of them had already changed and were dressed in matching warm-up suits that Annie had bought them last Christmas as a gag.

"I'm leaving now with Aunt Maggie," Bella said through the screen door. "We're going over to her house and we're going to stay up all night and watch old movies and eat popcorn.''

She opened the screen door and bounced outside, the late hour not even fazing her. ''We're going to have fun, fun, fun!''

Annie lifted her eyes to Maggie. ''Are you sure you're up to this?''

''I can handle it,'' she said drily. ''As long as the honeymoon doesn't last past tomorrow morning.''

In the darkness, Annie felt her cheeks immediately flush. ''I've got sixteen mystery writers checking in tomorrow afternoon. The honeymoon will definitely be over by then.''

''All right, then, let's go, sweetie,'' Maggie said, looking down at Bella. ''I think it's time for us to hit the road.''

Annie kneeled down and Bella hopped over. Kissing the little girl's cheek, Annie held on to the small, warm body a second longer than usual, her heart finally secure in the knowledge that she wouldn't be losing her daughter. *She'd done it. She'd actually done it.* And now Gray could never leave and take her with him. Annie released her, and Bella skipped toward Gray.

She held out her arms in the very same way, as if she'd grown up around the man and had known all along he was her father. He opened his own arms and hugged her tightly. ''Take care,'' he said, his lips against her hair. ''And we'll see you in the morning. Okay?''

She pulled back and grinned. ''Okay.''

And a second later they were gone.

Annie and Gray were all alone…and it was their wedding night.

He held his hand out toward a table on the terrace. ''What do you say we sit down and relax just a bit? I hid a bottle of champagne before all this started. You take off your shoes and I'll go get the bottle.''

She started to refuse, then asked herself why not? The alcohol might reduce the tension—or whatever it was—that was still humming around her. "That sounds good." She looked up at him and met his eyes. "In fact, I think it sounds real good."

In the soft moonlight, his eyes darkened perceptibly, then without a word he turned and walked back to the kitchen. Annie sank into one of the nearby cushioned chairs and tried to make her mind go blank.

But it wouldn't. It filled, instead, with images of Gray. Images of him standing in her kitchen wearing an open shirt and low-slung jeans. Images of him and Bella...images of him in a perfect tuxedo...

He came out the back door a second later, the bottle of champagne in one hand, two glasses held in his other. With efficient, graceful movements he removed the cork and filled their glasses. Handing her the first one, he took the other and touched the rim to hers. "Cheers," was all he said.

She nodded then brought the flute to her lips. The wine was cold and sharp. In silence they sipped their drinks and slowly she began to feel the tension ease. He filled their glasses a second time, then stood up and moved behind her. His hands were warm and heavy when he put them on her shoulders and began to rub them.

"You need to relax, Annie." The rhythm of his words matched the movements of his hands. "I'm not going to bite you, you know."

Letting her head fall back, she closed her eyes and let her body move under his touch.

"Unless you want me to, of course," he added, his voice suddenly lower and husky. His hands stopped. "I'll do whatever you want. Anything. You name it."

Can you make me not love you?

Annie pushed the question away, and let the heavy sensuality of his voice caress her.

"Tell me," he said. "Tell me what would make you happy."

"I'm not sure I know anymore," she said hoarsely. "I thought I wanted…"

Her voice died out in the midnight silence. The river sounded faintly in the background and beyond that, somewhere in the distance, an owl cried.

Gray's fingers stilled. Without taking his hands away, he came around to face her, his fingertips trailing above the neckline of her dress against her bare skin. She opened her eyes in time to watch him kneel before her, his hands going down her sleeves to come to rest at her wrists, pinning her in the chair, her knees pressing into his chest. He kept his eyes on her face.

"What?" he said. "You thought you wanted what? Just tell me…"

"I—I can't say." Her breath caught in her throat, hot and heavy.

"Can't or won't?"

"Does it matter?" Her pulse pounded at the base of her neck, roared in her ears. "What's going to happen is going to happen, regardless of what I say."

"That's not true," he answered. "You have a say in all this. I'm not going to make you do anything you don't want to do. You should know me better than that by now, Annie." His hands tightened against her wrists. "So tell me…tell me what you want…tell me what you like."

"I…" She simply couldn't say anything else. Her throat seemed paralyzed.

He stared at her for what seemed like a very long time, almost as if he was trying to read her mind, then finally, he rose slowly, his hands gliding back up her arms. With

his touch warm and sensual against her breasts, he bent
over and whispered in her ear, his breath caressing her.

"All right…if you can't tell me…then I'll tell you…."

The words that followed she'd heard before…but never
like this. And then he proceeded to show her *exactly* what
he meant.

Chapter 13

Afterwards, Annie had no idea how they got from the terrace to the bedroom. All she knew was that she was in Gray's arms and they were standing beside the big four-poster bed in the center of his room.

The windows were open and the drapes billowed into the room with each breath of the wind. The faraway sound of the chimes down by the river added to the sense of isolation she felt. Gray hadn't turned on the light, and she was glad. Light would make her see, see why she shouldn't be there, and for the moment all she wanted to do was feel. To feel, and to finish what he'd started out on the terrace.

His fingers came to the row of buttons on her jacket and as he began to undo them, one by one, his lips covered hers in a kiss so light she could barely feel it. He spoke and kissed at the very same time, his breath caressing her as much as his mouth.

"So beautiful...so soft...so sweet..."

Down her neck, then on the sides of her shoulders, his mouth dropped feathery touches, warm, bare kisses that were there and then gone. When her jacket was completely open, he slipped it off her shoulders, but held on to the edges of the fabric while taking a step backwards. With her arms trapped in the sleeves and the neck of the jacket taut around her hips, she found herself in a silken restraint. Even if she'd wanted to, she couldn't move. Gray was in complete control and once again, there was nothing she could do, nowhere she could go. He held the power. A flash of panic, a final question, then Annie let her thoughts burn up in the heat of her desire.

There was nothing else she could do.

He made no move at all to reach for her. In fact, he touched her with nothing but his eyes, the dark and burning gaze deliberate and intense. She shivered but couldn't look away as his stare raked her lacy bra, lingering at the curve of her breasts, pausing at the shadow of her cleavage, stopping finally on the dark center of her nipples still partly hidden by the lace but rising and growing hard.

His gaze was the most erotic, the most provocative, the most incredible phenomenon she'd ever experienced. When he'd touched her outside, she'd thought she was going to die. But this…this was even worse because now she knew what he was holding back and it made her want it even more.

Her pulse began to throb at the base of her neck. A second later, a low moan escaped from somewhere deep in her throat. The sound broke the thick silence of the room, and he lifted his eyes to hers. Her lips parted in automatic response.

Tightening his hold on her jacket, Gray pulled her slowly toward him, the ends of the silk whispering a false protest as he reeled her in. His gaze never left her face. And still they didn't touch. When she was close enough to see the individual lashes ringing his eyes, to feel his breath warm against her cheek and to smell the hint of soap that lingered on his skin, he dropped his hold and released the silken binding. Released *her*.

But by then, it didn't matter.

Annie was trapped as surely as she had been the moment before. She was trapped by her own desire and by the desire that was mirrored in the depths of his eyes. She had no power, no power at all. The forces sweeping over her scared her, but at the very same time, freed her. What else could she do but give in?

His hands came up, and slowly, with the utmost delicacy, he released the center clasp of her bra. Edging the straps over her shoulders, he let the garment fall to the floor.

She stood there for a second, almost afraid to breathe, almost afraid to think. Then, with fingers that trembled, she lifted her hands and began to unbutton his shirt. When it was open, he too stood unmoving. She slid her hands inside his shirt and flattened her palms against his chest.

It was a moment she would never forget.

Gray closed his eyes and drew a deep, shuddering breath. Beneath her fingertips, she could feel his chest rise and expand, the warm smoothness of his skin providing a contrast to the triangle of black hair that curled in the center.

For two long heartbeats they stayed that way—motionless, silent, tied by their desires—then Gray opened his eyes and looked down at Annie. When their gazes collided, she had one last thought: her life would never be the same.

Instantly, explosively, he pulled her toward him, the last few inches that had separated them disappearing in the volatile heat erupting between them. His fingers bit into her arms and his bare chest pressed against her breasts while his mouth claimed hers, his tongue hot and insistent as it parted her lips. Annie wrapped her arms around his waist and kissed him back, pulling him toward her just as he pulled her toward him. She couldn't get close enough, couldn't feel enough of his skin against hers.

In a flurry of movement, they discarded the rest of their clothes. Gray lifted Annie and deposited her in the center of the bed, the old, soft quilt billowing up around them. His hands never left her body and Annie gave herself up to the feel of him, the smell of him, the warmth of him. Without his clothing, he seemed more solid, more substantial, and at once she knew the reason why. Clothed, he was tall and almost lean. Naked, he was powerful and taut. The muscles burning under her touch were all tight and strong. There wasn't an ounce of unnecessary cushioning—Grayston Power's body fit his personality perfectly. He had nothing extra, nothing he didn't need, yet everything he did have, he used to the fullest extent.

His hands continued to caress her, sliding over her breasts and arms, her shoulders and legs, as if he already knew her body, already knew what would please her. It was a new experience for Annie, and she gave herself over to it, reveling in the total concentration Gray had for her. The intensity that hung over him like a cloud never left him—and now she was grateful for it.

His mouth covered hers and he began to kiss her once more, his hand caressing her breasts and then her stomach, the touch light but demanding. She let her own hands begin their exploration, feeling as though this was the first time for her, experiencing everything through a haze of sensations and impressions. When his hand slipped between her legs and he began to stroke her, she opened herself to him without thought, without hesitation.

Her every sensation focused on the feeling building up between them. When Gray moved over her, his solid body blocking out everything for her but his existence, she wrapped her arms and legs around him...and opened her eyes.

He was watching her, *had* been watching her, she realized at that point, and when she met his gaze, he spoke for the very first time. "Are you sure?" he whispered.

It wasn't really a question, because they both already knew the answer. She gave him the answer he seemed to need, though, and he entered her a moment later.

The last shreds of her control evaporated. Gray sensed the flight as well, and as he thrust against her, his every movement brought her closer and closer to a final freedom. For countless moments they seemed to be suspended at the top of a very high place, then they both cried out.

And in that moment, that crystalline moment, Annie knew she'd made the biggest, most terrible, most unforgivable mistake of her life.

She'd not only slept with her enemy—not only married him—now she loved him, as well.

When Gray woke up the next morning, Annie's side of the bed was empty. Empty but warm. With his hand on the spot where she'd lain, he thought about the night before. The sex had been unbelievable, but more amazing than that were the feelings racing around inside him now. He'd never let a woman get so far under his skin. He'd told her everything about himself, and now that they'd made love, the circle was complete. She knew him—inside and out.

It was a scary thought.

He turned his head when he heard her emerge from the bathroom on his right. She wore the robe to the negligée she'd never had a chance to wear the night before. Her curly hair was tousled, her lips swollen from the kisses they'd shared. She looked like some kind of fallen angel and he immediately wanted to pull her back into his arms, his desire rising like a teenager's.

Her blue eyes flickered to his, then down his bare chest, revealed by the fallen sheet. "I...,I'm going down to make coffee," she said in the suddenly awkward silence. "W-would you like anything?"

"You don't have to wait on me." The words were automatic.

Her voice turned sharp. "That wasn't my intention."

He stared at her a moment. Every line in her body was tense, on edge. She'd clearly not enjoyed the night as he had. "Fine," he replied. The irritation that washed over him was more than just annoyance. It felt like something akin to disappointment, but he told himself how ridiculous that was as soon as the feeling came over him.

Sensing his attitude, she spoke once more, her words breaking the moment. "I—I just meant that I'd fix you something to eat if you liked."

He hardened his heart and spoke precisely. "That won't be necessary. I'll be there in a moment and get a cup of coffee." Then he climbed from the bed and stalked toward the bathroom without giving her another glance.

Annie mumbled curses all the way down the stairs. Why couldn't she think of anything else to say to him? Why had he just turned around and left? Any other woman would have been witty, frivolous, sexy, even, after a night like they'd shared, but not her...oh, no...she'd treated him like one of her guests and offered him breakfast. She felt like a fool. She stalked into the kitchen and began to bang the cabinets open, looking for a new package of coffee filters.

She knew the answer to the questions, of course. She couldn't think of anything to say and she couldn't be any of those things because she was scared. Scared to death.

When she'd awakened and glanced at Gray across the huge king-size bed, sleeping soundly, his dark hair falling over his forehead, all she could think about was that they were married. They were married, and he didn't love her.

She'd continued to stare at him and let the enormity of the situation come over her. He was naked, she was naked, they'd made love all night long. Even if she'd wanted to, she couldn't have ignored the reality of that. Her lips were bruised and reddened and an aching weariness had robbed her body of any energy it might have had left after the wedding.

They'd made love and she'd opened herself to him in a way she'd never done for anyone. She'd let him take control of her mind...and her body...and there was no stepping back from that. She'd relinquished it, given it up... Leaning against the kitchen counter weakly, she clutched the cold can of coffee she'd dug out of the refrigerator and told herself she'd do it all over again in a heartbeat, too.

How had this happened?

Over the next few weeks, Annie and Gray fell into an uneasy routine. He did most of his work from his office on the Square, and Riverside filled up with guests. They were two polite strangers, courteous and distant. After their wedding night, Annie didn't know how to act...didn't know what was expected of her. The passion that had exploded between them had been so intense, she couldn't deal with it rationally. If they were to repeat it, where would it lead?

So when the bedroom door closed, she stayed on her side of the bed and pretended to be asleep. She just tried to forget they'd ever become lovers. Lovers who couldn't get enough of each other. Lovers who hated to see the sun edge up over the river. Gray didn't have any real feelings for her, and after that one night it was more than obvious he didn't really want a real marriage, anyway.

She wanted to ask him about the situation, but what would she say? *I know we're not really husband and wife but I thought…* Suddenly life seemed even more complicated than it had a few months before—and then it had been crazy, to say the least.

There was only one thing she was sure about, and in the end, as she'd told herself a hundred times, it was the only thing that mattered. Bella was growing closer and closer to her father, and Annie finally began to accept the fact that she really had done the right thing. Maggie had been right—the little girl *had* needed a father and until now, Annie had been blind to how much Bella had been missing.

Friday afternoon confirmed that as nothing else had before.

Bella came bouncing into the kitchen, Maggie trailing behind her. "Where's Daddy?" the little girl demanded immediately. "I need to see him. Right now."

Annie glanced up from the shopping list she was making as Maggie dropped her keys and purse on the desk beside her. "Well, hello to you, too," Annie said. "Don't I get a kiss and a hug?"

The kiss was perfunctory and the hug so brief Annie barely felt it.

"I need my daddy. Is he here?"

A tug of jealousy shot through Annie but there was nothing she could do about it. She had to share Bella now. It was tough to remember that, but whenever she had a problem with the situation, she reminded herself how lucky she was to even have the little girl around at all.

Running her hand through her hair, Annie leaned back in her chair. "He's at work. You're going to have to wait until he gets home…unless it's something I could help you with.''

The six-year-old's chest puffed out. "Nope. This is a daddy job. The Brownies are having a father-daughter banquet next month. I have to invite him.''

Last year Annie had gone. It hadn't seemed to bother Bella that Annie was the only woman there, but she obviously wanted something different this year…and that was only right, Annie told herself. That fact didn't take away the sting. "I'll tell him the minute he gets here that you need to see him."

"Very good,'' Bella said importantly. Her seriousness evaporated and she grinned. "Can I have some chocolate chip cookies?''

Annie laughed and reached into the cookie jar beside her. "Here,'' she said. "Have two on me.''

A second later, the screen door banged and the little girl disappeared, Beau running along beside her.

Annie watched them through the screen. "Father-daughter banquet…'' she murmured.

"I had no idea that's what she was so pumped about.'' Maggie reached into the cookie jar Annie was still holding and pulled out two cookies, keeping one and handing the other to Annie. "She came tearing out of the schoolhouse like it was on fire, then jumped in the car and said 'Beam me up, Scotty.' I couldn't get here fast enough for her.''

Maggie crunched the cookie, catching the crumbs in her hand. "She didn't tell *me* why, of course. No one tells me anything around here anymore. I'm just the poor stepchild of the family…the cousin that nobody wants, the old maid aunt who's in the dark all the time—''

Annie rolled her eyes. She'd been waiting for this and was actually surprised Maggie had managed to hold out this long. "Okay, okay,'' she said, lifting her hands in a gesture of defeat. "What is it you want to know?''

"Why...nothing, of course." Maggie opened her eyes in a parody of innocence. "Your marriage is your business. If you don't want to share anything with me, I understand. Once that door is closed, it's closed. I'm sure you and Gray are enjoying a completely platonic relationship that has absolutely no elements of lust or sexuality in it. Just because we used to share everything, and now you don't tell me a thing, I understand—"

"Oh, for heaven's sake, Maggie." Annie made a face and started to tell her sister to get a life, then suddenly she caught a shadow of something in Maggie's eyes. A shadow of something that almost looked like sadness. Surprise came over Annie, and then it was quickly replaced with remorse. She'd been so wrapped up in her own problems lately she hadn't even stopped to think how the whole situation must have appeared to her sister. Her lonely, twice-divorced sister. Her sister who had *always* been there when Annie had needed a shoulder to cry on.

A part of her must have known, must have realized how Maggie felt, Annie realized belatedly. She had always shared everything with her sister until now, so she must have subconsciously been sparing her the details of that long, loving night. A second part of Annie knew there was another reason she hadn't said anything, though. A reason she didn't want to think about. A reason that involved facing the truth.

She met Maggie's gaze now. "I—I haven't said anything because I...I..."

Maggie's expression shifted instantly. "It's okay," she said softly. "I was just teasing you. Really."

Annie looked down at her hands. "No...it's not okay. I—I need to talk, but I just don't know what to say, that's all. I'm confused."

"Well, I can definitely see how you would be. Gray seems to have that kind of power."

Annie's head came up. She held out her hands help-lessly. "He's so very..." The words died off.

Maggie nodded with understanding. *"Very,"* she agreed. "Very, very."

"How can I fight that?" Annie twisted her hands. "How can I not give in to a man like him?"

"Who says you have to fight him?"

"He doesn't love me."

"So? You don't love him, either." Maggie raised her eyebrows. "Remember? You told me that very emphatically. YOU. DID. NOT. LOVE. HIM. Remember that conversation?"

"Yes, I remember," Annie shot back. "But..."

"But?"

"Well, that was before we'd slept together. Things change after that, you know."

Maggie crossed her arms and leaned her hips against the island in the center of the kitchen. "Sex *does* do that to a situation," she agreed.

"But it wasn't just sex." Annie said the words so softly they could hardly be heard over the hum of the refrigerator. "It was...more."

Silence filled the room.

She struggled, the right words as elusive as the leaves now dancing over the terrace outside.

"Feelings?" Maggie supplied.

Annie nodded.

"Strong feelings?"

Annie nodded.

"Feelings that almost feel like..."

"Like love," Annie whispered. She lifted her eyes to her sister's face. "Like love...but they can't be."

"Why not?"

Annie's eyes filled up. "I can't fall in love with this man, Maggie. I can't—"

"I've heard this argument before, and it was stupid then and it's stupid now. You aren't going to give me that song and dance about him being cold and hard and all that malarkey that Monica dreamed up, are you? You know that's not true."

Annie just shook her head.

"Then what?"

"I can't love him," she said woodenly, "because he doesn't love me. The only reason he married me was so we wouldn't be in court constantly, fighting over Bella. If I told him now I was in love with him, what do you think he'd think?"

Maggie's eyebrows went up, making two question marks over her eyes. "Jeez, I don't know...maybe that you'd fallen in love with him?"

"No," Annie cried. "He'd think it was some kind of trick. Something else I'd dreamed up to do just so I could somehow get my hands on Bella. Something to get him off guard so I could take over again."

"Oh, Annie!" Maggie threw her hands up. "Do you really think that's what would happen?"

"Yes, I do. He'd never believe me if I told him I loved him. Not now. He'd never think the emotion was real or that the love actually existed."

"Gray's not a stupid man, Annie. Give him a break, please!"

"I'm not talking about brains." She took a deep breath. "I'm talking about heart. Even if I hadn't done the things I've done, it'd be impossible for him to love me. Gray doesn't trust enough to love. His parents taught him that, Monica reinforced the lesson, and everything I've done told him it was true, too." She shook her head, sadness filling her heart for the way things had turned out. "It's too late, Maggie. It's just too late."

Her sister stared at her with hazel eyes. "It's never too late for love."

When Gray got home that night, Bella was bursting with news. The Brownies were hosting a father-daughter banquet next month. He could come, couldn't he? With love swelling in his heart, he stared at her and said he wouldn't miss it for the world...and realized he meant it. He found himself wondering how he'd been able to stand his life before. He'd been so lonely...and never even known it till now. His relationship with Bella had opened a whole new chapter in his life.

Annie, though...that was another story. When he walked into the room, she walked out. When he turned right to go into the hall, she went left. At breakfast, Maggie would serve him, and when he returned to Riverside in the evening, Annie would disappear into her office and close the door. At night, when they both climbed into the bed, her nearness tortured him, but what could he do? She'd made it more than clear she didn't want anything else to do with him, and he had to respect that. Despite his demand their marriage be a normal one, he wasn't about to force her.

But the feelings persisted, and he didn't understand them at all. He found himself thinking a lot about the evenings he'd shared with her before everything had blown up—the night they'd grilled fish, the evening at Tia's, the kisses when he'd held her in his arms. He couldn't get them out of his mind, and even when he and Bella were together, there was an edge to his emotions, as if something was slightly off. A part of him knew what it was— it involved Annie—but another part of him refused to acknowledge what that really meant.

At the end of the month, Bill called. "I've got some papers that need your signature," the assistant said. "Do you want them overnighted or could you come into the office? There's some other details I'd like to go over with you."

The man's voice was as professional and courteous as always, but Grey heard the undercurrent of concern in it just the same. "Is anything wrong?"

"Absolutely not," Bill said. "But..."

"But what?"

"Well." He hesitated, then plunged ahead, his words coming out in a rush. "I hated to bother you with this because I know you've got a lot going on, but it's that Number Four well in Indonesia. We've got some problems with it again."

Gray held back a curse. The well had given them more grief than he wanted to think about. He'd already been over there twice in the past eighteen months and the trip was a bear. "What's wrong with it this time?"

"I'm not too sure, but I think it might be playing out."

Gray ran one hand through his hair and shook his head. "It can't be. It's way too soon."

"Then something else has happened. The pressure's dropped to way below what it should be, and we're getting lots of water. The boys in Jakarta are getting nervous."

Gray sighed. "Then I need to calm them down. Set up a conference call for Wednesday afternoon. I'll come in tomorrow and you can review the details for me before we talk." He paused, then plunged ahead before he could change his mind. "And Bill?"

"Yes?"

"Call my housekeeper and tell her I'll be there tomorrow. I'll be bringing my daughter...and my wife."

He hung up the phone slowly and wondered what he'd done. A few seconds later, when he went downstairs and began to explain, he found out.

"Go with you to Dallas?" Annie reached for the kitchen

towel lying beside the coffeepot and began to wipe her soap-covered hands with it. "Absolutely not. I can't leave Riverside."

"But it's the middle of the week," he said patiently. "And it's only for one night. I'd really like you to come."

She raised her eyes to meet his. He was shocked at the ripple of unexpected pleasure her blue gaze brought him. It was like falling into a river after crossing a parched desert. "Why?" she said.

There were several answers that ran through his mind, all of them reminiscent of the night they'd spent together, the night he'd been trying to forget about ever since it had happened. He pushed all of them aside and gave her the first one that came into his mind.

"I'd like Bella to see my house in Dallas. I—I want to share that with her."

"She's just a little girl. She doesn't care about things like houses. *This* is her home."

"I know that," he said, containing his irritation, "and I've tried to be as understanding as I can, but I need to go to my office, Annie." He explained about the well, then spoke again, this time with more determination. "I'm going, and I'm taking Bella. Do you want to come or not?"

"What about her school?"

His anger melted when he saw the fear in her eyes. Did she think he was going to snatch the little girl and run away with her? Didn't she realize now she had nothing to be frightened of? The question ran through his mind that maybe that wasn't her fear—maybe she didn't want to be alone with him, alone on his turf, in his house—but he dismissed the thought as crazy.

"Missing one day of kindergarten is not going to keep her out of Harvard."

Her jaw tightened. It made him want to take her into

his arms and tell her everything would be okay...but something held him back.

"All right," she said in a quiet, tense voice. "But just for one night. That's it. After that, I have to get back here."

He couldn't help himself. He reached out and touched the side of her cheek with a single finger. The skin beneath his touch was so warm, so soft, it almost made him groan. "I'll bring you back," he said. "You and Bella both. I promise."

Chapter 14

The trip took longer than Annie had thought it would.

The big Mercedes ate up the miles quickly, but with every whirl of the wheels all Annie could think about was being alone with Gray. Her resolve would weaken, and they'd end up making love again, she was sure of it. And she just didn't want that to happen. It was torture. She looked out the window at the rolling green farmland passing by. If he really loved her…it would all be so different.

She cut her eyes across the leather seat to take in the man behind the wheel. He and Bella had a big conversation going.

"You'd love going to Dubai," he was saying to the little girl. "They have beautiful shops full of gold and you can wander up and down the street and see people from everywhere in the world. Along the dock there are ships called dhows. They're made out of wood and at night, you can see the sailors who live on them sleeping on deck."

Her green eyes were huge. "Are there elephants there?"

Laughing, he answered her question with a shake of his head. "No, but camels wander all over, once you go into the desert outside the city."

Bella rattled on with more questions as Annie turned back to the window. What in the hell was she going to do? She'd hated him with a passion and now she loved him equally. And there was no way she could tell him. Ever.

She thought about the dilemma for as long as she could, but there didn't seem to be a solution. Finally, between the rhythm of the car and the soft hum of conversation from across the seat, Annie felt her eyes grow heavy and close.

The next thing she knew, Gray was shaking her shoulder gently and she realized the car was parked. She opened her eyes just in time to see Bella disappear up the steps of an absolutely enormous house.

"We're home," Gray said, tilting his head toward the stuccoed house. "This is it."

"Are you sure?" she asked automatically. "I think we took a wrong turn and ended up at the Mansion on Turtle Creek."

He laughed lightly at the name of the famous Dallas hotel, but his voice was thoughtful when he answered. "Yeah—it does look a little like that, doesn't it?" He shrugged. "It was Monica's choice. I didn't have much to say about it."

She turned in her seat. "Why'd you keep it? After the divorce, I mean."

"I don't know." Then breaking the empty silence, he spoke again, reversing himself. "Yes, I do, " he said. "It was the simplest thing to do. Selling it would have been an enormous hassle and finding another place to live would have been even more work. It was easier just to keep it."

The answer was interesting for what he didn't say, she

thought instantly. He didn't say "it was home." She wondered for a minute if he'd *ever* felt at home.

They climbed out of the car and crossed the graveled driveway. A woman in a light pink uniform waited for them at the door. Gray introduced her as "Mrs. Martini, the woman who keeps me in line."

The house was even less personal on the inside, Annie discovered, as she followed Gray through an enormous marbled hall and into a vast living room that would have easily held fifty or sixty people. From the pristine white sofas to the gilt-edged consoles under the windows, the room, and everything in it, was perfection. The only thing missing was the personal touch that would have made it a home. There were no photos, no books, nothing that made you think any real people lived in the house.

He threw his briefcase down on a Louis XIV desk in one corner and picked up the nearby portable phone. After punching out a number, he covered the mouthpiece with his hand and spoke to her. "If you'd like, ask Mrs. Martini to get you something to drink. I'm probably going to go into the office after this— Hello? Bill?"

She turned away as he began his conversation, and moving toward the French doors that made up one end of the room, she spotted Bella, who had already discovered the small, sparkling swimming pool that sat, like a jewel, in the center of tiled terrace just outside. She lifted her hand and waved as she saw Annie at the door. Annie waved back and appreciated the fact once again that Gray could give the little girl the world. Everything Bella could possibly want or need, he'd be able to provide—without even thinking twice.

And he loved her as well. Bella would have everything, absolutely everything.

So why did the hole inside Annie grow even larger?

She realized Gray had hung up the phone and silence

had returned to the enormous room. She turned around and looked at him. He, too, was staring at Bella as she skipped around the edge of the pool. All at once, Annie found herself wondering if he'd imagined having children in this house when he and Monica had lived here.

If he suspected what she'd been thinking, he chose to ignore it when he turned and met her eyes. "I need to go into the office. Will you two be all right here?"

Annie couldn't stop her ironic smile. "I don't know, Gray. It's a pretty shabby place.... Are you sure the neighborhood's safe?"

He smiled back, and when he did, it was clear, all at once, what a mistake it was to let down her guard, even for a second. His expression reignited the flame she'd been guarding so carefully. It flickered and curled somewhere deep inside of her.

"I think you'll be okay," he said, his eyes, as intense and black as ever, going slowly over her body. "Just don't open the door for any strangers."

Strangers? Standing beside her was the man who poised the most danger to her heart. Who cared about strangers?

She nodded but didn't trust her voice to speak. With one last look, he turned and headed for the doorway, his footsteps clicking against the parquet floor.

He'd decided on dinner at the house, and now he was glad. With Annie sitting on his right and Bella chattering away at his left, the huge dining room, where he had always eaten by himself, seemed infinitely friendlier, warmer. Banished by the candles Mrs. Martini had lit, the shadows had disappeared into the corners...even the shadows in his heart.

Bella's nose glowed pink after a day by the pool, and she hadn't stopped talking since he'd gotten home. Now, although she continued to talk, every other word was hidden behind her hand as she tried to stifle her yawns. Her eyelids were heavy as well, and once or twice, he'd caught her nodding and jerking herself awake. After Mrs. Martini cleared away the ice-cream dishes, Gray glanced toward Annie. "Should we put her to bed?"

"I think we'd better. Before she falls off the chair."

Gray nodded, then rose, and without even giving it any thought, he picked up Bella and started from the room. Her arms curled sleepily around his neck, and when he heard Annie falling in behind him, a sweet sense of peace—like nothing he'd ever felt before—came over Gray. It was strange and wonderful and totally unexpected.

Annie led the way to the bedroom Bella had picked as hers. Mrs. Martini had already turned down the sheets and an inviting night lamp, just the kind to keep away nightmares for little girls in strange places, had appeared on one edge of the dresser. Gray laid Bella on the bed and with a swiftness and ease that impressed him, Annie quickly removed her play clothes and replaced them with a nightgown—all without waking her. A moment later, Annie was pulling the pressed sheets up and tucking them under Bella's chin. They stood beside the bed and looked down at the sleeping child.

"She's so beautiful," Gray said without thinking. "Was Monica that perfect when she was that age?"

"I saw her with a child's eyes, and thought she was the most beautiful person I'd ever known. The other kids made fun of her, though. Her hair, her eyes…" She glanced up at him. "Do you see any of yourself in Bella?"

"Not really," he confessed. "Except maybe for her stubbornness."

"That's not always a bad trait," she said. "If you call it persistence instead."

He turned back to look at his daughter. This was what he'd always imagined a family would be like. A mother and father standing over a sleeping child. Soft conversation, warm feelings, emotions that were close to the surface. He'd never believed this would have been possible for him, had given up that dream so long ago he couldn't even remember when it had become nothing more than imagination. Now, even as he was experiencing it, something else was going on as well. He closed his eyes for a moment, but no matter how hard he tried, he couldn't imagine having this experience with anyone but Annie. Frightened by the realization, Gray opened his eyes and stared down at her.

She was looking back at him. Dim light spilled into the room from the hallway, shimmering against her hair, shadowing her face. Her gaze met his and locked. He reached out and cupped her cheekbone. It was warm, as if she'd just come in from the pool where he'd found her and Bella when he'd returned from work. He'd stared at them a few minutes through the French doors and had let himself pretend.

He knew it was dangerous, but he couldn't help it. He wanted to pretend just a little bit longer…pretend that he had a real family, pretend that everything was just as it seemed. Pretend that he could be a good father and husband even though he didn't know how.

A second later, they were in each other's arms.

Annie woke up early, slipped out of bed and put on her robe. Opening the door to her room, she glanced down the elegant hallway but she knew immediately that Gray had already left for work. The house had an empty feeling that told her he was gone. She felt a mixture of relief and disappointment. Walking down the hall to the room where Bella had slept, Annie opened the door and spied the small mound still under the covers. She'd been exhausted last night. No wonder she was still asleep.

Tightening the belt on her robe, Annie proceeded down the hall to descend the stairs. Last night had been incredible, just as she'd known it would be. There was something between her and Gray that she couldn't explain, couldn't understand. She'd never thought she could sleep with a man who didn't love her, but he made it impossible not to when he touched her.

Her confused thoughts were broken by the sweet smell of fresh coffee. Turning left and letting her nose lead her, she headed toward the back of the house. A moment later, a double set of swinging doors appeared on her right. She pushed through them and stepped into a kitchen she would have killed for.

Mrs. Martini looked up in surprise from the tray she'd been working on. It held a miniature silver coffee service, a china plate with what looked like an omelet, and a crystal vase with a single red rose. "I was just about to bring you breakfast," the housekeeper said with an open smile. "Why don't you run back up and pretend you're still in bed?"

"Oh, no. I don't think I could do that. I'm too accustomed to being on the other side of that tray."

"Well, all right then," she said agreeably. "Go on into the dining room and I'll serve you in there."

"Oh, Mrs. Martini, I—I'd just as soon eat in here if it doesn't bother you." Annie tilted her head toward the formal dining room. "I don't think I could stand being in there all by myself."

This time the housekeeper's smile was sympathetic. "I understand completely," she answered, "and I'd love the company. You don't know how lonely this big, old house gets...but please, call me Mary."

Annie pulled out a chair at the table and the older woman set the tray down in front of her. Two minutes later Mary Martini had her own cup of tea beside her and she was slathering a triangle of toast with strawberry jam.

Annie tasted her coffee. It was perfect. Almost better than what she served at Riverside. She didn't want her thoughts wandering back to the night before, so she spoke to the housekeeper. "How long have you been here, Mary? With Mr. Powers?"

"Quite a few years," the older woman said.

"Did you know his wife, Monica?"

"No. I came after the divorce. Actually his assistant hired me and I didn't even meet Mr. Powers until I'd been working for him six months." She raised her jam-covered knife and pointed over her shoulder. "I live here, you know—in the back over the garage. It's a wonderful place, and I'm thrilled with the work." Despite her words, though, her gaze dropped and Annie knew something was wrong.

"But..." she prompted.

The housekeeper looked up slowly. "But I wish he had more of a life," she said quietly. "He's a wonderful man, but it's sad here. All the time. When he's gone, the house is empty and quiet and when he's here, it's hardly any different. It breaks my heart. I've always thought he deserved better."

Annie's heart cramped instantly. The image of Gray sitting down to a lonely meal in that huge dining room was painful.

"It'll all be different now, though, won't it?" Mary's eyes warmed. "I'm so glad you two are married. And it's so obvious he loves the little girl and—" She broke off abruptly.

"And?" Annie prompted.

"Oh, nothing, nothing. I talk too much." The housekeeper averted her gaze. "Would you like more coffee?"

Mary Martini was an honest woman and she'd realized

instantly she was going too far with her chatter about Gray. That's why she'd broken off so abruptly. It didn't matter, though. The unspoken words hung in the bright, beautiful kitchen like an unwanted guest. Annie didn't need the older woman to voice them because she'd heard them in her mind a thousand times: It was obvious—Gray loved Bella.

And just as obvious that he didn't love Annie.

Gray didn't know what in the hell to do.

After their trip to Dallas, he couldn't seem to stay away from Annie. She had some kind of hold over him. It was like nothing he'd ever experienced before. Every night he had to force himself not to reach for her. All he could think about was slipping the silk from her shoulders and caressing her body. He knew he was getting in way over his head, but every time he tried to pull back from her, he found himself doing just the opposite. It was driving him crazy.

Sitting on the terrace of Riverside on Saturday morning, watching Bella and Rose play in the yard, he felt a twinge of panic rise up inside him. What was he going to do? This wasn't turning out as he'd thought it would. Not at all. He'd thought that by marrying Annie, he'd be able to control the situation. Instead…it was controlling him.

The screen door banged and, thinking it was Annie, Gray turned. Instead, it was Maggie who was crossing the yard, a tray covered with glasses and a pitcher of lemonade filling her hands.

He jumped up and took the tray from her, and she called out to the girls. They ran up to the table, swigged down two glasses apiece then bounded back into the yard.

Maggie filled a glass for him, then one for herself. "Here's mud in your eye," she said with a smile, then downed the golden drink.

Gray smiled back but knew the expression didn't reach his eyes.

They watched the children play a second longer, then he felt Maggie's gaze turn on him. "It's got you going, hasn't it?"

Startled, he met her look. "What are you talking about?"

She guffawed. "What do you think I'm talking about? You and Annie. You don't know how to handle it, do you?"

"Everything's just fine between us."

"Sure. Everything's perfect. That's why you have those lines across your forehead and a perpetual frown in your eyes."

Anything he could think of to say would only confirm her suspicions, so he remained silent. She looked across the yard toward the playing children.

"I've been married twice," she said quietly. "Each time I goofed up. Relationships stink, don't they?"

"I'm sure you didn't goof up all by yourself. It takes two people to do that."

"True," she conceded, "but I seem to have extraordinary talents in that department. I always manage to complete the destruction without any help from my partner."

He laughed lightly and took a sip of the lemonade.

"Annie, on the other hand, isn't like me." Maggie's gaze suddenly drilled him. "She's usually right on target with her feelings and emotions. Most of the time, she knows exactly what she's doing when it comes to people." Silence rose up between them. Maggie let it stay for a moment longer than Gray felt comfortable with, then she spoke again. "That's why I'm so concerned about her right now."

He turned his head to look at her, his gut tightening.

Her expression was serious, the fall breeze picking up her hair and brushing it across her shoulders.

"Her life wasn't perfect before you got here, but at least things were calm. She's so upset these days she doesn't know which way is up." She paused for a second, then went on, her voice slower, more thoughtful. "Which is okay, I guess, if you're in love. Are you?" she finished bluntly.

He hadn't expected her to be so open, then he remembered another conversation they'd had. The conversation they'd had when the DNA report had arrived, the conversation when she'd told him what her sister needed more than any thing in the world.

Love.

When he didn't answer, she went on. "Annie means a lot to me, Gray. She's more than a sister. When we lost our parents and went to live with our grandmother, Annie was the one who protected me, who slept with me when I woke up crying, who held my hand when we walked to school. She understands me like no one else and she accepts me like no one else. I don't have to explain and I don't have to make up excuses...even when I do something stupid. She loves me. And I love her."

Do you love her, too? The question sat between them like a boulder.

He let his eyes go back to the children. Against a backdrop of maroon mums that lined the low wall between the yard and the river, Bella and Rose were skipping rope, calling a cadence out to each other that reminded him of a childhood he'd never had. As if he was watching a scene from a movie where everything was perfect, he took in the little girls, the landscaped yard, the sound of their voices, even the pitcher of golden lemonade on the terrace table. He let the image burn into his consciousness and take form because he suddenly realized what he'd known all along.

It wasn't real.

None of it was real.

And it couldn't last if it wasn't real.

He'd come to Riverside looking for a dream, thinking anything was possible. He'd let himself buy into the idea that he finally could have a family, finally could have love. Bella had been there, it'd been proven she was his.

He'd taken it from there like a freight train, barrelling down the tracks, too determined and focused to see anything other than his own intentions. All he'd wanted to do was control the situation…control the situation *and* Annie.

And what he'd really done was ruin her life.

Because he could never give her what she needed.

The woman beside him spoke again. "Hello—are you with me here, Gray?"

He pulled his gaze away from Bella and swallowed hard. "I'm here." His voice was stony and he felt his heart turning the same way.

She locked her eyes on his. "I don't want to see my sister hurt."

"I never meant to do that."

"And I know that. So the time has come for you to do what you need to do—"

He rose abruptly, so abruptly the chair behind him rocked back and forth and threatened to overturn. "I understand what you're telling me, Maggie. You don't have to spell it out. You want me to tell you I love Annie and that I'll always take care of her and give her the good things she deserves."

"That's right." Maggie jumped up. Unlike Annie, she was almost as tall as Gray. She had no trouble looking him in the eye. "That's exactly what I want to hear and so does she. She needs to hear those things, and you need to tell her."

The wind picked up and sent the wind chimes down at

the river humming. On the breeze, Bella's voice sounded, the rhythm beating inside him. "Along came a funny man, riding on a horse..."

He stared at Maggie, his heart closing down inside him. "She may need to hear them, but I can't say them because they wouldn't be true. I've been wrong to ever think that I could make this work. It was a mistake on my part to even consider it." Maggie's mouth dropped open and her hazel eyes turned round with surprise. This clearly wasn't what she'd expected. He cut his gaze away from hers and directed it toward his daughter, a tight band of grief and disappointment wrapping itself around his heart and mind.

There was only one way out of this and no matter that it would kill him, Gray knew what he had to do.

Annie thought she'd never get home from Austin, and she began to question why she'd even gone in the first place. She'd wanted to buy fall plants for the garden, but she could have just as easily gotten them in Timberley at the small nursery on the edge of town. She wondered if she'd just needed the space and time away from Gray's overwhelming presence in the house. They were going to have to do something, but she had no idea what. All she knew was that she couldn't live like this for the rest of her life, that was for sure.

She gripped the steering wheel with both hands and felt the tension rise inside her. To top everything off, a Northern had decided to blow in, bringing with it gusts of rain that had dropped visibility to zilch. The windshield wipers clicked as fast as they could, but it was a losing battle. She pulled the Jeep into the driveway of Riverside an hour later than she'd planned.

Shaking raindrops from her hair and collapsing her umbrella, Annie ran onto the front porch. The door opened just as she reached for the handle and Gray stood in the doorway. The light streamed around him, preventing her from seeing his expression, but suddenly she realized she didn't need to see his face to know what was going on. The suitcases he held in his hands told her everything.

"Wh-what's going on?" she asked anyway, her heart thumping.

"I'm leaving."

"Leaving? We just got back from Dallas...is there another problem with the well in Jakarta?"

"There's a problem...but it's not with the well." He held the door open wider. "Why don't you come on inside?"

She almost didn't want to. A part of her brain was screaming *Turn back! Leave now before you hear this!* But sensing it was inevitable, she stepped into the foyer. He helped her out of her raincoat and draped it over the oak coatrack to the left of the door. When he turned and met her look, his eyes were darkly impersonal.

"I'm moving back to Dallas, Annie. I—I don't think this arrangement is going to work out."

Shock replaced her tension, anxiety turned into disbelief. For a moment, she was sure she hadn't heard him right, but his hardened expression told her otherwise. She opened her mouth but nothing came out. Swallowing once, she tried again and managed to stutter out the words. "You're—you're leaving...for good?"

A dark lock of hair fell over his forehead. Almost automatically, she felt the urge to reach out and smooth it back—and knew she couldn't.

"I think it's best for Bella if the break is clean. Anything else would confuse her."

Without thinking, Annie sat down heavily in the old church pew she kept along one wall of the entryway. "I—I think I'm confused, too. Are you saying you've changed

your mind? That you don't want anything to do with her?"
With me?

An expression shot into his eyes, an expression so full of pain and suffering that Annie's heart clutched at the sight of it. It disappeared a second later, confusing her even more. Had the look been real or her imagination?

"I'd thought this arrangement was the best, but to-day...I realized what a mistake it really was." His hands were fists, then he relaxed them as though he had just realized what he was doing. "I can't run my business from Timberley. I need to be in Dallas."

"Your business?" Annie felt her mouth hang open. She snapped it shut. "But...but...what about Bella? She loves you."

His forehead knit for a second, then went smooth again. "She'll forget about me eventually. I—I'm really just a stranger to her still. You're the one she depends on."

"That may be true, but—"

He interrupted her. "We'll divorce and I'll see that you get complete custody. If you still want to adopt her—to make her yours even more—then I...I won't stand in your way."

Astonishment rippled over her at his words. She started to tremble even though she was sitting down. Divorce? Full custody? She couldn't believe it. "But what about the father-daughter banquet?" she asked idiotically. "I—I thought you were taking her to that."

"I think it'd be best if you went."

Annie shook her head slowly. "I don't understand, Gray. I thought we..."

His expression turned into granite. "This is for the best, Annie. Our...relationship wasn't a real one, and frankly, I don't think it ever could be. I was foolish to believe we could fool the world, and even more foolish to think we could fool ourselves."

Her heart cracked slowly, a long, painful movement that shook her all the way to her toes. She'd known he hadn't loved her, but part of her had always hoped, she realized now. Hoped that things could be different. Hoped that they could really be a family.

He turned his back to her and looked out the front entry. The rain was really pounding down now. It reminded her of the night the electricity had gone out. The night he'd stood beside her in the darkness and made her so aware of him as a man. She looked at the bags beside him. "Were you just going to leave?" she asked in a wooden voice. "Leave and not tell me?"

He spoke without turning. "I left you a note."

"What's it say?"

"It's upstairs. It'd be better for you to read it."

Unexpected anger washed over her. "I thought you liked to face your problems head-on. Didn't you accuse me of being the one who put things off? Who didn't face the music? I don't think leaving me a note is facing your problems, is it?"

He turned slowly. His eyes were two black coals. "I've faced every problem that came my way with this one, Annie, so don't you dare accuse me of doing that. In fact, I'm facing it even more by leaving you. I'd think you'd have the sense to realize that."

"I have the sense, all right. I have the sense to understand that you're running out. Just like you ran out on Monica."

His face blanched at her words, and she wished instantly that she could take them back. God, he was giving her everything she'd fought him for and now she was giving *him* a hard time in return. What was wrong with her?

"There's other ways of looking at it," he said, his teeth clenched in an effort to control himself.

"Like what?" she asked softly. "Tell me how else you could read this one?"

"Maybe you could say I've realized some truths I didn't see before," he answered. "Some truths I was trying to ignore but know now I can't."

She knew instantly what he was talking about. He didn't love her. He'd thought he could make himself, but now he knew he couldn't. She started to say something along these lines, then closed her mouth as he turned his back on her. What was the purpose? What was the use?

She couldn't make him love her. It just didn't work that way. She rose from the bench without a word and started up the stairs. Now she understood the term 'empty victory.' She'd won Bella...but she'd lost her heart.

Gray turned around when he heard her footsteps. She was going up the stairs. Neither of them had turned on the lights and with the storm raging outside he could barely see her form in the dimness.

His voice stopped her, but she didn't turn around.

"Annie?"

"Yes?" The voice was strangely wooden for a woman who'd just gotten everything she'd wanted.

"Will you explain to Bella for me?"

She turned around slowly. "What would you like me to say?"

"I—I don't know," he said gruffly. And he didn't. Didn't know how to put into words the decision he'd made. The decision to set both of them free of him. He could never give Annie what she really needed, and he'd been ridiculous to think that he could. But, of course, he hadn't been thinking during this entire episode. That was the problem. He'd only wanted to control her, to control the situation. Now he cared too much. And the only answer was to give her up. To give them *both* up. It was strangely ironic, but he didn't have the heart to examine that right now.

"I'm sure you can come up with something, can't you?" he said. "Something that makes sense?"

She looked at him through the dimness. "Nothing about this makes any sense, Gray. Nothing at all."

He watched her go up the stairs and knew in his heart she was telling the truth. But he had no other choice. He couldn't do to Annie what Monica had done to him, and that was something else he just couldn't explain. As much as it hurt, Annie was right on target with her comment about Monica. She'd forced him to marry her, and look what had happened there. Without learning the lesson, he'd done the very same thing to Annie.

It was the biggest mistake someone could ever make, but he couldn't explain that because that meant admitting that he loved her. And Gray couldn't do that because love wasn't part of him. It wasn't how he'd grown up or what he'd known in his marriage, and it wasn't something he could experience now. All he could do was make sure his daughter had love, and by living with Annie, Bella would always know that feeling.

It was the least he could do for his daughter...and for Annie.

Chapter 15

Annie couldn't do it. She just couldn't do it.

She looked into Bella's bright green gaze and swallowed the faltering words she'd so carefully prepared to explain Gray's abrupt departure. She'd managed to say he'd gone to Dallas and that was where the explanation had stopped.

"It's okay," the little girl said, patting Annie's hand. "I know daddies have to travel. Rose's daddy goes to Austin all the time for his work. He always brings her something special back, though. Do you think Gray will bring me something?"

The weight on Annie's chest was crushing: "I—I don't know."

"Did he say when he's going to come back?"

"Not...not exactly."

"Well, he'll be back by next month," Bella replied with confidence. "He has to be. That's the father-daughter banquet. He wouldn't miss that."

"I'm sure he wouldn't want to," Annie said faintly. "But sometimes things come up...."

"Not this time," Bella said. "Not with Gray. He knows how important it is, so he'll be there." As if she sensed Annie's feelings but didn't quite understand them, the little girl stepped closer and wrapped her arms around Annie. "It's okay, Annie. Don't be sad. He'll be back."

Annie hugged Bella, her arms tight around the slight form, tears filling her eyes. Gray wasn't coming back...but she couldn't tell her that. Not yet. She hadn't even accepted it herself.

Not even his note could make her accept it. As the door had closed downstairs, she'd picked up the single sheet of paper lying on the bed.

Dear Annie,
I've come to realize that our marriage isn't going to work and it was a mistake to ever think it would. My business is suffering and I need to return to Dallas, as well. My lawyers will be contacting you.

The words were as cold and as curt as Monica had said he was and as Annie had once believed him to be. But now, knowing him as she did, the letter almost didn't seem real. She told herself she was being foolish, but she half wondered if he was trying to *act* like the person she'd thought he was. It was a silly question, but it haunted her.

Regardless, one by one, the days dragged by. She alternately missed him and hoped she never saw him again. Bella went on her way, certain in her ignorance that he would turn up by the time she thought he would. After three weeks had passed, Annie knew she had to tell the little girl the truth—or at least a version of it—but still she just couldn't bring herself to it.

She was sitting in the kitchen trying to think about how to do this when her hand inched toward the phone and she found herself dialing the number of the house in Dallas.

"Powers Residence, Mary speaking."

"Mary—this is Annie, Annie...um...Powers."

"Oh, Annie! How are you, dear? I've been thinking so much about you." Her voice dropped and Annie could hear her moving about the huge kitchen. "He's in his study—do you want to talk to him?"

"N-no." Annie spoke the word so fast, she stuttered over it. "I...I just wanted to call, that's all," she finished lamely.

"I understand," the housekeeper said.

Then explain it to me, Annie wanted to say. *Explain to me why I can't sleep and I can't eat and I can't do anything but think about a man who doesn't love me.* "Is...is he okay?" she said instead.

"No," the housekeeper said bluntly. "He's not okay. He works constantly, he's never at home, and when he is here, all he does is stare at papers he's brought with him from the office. He doesn't read them—he just stares at them. It's like he's..."

"What?"

The housekeeper sniffed audibly. "Like he's remembering when you two were here and swimming and everything. It's the saddest thing, Mrs. Powers. I can't believe it."

Annie felt her own heart crack open a little wider. "But he made the choice, Mary. *He's* the one who left."

"And don't you know why?"

Maggie had told Annie all about the discussion she'd had with Gray. Oh, yes, Annie knew why. "He...he doesn't love me, Mary. That's why he left."

"Doesn't love you? Why that's the biggest bunch of hogwash I've ever heard. The man's head over heels in love with you."

Annie clutched the phone and closed her eyes. "No. He doesn't love me. He made that more than clear. He said it wasn't going to work, and he had to return because of his business. He not only explained it to me, he told my sister, too. It's the truth, Mary.''

"Hah! He may have said something, but it wasn't the truth. That man misses you. And he loves you. I wasn't married for fifty years not to know that myself. If you know what's good for you, you'll get yourself to Dallas and straighten him out as soon as possible.''

Mary's words rang in Annie's mind for the rest of the week, but she just couldn't bring herself to call Gray. He'd left. He'd made the choice. Obviously Mary was wrong.

Gray stared out over the turquoise swimming pool. It was cold and gloomy. A biting wind whistled around the corner of the house and sent a barrage of oak leaves shooting into the water, rippling the surface. In his mind's eye, he saw a different day, a different time. Bella was splashing in the pool, and Annie was seated on the edge, dangling her feet in the water. They called out to each other and when he opened the French doors and went out to join them, they both looked up and smiled, sending a wave of happiness over him.

Turning away from the window, he tried to turn away from the memories as well, but it was a hopeless task. Like a thief sneaking into a house, a second image came into his brain. The image of Annie in his bed that night. She'd wrapped her arms around him and given herself to him so completely, he'd known it was the point of no return for both of them. After that, it seemed like someone had thrown open the dam gates and nothing they could have done would have stopped the passion between them. An aching loneliness came over him and, closing his eyes, he almost groaned. He missed her. He missed her and he was miserable...and he loved her.

His eyes came open and he stared sightlessly out the

beveled glass. *Love?* Who in the hell was he trying to fool? Himself? That was pointless. He *knew* better. He wasn't the kind of man who loved...not anymore. When he'd been younger and more foolish, maybe, but now? That time was past, and he'd accepted that fact when he'd left Riverside.

Hadn't he?

He'd left because he couldn't give Annie what she needed. He didn't have it to give.

Did he?

He walked across the cold, formal living room and sat down on one of the ivory couches that faced the marble fireplace. There was a fire going—Mary had prepared it— but the flickering flames gave no warmth to the room. It was totally devoid of anything homelike and he'd never noticed it until this very moment. No photos, no blankets on the couch, no half-filled glasses or magazines lying upside down. The room existed, but it was just that...a room. It held no love, no memories, no emotions. Nothing could give it those things but people. And not just any people, either, he realized slowly. Nothing in the house was alive, including himself, because Annie and Bella weren't there.

Since he'd walked out of Timberley, he'd felt like a zombie.

He stared into the flames. Was this how the rest of his life was going to be? Alone? Empty? He gave a short bark of a laugh at the irony. When he'd found Annie in the park after she'd sent Bella to school that first day, he'd thought he'd never seen anyone so desolate, so alone. If he'd taken Bella, Annie would have been all by herself with no one to love. She'd been terrified of that possibility, and told him. He hadn't understood.

Until this very moment.

The cafeteria was huge, noisy and smelled of endless school lunches. Tonight's banquet menu—mashed potatoes, meat loaf, candied carrots and blue Jell-O—hovered in the thick, stagnant air as well. Annie and Bella moved through the crowded room, their hands clasped together. Bella's uniform was pressed to a starchy perfection, but Annie's red slacks and white silk blouse stood out against all the darker suits and blue jeans on the men who filled the room. Over their deeper voices, Bella said something, but Annie couldn't understand her. She led the little girl to one of the walls, then kneeled in front of her.

"What'd you say, sweetie? I couldn't hear you."

"I *said,* how is Gray going to find us with all these people here? He'll never know where we are." The last words ended in what threatened to be tears.

Annie's heart felt as if it had a band around it, and Bella was tightening it. "He's not coming, Bella. Don't you remember what I explained yesterday? He has to work. You told me you understood."

She just hadn't been able to tell the little girl the whole truth. That Gray wasn't coming back. That he didn't love Annie. That they were going to be on their own. In her heart she knew she'd kept quiet because she hadn't been able to accept it herself. A wild idea had begun to form in her mind just last night...a wild idea that maybe he wasn't telling her the complete truth. That maybe she should go to Dallas and ask him point-blank. Try one last time. Tell him the truth and see what happened. She was fighting the idea.

Bella's red hair trembled with indignation as she shook her head. "I understood," she said stubbornly, "but you're wrong. Just plain wrong. He *is* coming. Gray is coming to my banquet."

A man jostled Annie in the crowd. She put her hand against the wall and concentrated on the little girl.

"Sweetheart—he's in Dallas. He's not coming. I'm

sorry, but that's just the way it is. Can't you be happy with having me here instead?''

Bella lifted one Reeboked foot and put it down firmly. It wasn't quite a stamp—she wasn't allowed to do that—but it was an expression of exactly how she felt. "He is, too, coming. He told me he loved me and he told me he'd be here, and I believe him." Her eyes zeroed in on Annie's face. "You're wrong. He's coming."

At the front of the room, someone began to tap on the microphone. "Can we take our seats, please? Brownies, fathers…can we take our seats now?"

Annie shook her head and tried one last time, even though her heart was breaking—for Bella *and* herself. "Look, I know this isn't how you wanted it to be, and…well…it's not exactly what I wanted either, but life is like that sometimes. We don't always get what we want. You're growing up now and that's one of the things you just have to accept. Bella…Bella, are you listening to me?"

The little girl's eyes had focused at a point somewhere over Annie's right shoulder. Despite Annie's words, she was searching the crowd, absolutely convinced she was right. Annie remembered her words to Gray that evening in Dallas…*perseverance…or stubbornness?* What did you call the trait?

"Bella, please. You've got to listen to me." Annie put her hand on Bella's shoulder and started to speak again, but the little girl's face suddenly lit up and she shot into the crowd. Without regard for legs and knees, she plowed into the men, pushing and shoving. Annie stood up and started after her, her heart cracking in two. All the men looked alike in their suits and jeans. The little girl wanted her father there so badly, she'd made a mistake, a terrible mistake.

"Gray, Gray!" she squealed over the noise. "I'm here. I'm here."

All at once, the sea of dark-suited men seemed to part and at the end of the aisle they'd formed, a man stood. Bella barrelled toward him. He bent down and she jumped into his arms. When he straightened, he met Annie's eyes over Bella's head.

The darkly intense stare of Grayston Powers locked on her face, and Annie's heart stopped.

"Let's settle down now. Let's settle down, please, people." From the front of the room, the microphone crackled again. "Please take your seats."

Bella turned in Gray's arms and beamed at Annie. "I *told* you he'd come," she cried. "I *told* you."

Annie's pulse was ringing in her ears, throbbing at the base of her neck. She felt hot and cold all at the same time. *He* looked cool and calm. "Wh-what are you doing here?" she said.

"I know it's a father-daughter banquet," he answered, his voice husky with emotion, "but do you think they'd mind if it was father-daughter-and-mother?"

"I—I don't see why not," Annie replied, her voice trembling as much as her legs. His eyes warmed instantly and her heart leapt.

"Then let's sit down," he said, letting Bella out of his arms, "and afterward…I want to talk to you."

It took a year to serve the meat loaf, mashed potatoes and Jell-O. At least that's how it felt to Annie. The whole time, she was going over scenarios in her head…he wanted Bella back…he wanted *her* back…he wanted them to be a family…. Annie's thoughts were so confused, so full of tension, she couldn't even choke down the sticky-sweet Jell-O.

When the meal finally finished, two hours later, and they

headed toward the car, Annie was practically sick with anxiousness. In the back seat, Bella felt none of the tension. She was asleep before they even pulled out of the school parking lot, clutching the certificate she'd won for having made the best vase out of a coffee can last week. Gray didn't say a word until the big car rumbled into the driveway of Riverside. He cut off the engine and stared across the leather seat at Annie.

She had no idea what he was going to say, and when he finally did speak, she was glad she was sitting down. Otherwise she might have fainted.

"I've been the biggest fool in the universe." His voice was quiet, deep, as intense as the look in his eyes. "I don't expect you to understand, but all I can do is hope that you'll listen and let me explain. Will you?"

Her stomach went into knots. Her heart raced. "Of—of course."

"My leaving had nothing to do with my business and I lied to you about that. I'm sorry." He lifted his hands from the steering wheel, then dropped them back down in a gesture of hopelessness. "I...I didn't do it deliberately. I just didn't understand myself what was going on."

"And what *is* going on?" Annie's voice was soft, questioning.

He met her gaze. "I love you. That's what's going on. I didn't realize it until I got back to Dallas and saw how empty my life really is without you and Bella. I know that I might not be the perfect husband, might not know how to be the perfect father, either...but I want to try again. If you'll let me."

"Oh, Gray..." Annie's throat closed, the tears building up and stinging. "I...I don't know what to say. Are you sure?"

"I'm very sure. I thought about it long and hard. I didn't believe, when I left, that I could give you what you wanted, what you needed, and then I realized that if I never tried, I would definitely fail." He reached across the seat and stroked her face with his fingers. His expression was tender. "Will you teach me, Annie? Will you teach me how to be a good father to Bella? Will you teach me how to love you?"

Annie's heart filled. She captured his hand with hers and kissed the palm of it, her eyes locking on his in the darkness. "I don't have to teach you anything," she said, her voice trembling. "You understand love. You came back here, didn't you? I think *I'm* the one who's just learned a lesson. I—I should have told you before now, but..."

"Told me what?" His voice was tender. It matched his expression.

"I—I love you, too. I have since the very beginning, but I was..." She took a deep breath and let it out slowly. "I was afraid you wouldn't believe me. Especially after we married."

His dark eyes widened with joy, then his expression turned serious again. "I probably wouldn't have believed you," he finally said. "I was too busy trying to control everything to let what was going to happen...just happen." He shook his head and grinned again. "Does this mean we can stay married?"

Annie nodded, a smile lifting her lips from one corner to the other. "Just for forever."

He pulled her across the seat and wrapped his arms around her. Kissing her deeply, he threaded his hands in her hair. A moment later, he lifted his mouth from hers and looked into her eyes, the intensity of his gaze burning into her. "Forever isn't long enough for me. It's got to go past there."

Annie nodded, a sense of joy and peace coming over her that she realized she'd been waiting for for a very long time. "I can handle it."

He kissed her again, and she knew he felt the same kind of loving quietness that she did. They loved each other—always had and always would. From the moment their eyes had met, she'd sensed it, but fought it. Now, for the very first time, she gave in to the sensation and let it wrap her with a feeling of strength and enduring love.

And from the back seat—interrupting the mood—a small, quiet voice piped up. "Does this mean we're a family now, for good?"

Epilogue

Ten months later

"They're almost here," Maggie cried. "Everybody get ready." She tweaked aside the curtain in the front window as the roomful of friends scurried around. "They're pulling into the driveway! Hurry! Hurry!"

Beside her aunt, Bella jumped up and down. "Can I go now? Now?"

Maggie grinned down at her. "Go now, but don't tell them we're all here. Remember, it's a surprise."

Bella nodded, then ran to the front hall. She threw open the door as the black Mercedes pulled up. A second later, Gray stepped out of the driver's side of the car and waved to her. She waved back, so hard her whole body seemed to move. He walked around to the other side of the car and opened the door. Annie stepped out slowly, a small form cradled in her arms, a huge smile on her face.

Bella flew down the sidewalk, her excitement too much to contain. "Oh, let me see!" she cried. "Let me see my new baby sister!"

Annie folded back the blanket and Bella stared at the baby in awe. She couldn't believe it—her own sister, her very own sister. Finally! Someone to play with!

She looked up at Annie and grinned. "You'd better hurry up and come inside. We can't surprise you standing out here!"

Annie lifted her eyes toward the windows of the house, then sent her gaze back to her husband. "Surprise? What kind of surprise?"

He shook his head, a lock of dark hair falling across his forehead. She reached up, with her free hand, and tucked it back. "I have no idea," he said solemnly. "The only surprise I've known about is the one you're holding."

"You're lying," she said with a grin.

"Yeah," he admitted with an answering smile, "but I love you...and that's all that really counts." Then he tucked his arm around her and his brand-new child, took Bella's hand, and led them all up the walk to the wide, open hallway where the sunshine always poured in.

* * * * *